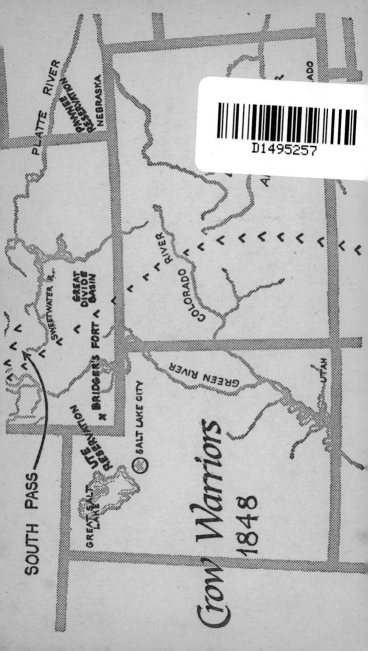

Prologue

The affair had actually begun the preceding December, Charles Madden mused. President Polk had assured Congress that the reports of abundant gold, while no doubt exaggerated in the telling, had nonetheless been verified by officers in the public service. With the announcement that gold had been discovered, the country was suddenly aflame with the idea that California was overflowing with the precious metal. And men rushed west, invading Indian lands.

A letter from Brigham Young had arrived two weeks after Polk's announcement. Pawnee raiders had kidnapped a white girl from a wagon train the previous summer, and the Mormons, reasonably enough, wanted her back. The letter, as Madden remembered it, stated the case quite clearly. Young and a man named Tommasen, the girl's betrothed, had apparently entered into an agreement with the Mormons' scout, an old mountaineer named Aloysius Benton, to retrieve the girl. But after a month without word from Benton, Tommasen had evidently prevailed upon Young to file an official protest.

Naturally, the case landed squarely in the hands of the commissioner of the Office of Indian Affairs. And the commissioner had seen fit to send Charles Madden west. He was to survey conditions among the Indians from the upper plains to the Rocky Mountains. More important, however, Madden was ordered to find out what had become of the missing girl. Madden understood clearly that he was being sent to placate the Mormons. Reconciliation with these people was something new to the federal government. As recently as 1838, the Mormons had been declared enemies of the state by the governor of Missouri, who had threatened them with extermination. Antislavers, blasphemers and polygamists, they had been called.

Their leader, Joseph Smith, had actually announced his candidacy for President of the United States. The bid ended tragically. Smith had been arrested and then killed when a mob stormed the jail where he was being held. That had happened in 1844. The following year, anti-Mormon outrages had forced the so-called Saints to leave their homes in Nauvoo, Illinois. Under the leadership of Brigham Young, the Mormons crossed the mountains and founded a city on the shores of the Great Salt Lake.

The location was strategic for westward expansion. With the Mormons established in the Great Basin, the United States government had chosen to intercede in their behalf.

But why hadn't the commissioner sent a younger man? Madden was forty-seven now, and nearly half of those years had been spent in Indian affairs.

"Charlie," the commissioner had said, "you know I can't send a boy to do a man's work. Look upon it as a paid vacation. With a proviso, of course. I expect a full and detailed report when you return. And you must appear to cooperate with Brigham Young and his band of fanatics, like it or not. Find out what has happened to that Cosgrove girl and return her to her people, if you can."

"You think she's still alive?" Madden asked.

The commissioner poured two glasses of brandy and offered one to the burly man with the thinning red hair. Madden accepted the drink and took a sip.

"Not likely, not likely," the commissioner replied. "Our friends the Pawnee aren't known for their compassion. But see what you can do. I have great faith in you, Charles."

Now, as he looked eastward across the swirling brown flow of the Missouri River, Charles Madden reflected on that final conversation. Before him, the area was crowded with covered carts and wagons. People milled about the riverside. On the west bank of the river, where Madden stood, Council Bluffs was covered with varicolored canvas tents. The clear, cold morning air was filled with the odors of cooking fires. The herd boys were moving about the hillside, urging their cattle and sheep along crisscrossed roadways.

Children were everywhere. Down by the river, their mothers washed white muslin, red flannel and particolored calicos, hanging their laundry on bushes to dry.

Settlers and livestock all would be heading westward soon, across prairie and mountain. Madden knew they were only waiting for a change of weather. After a winter of heavy rains, today was the first day of sunshine in two weeks. Mormon people, New Englanders, Southerners, New Yorkers, men mad to get at the gold fields of California—all crowded the shores of the dun-colored river.

And this, Madden thought, is the grand destiny of our nation. This irreversible push across the continent to the Pacific is our national fate. We are in the hands of fools and zealots, all eager to cross the Shining Mountains, all hoping to find Eden. And it's greed that drives them onward.

Years of trouble lay ahead, Madden was certain. Crossing the lands of the Indian nations of the high plains, emigrants would leave indelible trails in the landscape. They would slaughter the buffalo and elk. They would demand army protection in their fight against the Indians. Conflict was certain. Eventually the buffalo would be gone, and the Indians would be forced onto reservations like the ones occupied by tribes east of the Mississippi and in the Southwest.

Whole cultures destroyed, Madden thought. Treaties would be broken, he was sure. The Indians were doomed to move on until no place remained for them to hide, preserving their traditional ways. What the white man wanted would eventually be his. The redmen would become slaves or wards of the state. . . .

What had started, back in 1824, as a casual job for a young man had become for Madden a life's work. His sympathies drifted ever more certainly toward the Indian peoples. Commissioners changed with the regularity of the national elections, but Madden, as a career professional, stayed on. He had witnessed unbelievable corruption, had weathered the numerous battles for institutional power that speckled his twenty-three years of service. From head officers down to individual agents the desire for wealth inevitably overcame all other considerations. And the federal government itself, changing its Indian policies with monotonous predictability, neither understood nor appreciated the people whose lives it presumed to govern.

A bad business all around. Why had he stayed with it? Was it a sense of idealism, a fatuous supposition that he himself might be able to see to it that the twin causes of justice and humanity were served?

Madden didn't know.

But he knew that today, February 27, 1849, a very long journey lay ahead of him. There was danger, of course, but danger had never deterred him. What did bother him was his official entourage. Escorted by a troop of bluecoats commanded by Lieutenant Edgeworth, Madden didn't know whether to be grateful or sorry.

Edgeworth was a young man in his early twenties, a man with sawdust for brains and a spit shine on his boots. This was his first command mission. And ahead of them lay thirteen hundred miles of Indian territory. Their destination was Salt Lake City, where Brigham

5

Young and his pioneers were grimly fighting off starvation.

Madden knew that a few of Edgeworth's regulars had been upcountry before. Their presence was reassuring. But Madden also realized that the expedition was too early. Spring thaw hadn't even ended. With good guides and considerable luck, Madden hoped they had a chance of making it to Salt Lake City alive. But he wasn't overly confident.

Chapter 1

August 1848

The late August sun was a smear of white in the immensity of blue. Aloysius Benton drew up on the reins of his pinto, snorted and spat into the dust. A hot, dry wind had been surging out of the west for the past two days and it left his throat feeling parched.

Directly ahead was Devil's Gate. A steady ascent along the Sweetwater River would bring him to South Pass. Beyond that, near Black's Fork of the Green River, was Bridger's Fort. From there it would be no more than a squaw's jaunt on down to Salt Lake—the so-called promised land where this crazy bastard, Brigham Young, was taking his grim-faced saints. Benton knew well enough there was no point in telling that bunch anything. They wouldn't listen. They paid him well enough as hunter and scout. And with the fur trade gone under, an old mountain coon like himself appreciated the work. But they sure didn't take his advice. When trouble came, Brigham talked to his God. Then he made up his mind and told his people what to do.

Benton thought of the long string of wagons fifteen miles behind him. The Mormons would be coming up on Independence Rock just about now, he figured. Most of the folks were riding in prairie schooners, but a few of them rode horseback with pack horses and cattle trailing behind them.

Goddamn children o' Israel, he thought. They're lookin' for a valley of milk an' honey. Well, this ol' hoss is thinkin' they ain't going to find it, not where they're heading.

And yet old Brigham Young had some presence you couldn't deny. It was almost enough to make a believer out of a sane man just to hear that leader talk. Benton recalled Young preaching to his flock just after dinner a couple of weeks back, telling them they had relied on God too much and on themselves not enough. Well, now, that was somethin' for a man of the cloth to confess. Good thinkin', under the circumstances. And Young had told his people they could prosper only by the constant effort of everyone's pulling together. Nature was just too powerful, he'd insisted, for any individual man to fight her. The Church would have to provide the leadership and the people would have to obey without question. A man's ambition would have to be the ambition of all, and not just his own. If all the people could work as one person, then by God they'd make the desert bloom. Young had concluded his speech with some scheme of constructing irrigation canals down from the mountain streams.

"By the blue Christ!" Benton shouted aloud. "If madness can do 'er, he's the coon as will make 'er work. But me, I'm goin' to head back to the Crow and chaw on hump rib. Salt Lake's goin' to be a hungry place, I'm thinkin', when the cricks freeze solid."

Benton pulled his pinto mare about, leaned forward with his old, short-barreled Hawken in the crook of his arm and clapped his heels to the animal's sides. The horse snorted, threatened to buck him off and then began plodding her way eastward. Benton felt the sun burning hot through his leathers. He was growing drowsy.

Something wasn't right.

"Feel it in my bones," he murmured. "Damn horse feels it too, just like me. I guess when a man and a critter have been together long enough, they even start having the same intuitions. . . ."

The pinto lay back her ears and snorted. Setting her hooves, she jerked her head back and forth.

"God curse ye for a swayback mule, Charbonneau!" Benton hissed. "Whatever she is, I feel 'er too. Keep movin', damn ye!"

Charbonneau lowered her head and Benton kicked the animal's sides. Grudgingly, the mare began moving once more. Benton leaned over close to the horse's ear and clucked softly.

What was it? A soft, easy, hot wind was blowing but it wasn't the kind of blow that brought a storm. No sign of hostilities. They were into the territory of the Ute, but Jim Bridger, good old Gabe, was married to one of them and had an understanding with those devils. The white men—better known as long knives to the

Indians—were allowed to pass through with their wagon trains. As long as the Mormons didn't linger in this territory, it wasn't likely the Ute would make any real trouble. Sometimes a horse or cow would disappear during the nights. But from what Benton heard, the Ute were behaving themselves these days.

But renegade bands were liable to get out of hand. All the nations had renegades. No matter what the head chief said, from time to time the young warriors simply went off on their own and picked up whatever they could. Sometimes they halted wagon trains and, if they could intimidate the travelers, demanded presents.

The Cheyenne, Pawnee, Prairie Gros Ventres and Arapaho were dangerous. But the trail stayed mostly to the north of them, touching only the southern end of Crow territory.

The Crow, Benton thought. Guess I'm one of 'em. They're the only family I've got, anyhow.

A strange people, the Crow. Back during the days when Rotten Belly and Long Hair were the two head chiefs, the Crow had seen the handwriting on the wall and had decided to be friendly with the whites. The peaceful approach had worked out well for them. They got favored treatment in their trading, or at least imagined they did, and during the years of American Fur Company's dominance along the Big River, the Crow were always well equipped with arms. The weapons gave them an advantage in their interminable battles against the Blackfoot, the Assiniboin and the Cheyenne. The warriors were good trappers when they weren't fighting and the chiefs enforced a taboo against the use of "arwerdenty," the medicine water of the Long Knives. In the mid-thirties, the black trapper Jim Beckwourth, called Medicine Calf by the Crow, led the Sparrow Hawk clan to the very peak of their power. A raging epidemic of smallpox had, for a time, broken the power of the Blackfoot and had finally destroyed the Mandans. Miraculously, no more than a few cases appeared among the Crow population. Back around the turn of the century, the Crow had experienced their own dose of smallpox, as Benton had heard from Chief Yellow Belly. The chief had been a small child at the time, but he could remember the death villages well— or else he was just telling stories that he had heard as a boy.

Now, thinking back to his days among the Crow, Benton remembered his Indian wife, Sweetgrass, as good a woman as had ever lived. The years had drifted by, and Sweetgrass had been dead for—how many years? For a moment, Benton wasn't even certain.

"Ten years," he said aloud, clucking his tongue.

Taken by the lung disease.

They had spent good years together. No children of their own, but they had adopted Big Dog when the boy was only nine. The boy's mother and father and two older brothers had all been killed by the Assiniboin during a night raid on the Judith River.

Big Dog was the one man on earth whom Benton was genuinely close to. At twenty-eight, Big Dog was one of the most accomplished of the Crow war chiefs. Benton had taught the boy to speak a decent sort of English so that Big Dog could speak without difficulty with white traders or mountain men. In fact, the young

Crow had been accepted as one of them. He was known and respected by such as Jim Bridger, Joe Meek and Nathan Wyeth. He was the Crow who spoke like a Long Knife.

Benton and Big Dog had trapped together during the last prosperous years of the fur trade. But now the prices had dropped to almost nothing. The beaver had nearly disappeared from the streams. All things considered, the days of the trapper were finished.

Aloysius, Benton wondered, what the hell ye doin', anyhow? Helpin' these damned emigrants to find their way across the mountains? Don't ye know that when there's enough of 'em, it'll all be gone. The mountains, the rivers, an' every speck o' land will be plumb full o' saints. Well, damn, but a coon's got to make a livin' somehow he consoled himself. Most of the old trapper boys are doin' the same damned thing. What old-timers haven't gone under are doin' their best to help the mountains get filled up with people. Damn! It's a bitchkitty if they ever was one. What this child ought to do is go back to the Crow an' live 'er out with 'em. Goddamn world's endin', an' I'm helpin' it along.

Charbonneau was sulking, plodding along, making a point of going slower than was necessary. Benton was tempted to curse the mare and kick her in the sides, hard, so she'd know he meant it. But once she got into a mood like this, even kicking her wouldn't do much good. Better to let her just keep going at whatever rate she chose.

"I've put up with you for fifteen years," he sang in the pinto's ear, "an' all you do is get stubborner and

12

stubborner. More like a mule than a goddamn horse, ye are!"

Charbonneau snorted and kept plodding along.

Benton watched a pair of golden eagles sweep across the sky, graceful on the wind. He thought about Big Dog, living with the Crow. Big Dog had gone with the Crow after Benton had taken the boy down to St. Louis, when Sweetgrass had died. The time in St. Louis didn't work out though, not for either of them. The young Indian brave was still a red devil, even if he could speak English and knew something of the ways of the whites. Those civilized city folks would never accept the mountain ways of Aloysius Benton. White men who had lived with the Indians, or so a lot of folks figured, were no better than Indians, and maybe worse.

A couple of months in St. Louis, and he and Big Dog had taken off for the mountains again. They had trapped together, wandering the big forests and had gone to the last few rendezvous get-togethers with all the other trappers. When they finally gave up trapping, Big Dog had stayed with the Many Lodges and the Kicked-in-their-Bellies, which were two separate clans of the Crow Indians. Benton had taken to being hunter and scout for the increasing number of settlers whose wagons came creaking over prairies and mountains destined for California.

Benton remembered the story of how his son had been given his adult name. Until he was sixteen, Big Dog was known as Bad Raccoon. One day a rabid wolf had wandered into the Many Lodges' encampment just after sunrise, and all hell broke loose with women and children scattering in all directions, screaming their heads off. The wolf had backed an old woman up against the rear of a lodge and was about to spring when Bad Raccoon pounced on the animal. Wrestling the beast to the ground, the boy strangled it, coming through the encounter miraculously, without so much as a scratch on him. The Dog Soldiers, the fraternal warrior society, had sung his praises that night and had named him Big Dog. Even at sixteen, Big Dog was taller than anyone else in the encampment. Wanting to be a Dog Soldier all along, he had begged Benton for permission to go on a war party.

The strangling of the rabid wolf had proved Big Dog's prowess. He was accepted into the society. It wasn't long after that the boy counted coup, or touched the enemy, by killing his first man, a Blackfoot, taking his weapons and his scalp. The older warriors were predicting a great future for Big Dog.

Then had come his capture by the Pawnee. The Dog Soldiers had gone south to steal horses from the people who were the greatest of the horsemen, and after a night skirmish about the Pawnee herd, Big Dog had been taken prisoner. He had been bound and taken to the Pawnee camp by Antoine Behele himself, the half-breed war chief. Why Big Dog hadn't been killed and scalped on the spot, Benton didn't know.

Big Dog was fastened with deer hide thongs to the trunk of a scrub juniper and guarded through the remainder of the night. With the coming of light, his captors forgot about him. Camp dogs circled him, sniffed and then backed off. From time to time children approached and threw stones at him. An old woman brought a bowl of soup, laughed at him, and flung the hot liquid into his face.

The midday sun beat down, but Big Dog was able to sleep, despite the numbness of his wrists from the too-tight bindings.

He awoke from a kick to his side.

"What is your name, Crow?"

It was Behele, his captor. Big Dog stared up at the half-breed and then spoke slowly, in English. Benton had told him to do this if he were ever taken prisoner.

"I am Bad Raccoon, the son of Aloysius Benton, the trapper."

"You're not Crow?" Behele asked. His voice betrayed surprise, but his face remained impassive.

"I am Crow, but Benton is my father."

Behele turned and walked away.

Throughout the afternoon, the women and children carried in armloads of wood, which was deposited at the center of the circled lodges. Big Dog saw what his fate was to be. When darkness fell and the fire was ignited, he sang his death song. The Pawnee began to dance, and from the shouts and stumbling about, Big Dog knew the Pawnee warriors were drinking heavily of the arwerdenty.

Finally Behele and several young warriors swaggered over to him.

"I think your name is Big Dog, the Crow warrior," Behele growled. "Or do the Crows have many men who are too tall for their horses? Speak, Crow!"

"I am called Big Dog, but my name is Bad Raccoon, and Benton is my father."

"How did you get this name, Big Dog?"

"It was given to me when I strangled a rabid wolf."

Behele translated for the Pawnee braves, who gestured in astonishment and approval.

"To wrestle the rabid wolf requires the bravery of a man, but you are just a boy, no matter how tall you are. Tomorrow we will test you. We will give you a chance to run against White Bear, the fastest of our warriors. I have decided not to burn you, Crow."

Finally the dancing subsided. Big Dog attempted to work his bindings loose, but to no avail. At last he slept, but was awake again with the first light. Once more the old woman brought him a bowl of soup but this time held it, making it easier for him to sip. He nodded and thanked her. Her face remained immobile.

The soup was hot and good, with seasonings and chunks of buffalo meat. But Big Dog had to fight a fierce sensation of nausea. If he were to be put to a test of endurance, the strength his body would draw from the soup would be essential.

Two hours passed. His leggings stank from the several times he had urinated.

Behele and a crowd of warriors approached, and Behele cut his bindings.

"You will run to save your life," Behele ordered. "You will be given no weapon. But White Bear will have a knife. When he catches you, he will take your scalp."

The returning circulation was prickling Big Dog's hands, but they were still numb. He flexed them slowly and nodded to Behele.

Suddenly, Big Dog dashed from the circle of lodges, and the race was on. He was being given a head start, and he did not look back. When he heard the shout go up behind him, he knew that White Bear had begun his pursuit.

Big Dog ran steadily, determinedly, surprised that his endurance did not seem to have been impaired by the long period of being bound to the tree. At the same time, he knew that the Pawnee would not have given him this chance if they had thought the young Crow genuinely had a chance of escaping. Big Dog crested a low ridge, glanced back now and saw the Pawnee coming upslope. The warrior was close now, very close. White Bear was indeed a strong runner.

Below, perhaps a quarter of a mile away, grazed a herd of several hundred buffalo. Big Dog ran directly toward the animals. He reached the herd and threaded his way in among the animals. The chance was slim, but it was the only one he had.

"Play the cards that Coyote deals ye," Benton had told him often enough. "Ye don't get no different ones. . . ."

Puzzled by this intruder in their midst, the buffalo began milling slowly about. One of the big bulls was bellowing.

Then White Bear was on top of him, arm extended, the knife blade gleaming. Big Dog twisted away, bounced off the ribs of a cow, and shouted at the top of his lungs.

Suddenly the huge brown beasts were moving, dust spiraling up from their churning hooves.

Big Dog leaped into a dry stream bed. Clinging to

17

the bank, he watched the flood of animals pass over him. Then they were gone, and Big Dog stood up, looking for his enemy.

The buffalo had trampled White Bear. The Pawnee lay contorted, both his legs broken.

As Big Dog approached the fallen warrior, White Bear slashed out with his knife. Big Dog stared down at his helpless foe. The fierce eyes awaited death, the terrible pride would still not give up without a final struggle. Big Dog shook his head and used sign language to indicate that he wished to help. He indicated that he would carry White Bear back to his people so they could set his broken legs.

White Bear stared up at the tall Crow warrior, hardly believing what the sign language was indicating. At length the Pawnee offered the knife, which Big Dog took, and then he submitted. Big Dog lifted his enemy in his arms and began to walk toward the distant Pawnee encampment. For all the young Crow knew, he was walking straight to his own death, and yet he could not leave White Bear where he was, most likely to die a horrible death by thirst. Perhaps the Pawnee would value this gesture of good will and would give him his freedom in return.

As he approached within sight of the village, Big Dog considered leaving his foe there. But the thought passed quickly, and he continued toward the Pawnee encampment, White Bear's arms knotted about his neck. A band of astonished Pawnee surrounded the pair and then slowly parted, allowing Big Dog to pass. He could hear the puzzlement in their voices, even if he couldn't understand the words. He saw Behele standing, arms crossed, before the thinly smoking remnant of the preceding night's great fire. Big Dog strode toward him and placed White Bear upon the ground at Behele's feet.

"His legs are broken," Big Dog said. "I have brought him back to his people."

Behele spoke to White Bear in Pawnee, then nodded to Big Dog. "The tall Crow is indeed a brave man," he said. "You could have killed White Bear and escaped to your own people, for we would not have followed you. We gave our word. Instead you have brought White Bear back so that he would not die. Big Dog, son of Aloysius Benton, the Pawnee give you safe passage back to your people. We will return your weapons and your horse, and we will grant you freedom to pass through Pawnee lands whenever you wish, so long as you do not come as part of a war party against us. If you do that, then we will kill you, and all the Crow who are with you as well. These are my words, and they will spread throughout the Pawnee nation. There will be peace between the Pawnee and Big Dog of the Crow."

Aloysius Benton clapped his heels to Charbonneau's sides, urging the mare forward at a brisker pace. Remembering his son's story had made the hairs prickle along the back of his neck.

"A dumb thing to do, I'm thinkin'," he muttered to the horse. "Charbonneau, old varmint, if the Pawnee ever capture you and give ye a chance to run for 'er, you run, you hear me? And don't be lookin' back, neither."

Charbonneau snorted and tossed her head.

Benton continued to think about Big Dog, about the years the two had spent trapping together, about their friendships with other mountain men, about the sense of doom that had hung over the final rendezvous.

He felt a sense of doom now. Not really of doom, perhaps, but a sense that something wasn't right, something with the wagon train.

Another six, seven miles, and he'd be back with the caravan.

"Prob'ly just a bad intuition," Benton told Charbonneau. "But keep goin' anyhow, damn your ears!"

Mormons, the least likely and yet the most likely of people to be moving across the mountains. Persecuted and with no one to turn to, stuck on their own crazy ideas about God and destiny, they were determined to build a city of God by Salt Lake—a land where winter came early and left late. It was certain their kind wasn't popular with the regular kind of settlers, especially with their special covenant with God and their doctrine that a man could have more than one wife. And that fool of a Brigham Young, his eyes fixed somewhere beyond the human race, always cocked his head as if he were waiting for God to say something to him. Well, the man had gotten some of his sheep out to Salt Lake already, the year before, and now he was bringing more of them, and it looked like there'd be yet more wagon trains during the years ahead. If Young realized his dreams, it meant an end to the wild country. But it wasn't just Brigham Young, and Benton knew it well enough. The emigrants were getting to be as common as sand fleas, their prairie schooners crowding the trails to Oregon and California. The clumsy four-wheeled wagons, drawn mostly by oxen, were capable of floating across rivers too deep to ford, made watertight by a sheathing of rawhide or canvas coated with tallow. And filled to the brim they were, with everything from a wood stove or a grandfather clock to playthings for children. They were crammed with plowshares and churns and shovels and scythes, bedsteads and violins, flour and seed and cross-cut saws and brassware and even chickens and fruit-tree cuttings. Sometimes, if the going was tough, if there were storms or floods, the goods were thrown out to make less weight for the animals to pull. As the wagon train of Mormons had made its way upcountry, across prairies and sandhills and high plains and along the North Platte to the Sweetwater, it had passed perhaps a dozen caches of household goods jettisoned by earlier pilgrims.

The Indians would find these cast-off belongings and take what they wanted. But it was sad to find a cast-iron stove or a chest or a mirror abandoned in this wilderness.

Sometimes there was a grave marker. Benton remembered one such grave, a recent one when he found it. It was that of a four-year-old girl, not properly overlain with rocks. Coyotes, or maybe wolves, had dug it out, had stripped the little skeleton almost clean. What they hadn't eaten, the vultures had, and the ants got the rest. Benton had reburied the remains, hauling rocks up from a gulch to protect what no longer needed to be protected. And he had cursed the desperation and the ignorance of the parents all the while he had worked.

But why was he feeling a sense of imminent danger now? Brigham Young's wagon train was a big one, huge by usual standards, more than a thousand men, women and children. In numbers lay strength. Even the God-awful Blackfoot wouldn't usually attack a party large enough to defend itself. Although the Mormon leaders were men of peace, they were well armed, and their preparations for the westward trip had been exceedingly careful.

Was it something about Chastity Cosgrove?

A hell of a gal, that one, Benton thought. She was a proud woman, one who wasn't going to give herself away easily. In fact, she had resisted marriage—still single into her twenties—and that was no mean accomplishment among the Mormons. They were people who hardly concerned themselves about individuals. They worried only about the good of all, and at the heart of the *good of all* lay the family, presided over by the menfolk.

Benton knew, of course, that appearances could be deceiving. The life of the Crow might look much the same as the Mormons' to people on the outside. Crow women did all the work and took care of the lodges while the men were off fighting or stealing horses or trapping or hunting. But the reality was quite different. Crow women controlled the villages, owned the lodges, and generally, one way or another, ended up making all the rules of the game. Revenge and horse mania might not make sense to the whites, but the Indians, men and women alike, accepted both as necessary to the way they lived. This fact, as much as anything else, had drawn Benton to the life of these people. His years with Sweetgrass, with Big Dog growing up, had been happy ones for both of them.

His thoughts drifted back to Chastity Cosgrove.

Chastity, the proud daughter of Samuel Cosgrove, a stiff, self-righteous man. He was well to do, as these things went, but empty inside. Having lost his first wife, he had only recently married a girl two years younger than his own daughter. Tillie Ann was a little mouse of a thing who never spoke up at all, just the dead opposite of Chastity, who had a mind of her own and a healthy temper to boot.

Benton had taken a fancy to her right off, and, as it had turned out, Chastity had taken a fancy to him as well. Tall and blonde and blue-eyed, she had a streak of the devil in her. She wasn't mean, though, and not exactly stubborn, but she knew what she wanted, and it wasn't to marry Elder Tommasen or to be a part of the Mormon city of New Zion at all. But it was hard to break out of a group like that, with everyone lined up against her, either looking on quietly and sternly or actually telling her how she should lead her own life.

"Not easy, bein' a woman, whether American or Mormon or Indian, I guess," Benton concluded.

But Chastity had agreed to marry Elder Tommasen when the wagon train reached Salt Lake, mostly to give herself a little more time and to keep her father and the others from being riled. What would she do when she actually got there? The wagon train was getting close now—another month and they'd arrive. Would she give in at last and keep her word? Or would she try to hook on with some other wagon train and head on up into Oregon country? It would be interesting to find out.

Benton called her "Cozzie," for Cosgrove, her last name. What he felt for this girl wasn't the longing of a man for a woman. It was true that, at fifty-one, he was certainly not much older than Elder Tommasen. But it was also true that he'd already had the only woman he could ever be married to. And in any case, fifty-one was a lot older for a man who had lived his life in the mountains and had seen so much. As a young man, he'd had numerous Indian women, short-term things mostly, during rendezvous and maybe a season after that. But with Sweetgrass he had found his permanent mate.

No, Cozzie was more like a daughter, and the very fact that they both knew there could be nothing man-woman between them made the whole thing just that much better. She'd sneak off in the evenings sometimes and visit him at his camp away from the main group. A couple of times he had taken her out hunting, and had shown her how to shoot. The first two or three times she had missed, but then she had hit a big bull elk and dropped him in his tracks.

Cozzie had been proud as hell of that.

He'd taught her how to ride, Indian style, astride the animal and bareback, and she'd picked it up right away. Then she'd gone helling into the big circle of the wagon train to show her father, and that was a mistake. Not ladylike—pagan—a proper young woman doesn't do that sort of thing!

"Marriage will tame you down," Samuel Cosgrove had declared. "If it doesn't, you're a lost soul, daughter. . . ."

She'd been ordered to bed after that, but it didn't stop her from coming out to talk with Benton again the following evening.

Chastity Cosgrove, age twenty-two. She was an old maid, by most standards.

Benton could see the wagon train ahead of him now. There were hours of daylight left, and the train wasn't moving.

"Sure as hell somethin's wrong," Benton exclaimed. "Come on, Charbonneau, damn your eyes, let's get on down there!"

Chapter 2

She was not one of them, and she knew it. Yet the conditions of her life seemed inexorably to draw her along.

Elder Tommasen, she thought. Does he have a first name?

Chastity dismounted, tethered the little mare, and walked along the riverbank. The trailing end of the wagon train was perhaps a mile ahead, toiling slowly, painfully along, the men shouting at the draft animals, the axles creaking and the steel-rimmed wheels crunching over stones and throwing up dust. Some of the women and children walked, and the cattle plodded patiently forward. The animals were thin from their long journey and often stubborn. The herd boys moved along behind them and to either side, calling out, lashing the ones who fell behind, singing to the cow dogs

27

who worked with astounding agility among the milling cattle.

She thought again of Tommasen.

"Marriage?" she muttered aloud, stopping to gaze across the summer-low river toward the mountains beyond. "Damned if I will be. . . ."

The courtship back in Nauvoo had been brief. Tommasen had come for dinner one night, and she and Tillie Ann prepared a meal far more elaborate than the usual—salad and pea soup and fresh-baked bread, a roast of mutton garnished with onions and pickled beets, deep-dish blueberry pie, two fresh pitchers of milk. She and her father's young wife served the two men before sitting down themselves, and then she had been asked to say the grace. The men talked of the coming migration, and the women ate slowly and silently. At the meal's conclusion, the men adjourned to the sitting room while she and Tillie Ann tidied up. After Tommasen left, Samuel Cosgrove told his daughter that he had given Tommasen permission to marry her.

"I won't," she had declared simply.

"Yes, daughter, you will—and be glad of it. You're already nearly past marrying age, and Tommasen's a wealthy man and a good one. When we reach the New Jerusalem at Salt Lake, you will be given in marriage. You'll get used to the idea. Women always do. I have no more to say on the matter."

No more to say!

Chastity had immediately made plans to escape the community, but dangers on the outside had frustrated her plans. So she had given the appearance of

acceding to her father's wishes while all the time plot-
ting some possible course of action that would free her
from all of them. Salt Lake was still a very long way
away, and so there would be time.

But now they were drawing close. Benton had
made it seem like no great distance at all when she
asked about the remainder of the trail ahead. She
thought about the old trapper. No matter what question she might ask, Benton always had an answer. He
was forthright if the questions had to do with practical
matters, about the rivers or mountains or the habits of
animals. But if she asked him about things that really
had no answer, he became a kind of poet, and invariably he'd tell her some story or legend he had heard
during the years he lived with the Crow.

But she liked this man, liked him immensely. Re-
bellious all her life, she was an outcast among her own
people. In general, she preferred being alone. There
were books to read, when she could get them. Old
Mrs. Thrasher, who had lived alone in Nauvoo had
given her books to read, and had warned her against
letting her father know she had them. They were forbidden books, books not approved of by the Mormon
people.

Some people had thought Mrs. Thrasher was a
witch, a lost soul who had fallen away from her religion after her husband died.

"The evil crone," Chastity mused. "The woman
no one had understood, the woman they feared and
hated."

Her father had finally forbidden her to visit the

old lady, but she had continued anyway. More than once she slipped out the rear window at night and visited the lady of the books.

When Mrs. Thrasher died, almost no one had attended the funeral. Her father prevented her from going, and she had felt a terrible sense of guilt and disloyalty. Only later had she managed to visit the cemetery, where Mrs. Thrasher's grave lay at a distance from the others, near the big willow trees, close by the river. Then she had apologized to the old lady and, strangely enough, felt that her words had been accepted.

Chastity remembered the books. They held a whole world of imaginings, stories of places far away, in England, in France, in Spain—magic places. But all the books were gone now, vanished in flames. The cottage itself had mysteriously burned to the ground a week after the funeral.

The men of Nauvoo, of course, had done it. The Mormons persecuted any among their numbers who were different, any who held to their own thoughts. And the Mormons in turn, were persecuted by those in the world outside. Smith, the man who had seen God and who had been given the holy words that became the Book of Mormon, was dead—arrested and then slain by a howling, black-faced mob. Were the people in the world outside really so evil? They burned, murdered, terrorized. They had driven the Mormons from the city they had built and where they had been able to live and prosper. Yet Benton was such an outsider, and Chastity sensed, knew almost from the beginning, that there was no harm in this man. He was fond of her, she knew that. And he had become the friend she so desperately needed. She could confide in him, and, in some way or another, he was her link to that world outside.

When she had asked him if he thought she should marry Elder Tommasen, Benton said, "Naw, Cozzie, shouldn't no woman ever marry that one. Ye asked me, so I'm tellin' ye. He's got water for blood, that one. You take my advice and find ye a young man with fire in 'im. Don't let these folks push ye into somethin' you'll regret for a lifetime, gal."

Aloysius Benton. His answers were simple and to the point, unless it had to do with why some wolves were black or why sometimes there were sounds down deep in the earth. Then it was always, "Wal, now, the old medicine man Ears-of-the-Wolf told me once. . . ."

Benton had taught her to ride and to shoot, and her father had been horrified. Even Tillie Ann had attempted to persuade her to stay away from Benton, to act more like a "decent woman."

Is that what life was all about? Follow the rules, keep to the pretenses, speak softly and work hard and never complain?

Brigham Young thought so, and whatever Brigham Young thought, everyone else ended up thinking the same.

But now Benton said they were getting close, and Chastity knew she was going to have to do something. But what? Marry Tommasen? She felt nothing for him, but perhaps that didn't matter. The one boy she had felt something for, and whom she had kissed several times one afternoon as they stopped in the shade by the big creek—Tommy Logan—was dead. Tom and five others had been gunned down by a raiding party of outsiders while they were cutting firewood a few miles north of Nauvoo.

"Tommy," she whispered, "I would have married you, Tommy. I wouldn't have been afraid to go to bed with you. I would have been your wife when you asked me. . . ."

It was all distant now, all like a dream. A thousand miles of plains and mountains lay between her and the cemetery in Nauvoo.

Her pinto whinnied, and Chastity was jolted out of her reverie. Was there an animal close by? But then the horse was quiet once more.

She should be getting back. Benton would return tonight, would probably come riding in on Charbonneau just about sundown. He would talk briefly with Brigham Young and then pitch his camp out beyond the wagons, kindle a small fire and eat alone. If she could, she would use the cover of darkness to slip away from her father and Tillie Ann and walk out to spend a few minutes talking with Benton.

She returned, through the light growth of willow, to her tethered mare. Mounting easily, she trotted to catch up with the caravan. The light wind felt good on her face, and she watched a pair of big birds, hawks probably, circling gracefully above.

"If I'm going to marry that man," she said aloud, "then by heaven, he's not going to have any other wives. If he marries another, then I'll leave—I'll go back to St. Louis or maybe even to California."

Joseph Smith was dead, but his doctrine of multiple wives lived on, and grew stronger. The women themselves spoke of it, with some against and some for. Already a few of the men had, in fact, taken second wives, and these women thought well of the situation. They insisted that with more than one woman in each family, the individual woman had it easier. Four hands could easily outwork two hands. And not the least of the advantages lay in the fact that a man with more than one woman made fewer sexual demands on each of them.

But herself such a wife, giving herself to a man she did not care for, bearing his children, raising those children and keeping house—and growing old, growing old and dying as her own mother had died?

"There has to be a way of escaping," Chastity decided.

A group of four coyotes crossed in front of her, their tails out. They were moving rapidly, the long-legged, easy run that was oddly different from the way dogs ran. "Wandering dogs," Benton called them. He wouldn't shoot one, not for anything.

Little Brothers, he called them. "Cirape's the song dog," he had said. "Crow think they're special kinds of spirits, an' this coon does too, the dogs of God. Old Man Coyote, he created the plains and the basins and the mountains, gal. An' I guess he put his little brothers here to kind of keep watch over things. I'll tell ye somethin' else, too. They're the smartest varmints old Aloysius has ever seen. Coyote people are smarter than anybody except the humans, an' I wonder about us sometimes. If a man just watches what the coyotes do, he'll mostly keep out of trouble. You see the song dogs runnin' by daylight, gal, and they's somethin' up, sure as hell. You remember that, now."

But there was no sign of any danger. Still, Chastity scanned the countryside, moving her eyes back and forth in quick little motions, the way Benton had told her to do.

She saw nothing, but her mare was nervous. Suddenly she wished Benton were with her. Chastity breathed in sharply and fought for her breath for half an instant. She chided herself for her foolishness, but she felt gooseflesh anyway.

She laughed aloud.

It was just one of Aloysius Benton's yarns, nothing else. Just some coyotes running somewhere. The day was warm and pleasant, and a soft wind was blowing. Benton's stories charmed the imagination, but most were just flights of fancy.

Chastity had urged the mare into a faster gait when she heard the first of the rifle shots.

It did not seem real to her, but there they were, the red and white paint splashed on faces and arms and chests visible even from a distance. They rode over the low ridge, their war cries oddly shrill, joyous, like happy children at play, Chastity thought. It was actually happening—the one thing the people of the wagon train had feared most, had feared over all those long miles upcountry from Council Bluffs. Yet there had been no trouble from the Indians until now, and indeed almost no contact at all. Only once a small band of warriors had ridden in early one morning, before the train had begun moving. They fired their rifles first and trotted in slowly, with empty weapons, the sign of peace. Benton had ridden out to meet them and talked with them for fifteen or twenty minutes. He had embraced one tall warrior. Returning to Brigham Young, he had reassured the Mormon leader. "My Crow," he called them, "on their way to borrow some Cheyenne horses, bless 'em."

But now it was happening.

The Indians swept down on the trailing end of the wagon train, scattering the herd of cattle with rifle fire. The braves swung to one side, low on their horses, and shouted. The cattle milled about and then broke into a run, moving off northward, away from the river. The raid, apparently nothing more than some playful harassment, was over within moments. The Mormons had been taken so completely by surprise that the first of their answering shots did not come until the Indians were out of range—coming toward her.

Chastity sat her horse as if transfixed. Within moments the Indians had encircled her and had drawn their horses to a standstill.

"Why do you not ride with the others?" the leader asked in rough English. "Will they not let you remain with the women who stay in the wagons?"

Chastity did not answer. Her voice was frozen in her throat.

"I am Gray Buffalo of the Pawnee Loups," the chief said. "We will rescue you from these people who make you ride behind in the dust of the strange little buffalo."

Gray Buffalo nodded, and a warrior rode forward. He took the reins from Chastity's hands, drew her horse toward Gray Buffalo, and handed them to him.

"You do not speak, Yellowhair? Have they cut your tongue out for something you have done? You will ride with us now."

Gray Buffalo gestured to his warriors and spoke a few words in the tongue of the Pawnee. The horses began to move all at once, with Chastity's mare surrounded by the Pawnee warriors.

All afternoon they rode without stopping, across the shallow river and away southward, over low ridges and through dry basins. The Indians spoke but little, and no words were addressed to Chastity. Gray Buffalo rode behind her, and she was forced along.

Would men from the wagon train follow? With all the excitement of having to round up the scattered cattle, how long would it be before they missed her? Her absence might not even be noted until the evening meal.

The sun dropped westward, and the Pawnee turned up a ravine that led into an amphitheater-like box canyon. Here, springs trickled from the hillsides and the grass was tall and green above the willow and aspen-lined stream that issued down from the high rocks. The cliffs seemed to burn with some interior light in the last red rays of the day.

The Pawnee dismounted, and Chastity was pulled from her horse. Two young warriors fastened her hands behind her, laughing as they did so, and motioned for her to sit down next to a dead cottonwood by the stream. After that the Indians kindled three small cooking fires. Withdrawing chunks of meat from their pack bags, they began to prepare their meal. They seemed to have forgotten about her totally, and she wondered if it would be possible to slip off in the near dark. But where would she go? There was no way to get to her horse, and no way to remove the bindings on her wrists.

Where was she? She had no idea, for her sense of direction, not certain in any case, had vanished completely.

How could everything have changed so utterly and so suddenly? Chastity wondered.

She was lost, helpless, and at the mercy of the Indians. They had not harmed her, but she was completely in their power and lost in an uncharted wilderness where her father and the others would never be able to find her.

Benton, she thought. Benton will come to look for me—he will follow the trail they have left, and he will find me.

Now, for the first time, as if finally comprehending the hopelessness of her situation, Chastity felt the sobs forming deep inside her. She stared at the flickering lights of the three fires, and the moisture started to her eyes. But she didn't cry. She felt stunned, numb. Crying would do no good.

They could do with her whatever they chose, and she was helpless to resist. Would they kill her? Rape her?

She tried to think rationally but could not.

At length Gray Buffalo came to her, and unfastened her hands. He gave her a chunk of cooked meat that smelled strange to her. As hungry as she was, she would not have eaten the food had she not sensed that to decline might serve to alienate the brave who, if not a friend, at least spoke English and therefore might be reasoned with. She bit off a mouthful and chewed slowly, the gamy taste nearly gagging her for a moment.

Chastity swallowed and asked, "What is it?"

"Wolf meat," Gray Buffalo answered. "Many long knives do not eat dogs, but it is good, is it not?"

Chastity fought back a gagging sensation.

"Yes," she answered, "it is very good."

"I thought you would like it, Yellowhair."

She forced herself to take another bite.

"What is your name?" the Pawnee war chief asked.

"Chastity Cosgrove."

"Why were you not with the other white women, in the wagons?"

"I wanted to look at the river," she managed.

"Did you have to shit?" Gray Buffalo asked, as if not quite understanding.

"No!" she blurted.

"Do you have to do so now? I have heard that white women are very private about such things. When you have finished eating and doing what you must do, come over to the fire. Do not attempt to run away, for we would find you anyway, and then my warriors would be angry and I might not be able to control them. They have never lain with a white woman, and they are curious. If you run away, they will take you by force, and I will not be able to stop them."

Standing with his back to the fire, Gray Buffalo's features were shadowed, almost indistinguishable. Was he serious in what he said? If she could see his eyes, she thought, she might be able to tell.

Then he was gone, striding back toward the firelight.

Chastity finished eating and then, rising and stepping back into the willows, she pulled down the leather breeches Benton had made for her and squatted, her hands on her knees. Birds rustled uneasily in the strangely damp-smelling brush about her, and somewhere farther off, perhaps at the head of the box canyon, a pair of screech owls were hooting to each other. She recognized their mating sounds. One evening Benton had called to the screech owls. They had answered him, and he had explained their different cries to her.

Benton. Would he be able to find her?

She did not linger among the willows. Remembering the words of Gray Buffalo, she breathed deeply, controlling her fear, and walked toward the firelight. She went directly to Gray Buffalo and stood beside him, uncertain what to expect next.

There was a sudden rattle of voices from the Pawnee warriors.

"You are my captive," the chief explained. "Now my braves wish me to make one of them a present of you, for otherwise, they will all insist on sharing you. You must accept my decision and do what I tell you, Yellowhair. That way you will be able to live. You will be a wife to one of my warriors and become one of us and live as our own women live. Do you understand me?"

"I do not wish to marry anyone," she managed.

"You are frightened now, but this will be better

than what I told you of. My warriors do not understand this language of the Anglo very well, but still we must be careful in what we say. Many of the warriors have traded with the Long Knives, and so know a few words. I can give you your life only if you will do what I tell you, even if it frightens you."

"I will do as you say, Gray Buffalo."

"Then take off all of your clothes. The warriors wish to know what a white woman looks like. They wish to know if you are like all other women."

"No!" she protested.

"Do what I tell you, Yellowhair. If you do not obey me, I will tell the warriors that they may all take their pleasure with you. Afterward they will cut your throat and scalp you. It is better to do as I say."

The fire-gleaming eyes of the men were upon her. What was being asked was impossible for her, she could never do it. Yet her hands, as if with a desperate will of their own, began numbly to do as they had been bidden.

She was no longer Chastity Cosgrove. She was nothing now.

In a few moments she stood naked, the chill air of the night flowing about her. Her eyes stared fixedly at the earth.

A babble of curious, excited voices rose about her. The men looked at her, pointed, laughed. One pulled at her hair, as if testing to see whether it was real, but she made no outcry. Others pointed at the hair between her legs, and nodded solemnly. Another reached out slowly, as if to touch the nipple of her breast, and then suddenly drew his hand back. There was a wave of uneasy laughter and then grunting and clicking sounds. The chatter increased in tempo and suddenly ceased.

"This is my captive," Gray Buffalo said in English and then spoke again in his own tongue, at the same time gesturing in sign language. Benton had taught her some of the sign language, the universal gestures used by all the tribes of the plains and mountains. She saw Gray Buffalo make the sign for marriage along with that for lying down together.

"I will give the Yellowhair to Crooked Knife, for he is the one who returned my Nez Perce horse that had been stolen by the Ute. Crooked Knife is a brave man, and he was wounded by Long Knife rifles two winters ago, when we were hunting along the Arkansas River." Gray Buffalo, having spoken these words so that Chastity might understand him, now spoke again in his own language, gesturing as he did so.

One of the warriors, a man with a jagged scar on his left cheek, a scar which he had accentuated with bandings of red and white war paint, grinned and nodded. The others grunted their approval.

Gray Buffalo ordered Chastity to dress herself and go with Crooked Knife, who now stepped forward. He placed a hand on either side of her face, and clumsily kissed her on the mouth. Startled, Chastity screamed and tried to pull away while the Pawnee warriors laughed and slapped their hands against their thighs. Crooked Knife grabbed her by the hair, drew her to him, and slapped her hard across the breasts.

"He is your husband now, and you must do as he wishes," Gray Buffalo barked. "Put on your clothing

41

and go with him. He will do no more to you than is
done to all Pawnee women. I cannot protect you anymore. If you do not do as he wishes, then he will kill
you, for that is his right."

Gray Buffalo turned abruptly and stalked toward
the other warriors, who moved aside to let him pass.

Her face flaming with outrage and shame,
Chastity quickly pulled on her clothing. Her new husband yanked her forward impatiently, and began leading her away from the others, toward the buffalo robe
he had spread on the ground. She bit her tongue and
stumbled along silently.

As he flung her down on the robe, the last of her
reserve slipped away, and Chastity cried out a long
wail. She began to sob hysterically. Her body shuddered and she gasped for breath.

Crooked Knife knelt over her, tearing at his
breechcloth. Then his huge, strong hands were at her
clothing. She kicked and fought silently and frantically.

"Yellowhair!" Crooked Knife growled. "You
stop!"

Then he struck her, hard, and little lights blazed
in her eyes.

She spit out the words, "Bastard! Bastard!"

The warrior brought his fist down again and
again, and she lapsed into half-consciousness. She
dimly realized her breeches were being pulled off and
her legs spread. Crooked Knife was speaking to her,
his voice low and less harsh now, his tone almost plead-
ing. She sensed weakness and, with all her remaining
strength, she jerked her knee upward. She caught her
Pawnee husband in the abdomen. He grunted heavily

and tumbled backward. Chastity tried desperately to get to her feet, but a crushing blow came down across her ear, and she flopped forward onto the ground. Her mouth was open, and she tasted blood from where her teeth had gouged into her lip. As she tried to regain her breath, she could also taste dry grass and dirt.

She was gasping now and her body was convulsed with sobs. She was only half aware that she was being rolled over, that her legs were once more being drawn apart.

The Pawnee was thrusting forward into her, and a tearing, stinging sensation pierced her loins. She tried to move, but Crooked Knife's weight was upon her. He was driving into her, kissing and biting at her face with each stroke. She sucked at the air, breathed raggedly, and tried once more to twist away.

"Damn Yellowhair!" Crooked Knife hissed. His voice droned on in a babble of words she could not comprehend until there was just one long sound, rising and falling, the cadence of the syllables spilling over her face and into her eyes and hair.

She was losing consciousness. And she knew there was no longer any reason to attempt resistance.

Defloration. . . .

She could see the word floating in the darkness before her, in the darkness, off beyond Crooked Knife somewhere. The letters were irregularly formed and pulsing with a faint blue light, drifting apart, coming together once more until they coalesced into a single point of blue light that flared out and then vanished.

Her very body seemed to melt, to disintegrate, to drift away from her. There was neither pain nor pleasure, but a raw, unreal numbness. She uttered a long wail in a voice that had no resemblance to her own, and then the darkness began to spin wildly and she was drawn down.

When Chastity awoke, the thin gray light of predawn was in the air. The nearly blue-black cliffs at the upper end of the box canyon were etched irregularly across the silver gray. Crooked Knife was kneeling beside her, looking down at her. His expression suggested both wonder and perhaps even concern. He spoke to her in Pawnee, and she nodded, even though she understood nothing of what he said. He pushed some strips of dried meat at her and gestured toward her little mare, now idly nuzzling some shoots of young willow. Chastity rose, pulled her clothing about her, and thrust the gamy dried meat into her mouth.

"Squaw make water," Crooked Knife ordered, pointing to the nearby clump of cottonwood. "Then we move."

Chastity did as her new husband commanded, then returned and stood waiting. Gray Buffalo and the others were already astride their ponies. Crooked Knife gestured with both hands, forming the sign for riding, and Chastity mounted the pinto.

Her husband beside her, Chastity rode forward, following the other warriors in the direction Gray Buffalo led, down out of the box canyon and then away toward the south.

The sun had begun to rim the low range to the east, emerging from behind the mountain like a small, intense globe of molten metal, as though the mountain itself were burning out from its core.

"You have made your escape," whispered a voice inside her. "You will never go to Salt Lake. . . ."

She was an Indian now, the wife of a Pawnee warrior. She would live this life, she would learn the ways of these savage people. If they came to accept her, if she could learn their language and become one of them, then they would not watch her so closely. One day her opportunity would present itself, and she would ride away from them, would find her way to some white settlement, to some people who would be willing to help her.

St. Louis, she thought. Yes, and then passage on a riverboat, up the Ohio or down to New Orleans. . . .

She rode silently, glancing over at the impassive face of Crooked Knife.

The morning air was full of strange smells, smells that she had detected before but which she had never really paid any attention to, and the sound of running water seemed louder than she could ever remember. Two jackrabbits bounded away before them, leaping in long zigzag patterns through the sage. On the low ridge ahead, she saw a group of pronghorn antelope warily observing their passage, ears forward, their heads moving slowly back and forth.

This is part of my fate, Chastity thought. This is part of an amazing destiny that awaits me.

She drew comfort from the idea. In the meanwhile, she was determined to do whatever she had to to survive. Benton had told her much about the ways of the Indians, and though he had spoken mostly of the

Crow, she concluded that the ways of the various tribes could not be completely different. She would become one of them, would cause them to accept her, for in that course of action lay the possibility of her eventual escape.

I can do it, she thought. It won't be so bad. . . .

Chapter 3

"Pawnee," Benton drawled once he had examined the arrow that a herd boy had removed from the hip of a resisting Ayrshire. "Ye see the way they notch the end of the shaft? It's Pawnee, for sure. A bunch of damned renegades, likely."

"Slaughter the animal," Brigham Young said brusquely to one of the younger men who seemed invariably to follow him about.

"Hell, Young, it's only a scratch. Bossy'll make it over the pass and down to your patch of desert. Ye've brought her this far, she'll make it the rest of the way."

Young shook his head and repeated the order. The young men led the cow away to a spot closer to the wagon train, a place more convenient for butchering.

At that moment, Samuel Cosgrove and Elder

Tommasen rode up and dismounted clumsily. Benton spat on the ground and shook his head. It would take more years than those two had, Benton reflected, for them to learn how to ride a horse in proper fashion. Right now they wanted assurance that Chastity was all right, that he had found her. But it wasn't the case. Benton and a group of young saints had searched along the river for three or four miles back. As they were returning, Benton had discovered hoofprints at the place where Cozzie had ridden from the cover along the edge of the river, right into the path of the Pawnee. With several hours' head start, there'd be no catching them, even if he went alone. Charbonneau wasn't as young or as agile as she'd once been, and even if he did manage to catch up with the thieves, what then? They were renegades or young warriors out looking for trouble. If they would kidnap a white gal from a wagon train, they weren't likely to listen to reason.

But he had followed them for several miles before turning back, and he had a good idea of where they might be heading. While following their trail, he had dreaded at every clump of cottonwood or willow what he might find. If it had been just mischief the Pawnee were into, they'd all have raped Cozzie and taken her scalp. And they wouldn't have wasted too much time doing it, either.

Either they figured to sell her back to the whites, or else she would end up a wife to one of the braves. Whichever it was, they would eventually wind up at a winter encampment, South Platte or Arkansas country, maybe even down on the Purgatoire River. There might be a way of getting Cozzie back, but Benton knew that he was going to need help to do it.

He thought first of Yellow Belly and Pine Leaf and his own son, Big Dog. A Crow war party could be gathered with enough guns to make it look respectable. The Pawnee owed Big Dog a debt. A small group, with Big Dog at the head, would be able to ride straight into the Pawnee camp and demand to see White Bear and Antoine Behele. It just might work, and Benton was convinced that nothing else would—not even if the federal government brought in five hundred bluecoats. If the Pawnee chose to fight, they could handle the bluecoats, and they knew it. If they didn't choose to fight, they would just disappear back up into the mountains and maybe they'd leave Cozzie's body behind them, stuck full of arrows.

"Aloysius, we pay you to keep this sort of thing from happening," Cosgrove said ponderously, his heavy jowls as red as if he were a man given to drink. Benton wondered if Cosgrove might not just have a secret stash hidden away in his wagon. Or perhaps it was just that the man's native pomposity produced the effect.

"Well, now," Benton responded, "Old Brigham here done sent me ahead to check over the trail up to the pass. Couldn't be in both places at once, now could I? Even a white man can figger that out."

"Damn it, man, we have to find her," Tommasen exclaimed.

"Elder Tommasen," Young interrupted, "this is hardly a time for profanity. What we need is clear thinking and a few prayers. If it comes to finding someone to blame, gentlemen, I shouldn't have to remind you that each man among us is responsible for looking out for his own. You, Samuel Cosgrove, should never have allowed the girl to ride off from the others. Our strength resides in the group as a whole, and nothing illustrates this necessary concept more dramatically than what has happened. Elder, as one who intends to marry the Cosgrove girl, your responsibility in the matter is also great. A man is required to husband the people and things he values, even as he must pray for them all and for the success of our undertaking."

"Question is," Benton asked, "what's to be done? You boys want me to track 'em down into Colorado? Cause that's where they be going, sure as buffler chips."

Young's eyes narrowed, and he glared at the mountain man. He thought about chastizing Benton for his language, as he had many times before, all to no avail. The man was a fine scout, whether he would eventually be one of the damned or not.

Benton coughed, spat again, and squinting one eye, returned Young's stare.

"Brigham, ye be lookin' more like one of them Old Testament patriarchs all the time, especially since ye've growed that beard. Damn me, it do look good on ye!"

"Aloysius," Young remonstrated, "you need religion as much as any man I've ever met. You may be one of the devil's own, but you've done us good service. Do you believe the girl's still alive?"

"I figger so, Reverend."

Young smiled. Benton was Benton, and there was no changing the fact.

"I say that something must be done," Tommasen sputtered.

"Benton can lead us," Cosgrove added. "We'll track the heathens down and offer them presents—reason with them."

"Just what this coon don't need," Benton answered. "Might be I can find her, but not if I'm nurse-maidin' a bunch of ye along at the same time. If I go, I go alone."

"What are the chances, Aloysius?" Young asked.

"Don't know, Reverend, but this old hoss'll do his flat best. Truth to say, I liked Cozzie better than any of the rest of ye, if you don't mind my sayin' so."

"If you hadn't encouraged her in her rebellion, Benton," Cosgrove said coldly, "none of this would have happened."

"Ye can't keep lightning in a bottle, Cosgrove. Now if you boys want me to take off after Cozzie, then let's stop yammerin', and I'll be headin' out."

"What about the trail ahead, Benton? How do you propose that we find our way to the Salt Lake?" Tommasen asked.

"Brigham knows the way, don't ye, Reverend? This is your third time across, and ye didn't have me along the other two. We're less than a hundred mile from South Pass, and from there it's another seventy, eighty, to Bridger's Fort. Just follow the wagon ruts, an' ye can't miss 'er. Tell Gabe Bridger I'll be along later. One way or another, I'm goin' after Cozzie."

"A reasonable solution," Young agreed. "I know

51

the trail well enough. Whatever happens, Aloysius, come to Salt Lake City. We must know what's happened."

"I'll be there, for sure. You folks owe me my wages and I aim to collect 'em."

"Benton," Tommasen said, "you've got— what?—two hundred and fifty dollars coming in wages. I will personally add a thousand if you can bring my fiancée back unharmed."

"I'd bring 'er back a lot quicker if I didn't know that Cozzie was plannin' on marryin' ye. But I take it I've got your word on the thousand?"

Tommasen nodded, though Benton wondered if the man had spoken without reflecting on the large reward. But Benton thrust out his hand, and the two men shook on the bargain.

"Young, you and Cosgrove be witnesses?"

"We are his witnesses," Brigham Young said. "The bargain is fairly joined, and you know that a good Mormon man always keeps his word. The word, once given, is our common law."

"Then I'll see you boys over on the Big Salty. Reverend, just keep followin' the crick until ye get up to South Pass. Don't get turned around and head off up into Canada. I'll be wantin' my wages after a spell."

"Good luck to you, Aloysius Benton," Young said, extending his hand also.

"You're all right, Reverend," Benton replied. "Mebbe these damned fools will even survive, as long as they've got ye to lead 'em."

The mountain man swung up onto Charbonneau. The mare shook her head and bit perfunctorily at the air. Benton snapped the reins across her neck, and rode slowly toward one of the supply wagons. He took what he needed, laying in a fresh supply of powder and supplies, which he loaded onto a pack horse. Working quickly, he cinched the bundles in place, and with the pack horse trailing behind Charbonneau, headed out southeastward from the Sweetwater.

Once beyond sight of the Mormon train, however, he drew Charbonneau about and rode toward Independence Rock to the north. There he would cross the Sweetwater and continue on up into the Rattlesnake Hills and the headwaters of the south fork of the Powder River.

To the west the sun was setting, its orange-red globe oddly distended, elliptical, flooding the sky with a luminous crimson glow. The twilight faded slowly, and the shadows rose up from the earth as Benton urged Charbonneau and the pack horse across the river and along a shallow ravine on the north bank. The moon, just past the full, would be up soon, but the old trapper continued to ride. Perhaps it was folly to keep going after dark. The terrain was growing steep and jagged, and there was always the danger of a horse breaking a leg or pitching its rider down a canyon side. But Cozzie was somewhere with the Pawnee, far away to the south by now, and the Indians would likely already have drawn in for the night.

Might be rapin' an' butcherin' her right now, Benton thought.

If so, there was no cure for it. Enough years in the mountains, and a man learned to accept death. Yet when it came, it was always so sudden and unexpected—a rockslide ripping loose from above, a rattlesnake coiled in the grass by a spring, even something like the smallpox that carried away whole tribes. Its presence was never easy to bear. It was the way of things, the whims of Coyote, the Creator.

This time, however, it was hard to be philosophical. Cozzie had become almost a daughter to him during the long trek upcountry. It was her presence that had made the whole business of taking down meat for a crowd of God-crazy settlers something that had been at least tolerable. And now Cozzie was gone, taken off by the goddamned Pawnees.

In his imagination, Benton heard the girl's screams. He felt the knife being drawn across her throat. He could see a Pawnee warrior holding up the bloodied mat of yellow hair.

Benton leaned forward and pressed his forehead against Charbonneau's mane. The mare fluttered air out through her lips. The scout's stomach knotted, and tears streamed down his weathered face and into his beard.

By the time the pale oval of the moon rimmed the high rocks to the east, Benton had composed himself. He was breathing in deeply, almost panting. Even the mare, sensing something amiss, was uneasy as she moved slowly forward, up the little canyon.

"Damn ye!" Benton hissed at the night. "There wasn't no need for it, no need at all. You hear me, Old Man Coyote? You listen to this old trapper now. If ye haven't already let 'em put her under, you keep her safe until I can get to Big Dog. Somehow or other, the two of us'll pull her out. Ye don't need to eat everything, Song Dog. Ye just don't."

At length he came to a small meadow where cottonwood and aspen grew thick along a trickling stream. Benton dismounted, turned the two horses to graze, unrolled his robes and built a small fire. He brewed a mixture of willow-bark tea and coffee, half-cooked a chunk of venison and ate.

His stomach full, he fell asleep hunched over beside the fire. The moon had risen to the meridian before Benton became aware of the chill. He awoke, rose to relieve himself, and then slipped in under his buffalo robes. He heard the long wail of a wolf somewhere back down the canyon. Then he slept soundly until the thin gray of false dawn had come.

When he awoke, refreshed after a few hours of slumber, Benton knew, without knowing why he knew, that Cozzie was still alive. He splashed cold water on his face, chewed a few mouthfuls of cold deer meat, and called to Charbonneau.

"Come on, ye damned old mule, we got a long way to ride today! You'll be wishin' ye was a vulture bird before this journey's over, I'll guarantee it."

Benton worked his way up onto the back of the Rattlesnake Hills. The domes and crags of weathered sandstone, cream-colored to brown-black, thrust upward from the sparse vegetation. Pinnacles and columns rose like the vast ruin of some ancient civilization, the rock formations slowly carved by wind and rain and periods of time so vast that he could not even begin to comprehend them. Here in the Gardens, as the mountain men called them, the mud and sandstones towered about him in a thousand configurations, desolate, lonely, inhuman—and safe. For no one but a damned fool like himself would cross over the range, neither redman nor Long Knife. It was a land of bad medicine for the Indians and a place of little interest to the whites because nothing was there. It had not always been this way, Benton considered, for long ago some vanished tribe of Indians had carved pictures on the sandstone towers. The stone images were barely discernible now as the process, whatever it was, that had created the columns continued its work of wearing them away.

Benton pulled up at the crest of the range and looked northward across the sprawl of hill and canyon and basin. Beyond and below lay the headwaters of the south fork of the Powder, the white-dust river. North of the Powder was the Bighorn River, and somewhere beyond that, perhaps at the confluence with the Shoshone, he would find the great encampment of the Crow. With his son Big Dog he would head south once again, trekking back to the Arkansas or the Purgatoire or wherever the Pawnee were. It was a long shot indeed, but no other course of action promised even the slightest hope of success.

If only the red devils haven't cut her up, then there's a chance, Benton thought. Cozzie, damn your rambunctious nature, anyhow! I don't suppose ye'll ever act like a normal white woman. It's safer to stick with your own and do what they want ye to. Buffler chips! It's my fault, most of it, if I hadn't encouraged ye, if I hadn't of stuck that wanderin' bug in your head. . . .

As Benton gazed down across the tumbled rocks of the Rattlesnake Hills, the old vision came to him once more—the vast extent of land from the Great Falls of the Missouri in the north to the Rio Grande and the Pecos southward. The great Tetons and Colter's Hell, the Seedskeedee River winding down into its unbelievable canyons. The Black Hills and the Sandhills, the Platte and the Republican rivers. One could sometimes hear great herds of buffalo deep down in the earth—the underground buffalo the Crow called it. . . . He could see it all, and he knew it all.

But now he could see the wagon trains moving westward. He could see the frontier creeping up the rivers, the white settlements being established. He could see the Indian people driven west of the Mississippi a dozen years earlier, the Trail of Tears.

There was apparently no stopping this tide of white migration, and he himself had become accomplice to it. What business had these God-crazy Mormons in the Salt Lake Basin? But that was only part of it—the goddamned United States was intent on having it all, farms and cities and settlements clear to the Pacific. There lay California and Oregon, the final westward limit, lands Benton himself had never set foot upon, lands that he still wanted to see for himself—the high spine of the Sierra Nevada, the white peaks of the Cascades, a couple of them still smoking and fuming, and the valleys of the Sacramento and the Willamette, the Columbia, the great river of the West, ten miles across where it hit the ocean, or so he'd been told.

If Ephraim the grizzly didn't get him, and if he could keep Blackfoot knives away from what was left of his topknot, he still had a few more years. He closed his eyes, shook his head and clucked his tongue.

"It'll last that long, anyhow," Benton told Charbonneau. "Ye won't be with me, old mule, 'cause bad-natured horses don't live that long, and you've just about run out your string. But I'll be followin' ye after a space, that's sure now, an' I guess if the Big Spirit don't have no better horse for me in the world beyond, I'll take ye back. But first we got to find Big Dog and then we got to find Cozzie—so let's get our old bones movin'. Long trail ahead of us, Charbonneau."

The mare lay her ears back, tossed her head and snorted.

"I said move, *damn* your eyes!"

Since there was no cure for it, Charbonneau obeyed.

And so the days drifted by. The two animals and the man continued northward to the Powder, downstream to Hell's Half Acre, a miniature badlands of wind-carved towers and caverns and spires of bright-colored shale and sandstone. Then on they journeyed into Crow country along the Bighorn. Perhaps another three days of riding lay between him and the Many Lodges, but he felt suddenly at home. He was back with his beloved Crow, and as he prepared camp by a small stream, he couldn't imagine why he had ever wanted to be anywhere else.

"Coon's got to make a livin', I guess," he told Charbonneau and turned her out to grass. He stood his ancient Hawken next to a scrub cedar, checked the load in his Texas Paterson, and thrust the pistol back into his improvised holster. Then he built a larger campfire than he had allowed himself since heading north from the Sweetwater. Benton set a quarter leg of deer to roasting—the animal had conveniently presented itself that afternoon—and then strolled over to a blackberry tangle. A good many of the berries were black-ripe and glistening in the waning light of sundown. Benton picked a few handfuls into his beaver, whistling to himself as he did so. Returning to the roasting chunk of meat, he boiled up a pot of his coffee and willow-bark mixture, and ate. He had intended to save a portion of the meat for the following day, but his hunger got the better of him.

Times be, he thought, when fresh venison tastes damned near as good as hump rib, and tonight's one of 'em.

After his meal, he stared into the flames of his campfire for a time and then rolled into his robes, his hand on the butt of the Texas Paterson. Off across the Bighorn, several coyotes were yapping and wailing. And up the draw a horned owl was hooting, a lonely cry, Benton thought: *whoo-whoo, whoo-whoo-whoo.*

"Hello, critters," the mountain man called out. "It's good to be back with ye, even if I can't stay for long."

He slept deeply, and he dreamed. He was back with Sweetgrass once more, warm inside their lodge. Outside a winter storm howled down from the mountains, but inside the cooking fire blazed brightly, and a large pot of elk stew was brewing. Big Dog, still a boy, sat on a pack of beaver skins and rubbed bear grease into the wood of his new bow. Benton spoke, first to his wife, and then to his son. But neither answered. Sweetgrass and Big Dog continued what they were doing, as if oblivious to his presence. . . .

Awaking with the first light, he reheated the cold coffee and drank it in gulps. He whistled to Charbonneau, and the mare trotted to him, the pack horse following behind. Steam rose in filaments from their mouths. Benton noticed a faint touch of frost on the grass and knew that the season was beginning to turn.

They were down on the Bighorn again when Benton sensed before he heard the approaching horses. He drew back under the cover of some junipers and watched intently. It was horses all right, four or five hundred of them being driven along, and in no great hurry, either. That only meant one thing.

"Crow," Benton laughed. "Just like they come to greet me. . . ."

He trotted down from his cover, drew Charbonneau to a halt and waited. He could see the riders now, all of them on Nez Perce mounts, the most highly prized ponies, for the Nez Perce were known to breed the finest horses. One warrior sat taller than the others, and one was a woman, her owl-feathered lance gripped firmly in her left hand. Benton drew his Paterson and fired off a single shot. The Crow answered in kind, and within moments the Dog Soldiers were milling about him.

"Perhaps Benton has come to help us drive these Cheyenne horses home," Pine Leaf said. "Your son has struck coup again and has many animals. I think he will let you have your choice."

Beautiful, Benton thought as he nodded to Warrior Woman. She was tall for a woman, lithe, quick as a panther, fierce, and with the air of boundless energy and cunning. She was worthy of her great reputation as leader of the Dog Soldiers. In her thirties now, Pine Leaf was seemingly oblivious to the passing of time. Other women might grow heavy and matronly, but not Pine Leaf—not, certainly, until the time when her revenge was complete—a revenge she had vowed years earlier, after the death of her twin brother. The story was well-known to all, and all agreed that her medicine for battle was unexcelled.

How many Blackfoot, Cheyenne and Assiniboin warriors dreamed of taking her scalp, but always the issue went the other way. Ten or eleven years earlier, Pine Leaf had been wife to Medicine Calf, the black fur trapper Jim Beckwourth, legendary war chief of the Mountain Crow. Medicine Calf had left his adopted people and was now, if rumor could be believed, in California. Pine Leaf had declined to take a second husband, always insisting that Medicine Calf would one day return. And in the ten years or more since Medicine Calf's departure, Pine Leaf had far exceeded the number of scalps she had sworn to take and had gone on to become the leader of the Dog Soldiers and a high counselor to Yellow Belly, head chief of the Mountain Crow.

Big Dog now drew up alongside his father, and the two men embraced warmly.

"I thought the Killer of Beavers was showing the crazy people how to get to Salt Lake," he said. "What are you doing here, Father?"

"A little trouble, a little trouble," Benton answered.

"He has come to ask Big Dog to show him the way," Pine Leaf laughed. "He has grown so old that he has forgotten."

"Naw, this coon ain't forgot nothing. We had a run-in with some Pawnee, is all. I could've scalped the lot of 'em, but I figured Pine Leaf and Big Dog would say I'd been selfish. So I come to get ye to share with me."

"What difference does it make if the Pawnee kill a few of the crazy Long Knives?" Big Dog asked. His eyes gleamed with the prospect of what he already suspected would be a war party with his father. "Are their numbers not without end, as you have always told me? More and more of them are crossing the mountains all the time."

"We should join these Pawnee," Pine Leaf added. "We should convince all of our enemies to join with us so that we might drive the whites out of our lands. What good is it to us that we are friendly to the whites? Soon they will wish us to stay in one place and never go on the warpath again."

Two-tail Skunk had now ridden up, and he too embraced Benton. Two-tail Skunk, about Benton's own height but much heavier through the arms and chest, and extremely strong, was Big Dog's blood brother. Hence, in the way these things went, he was also Benton's son.

"Our father has returned to us," Two-tail Skunk grinned. "Now he will want us to put steel traps into the streams again, as in the old days, and we will all have to get our feet wet in the cold water of winter. I

am glad to see you, Aloysius Benton the Beaver
Killer."

"I was just telling Pine Leaf and Big Dog," Benton answered, "some Pawnee came down on the wagon
train I was working with, and they kidnapped the prettiest yellow-haired gal you've ever seen. I figger they've
taken her off to their big encampment, maybe down on
the Arkansas—Behele and his Loups. So I came back
to the Crow to get up a war party. I thought maybe a
few of ye might like to ride with the old man."

"Big Dog has medicine with the Pawnee," Pine
Leaf reminded him. "You must go with your father,
Big Dog. Two-tail Skunk must also go. How many
warriors do you need, Benton? We would all ride with
you, but we must take these horses to the Many
Lodges and the Kicked-in-their-Bellies, for our pastures are so thick with grass that we can hardly see
our lodges anymore. These Cheyenne horses will help
to eat the grass."

"The Pawnee will let me ride into their encampment," Big Dog said. "White Bear owes me a debt,
and Antoine Behele has given his word. Father, how
do you know the Pawnee have not killed the girl?"

"Once ye take a look at her, you'll know why
they ain't going to kill her. She's the prettiest varmint
ye ever saw, my son."

"Killer of Beavers wishes to take a new wife?"
Pine Leaf asked, smiling.

"No, it ain't that way at all. We took a liking to
each other, that's true. But she's not much more than
twenty winters, and I'm an old man."

"Twenty winters would be good for you, Father,"

Two-tail Skunk replied. "When a man grows older, he needs a young wife. Or maybe you wish to give this one to Big Dog, for he has never wanted to marry. I must always make my wives go to sleep with him, even though they hate it. Big Dog should have the yellow-haired one for a wife. Is this what you have in mind, Father?"

"I want no white woman for a wife," Big Dog said. "Benton is my father, and I am his son, but my blood is Sparrow Hawk. When I take a wife, she must be one who is of my own blood."

"When we capture women from the Cheyenne or Blackfoot, they become Sparrow Hawk Crow. As the generations go by, how do we know whose blood is all Sparrow Hawk and whose is not?" Pine Leaf asked. "Perhaps your blood is not all Sparrow Hawk even now, Big Dog, and perhaps mine is not either. And yet we are both wholly Sparrow Hawks, for the Sparrow Hawks are our people. Killer of Beavers is also a Sparrow Hawk, for he has lived among us for a long time, and we are his people. Big Dog does not wish to have a wife. Maybe he prefers to meet with the young women out among the willows but still keep his own lodge. This way the rest of us invite him to eat with us, and all he must do is hunt with the other warriors. Some do not wish to be married. I was not married for a long while, even though I loved Medicine Calf, and he kept asking me to be his wife."

"Yellow Belly also wanted you to be his wife," Big Dog said. "It is so even now. This is something we all know."

"I will wait for Medicine Calf to return. But now

we must decide what to do. Benton, what is it that you want?"

"I've got to go to the Pawnee an' buy the Yellowhair from 'em," Benton replied, "an' then get her back to her people. She's promised to marry one of 'em. This gal, Chastity Cosgrove, is a friend of mine, an' I don't want 'er to stay with the Pawnee against 'er will. I've promised the leader of the Mormon people that I'd try to bring the gal to the Big Salt Lake, where they've made their settlement, in the lands of the Ute. They'll pay me for what I've said I'd do. Then I'll give gifts to my sons Big Dog and Two-tail Skunk, if they're willin' to ride with me."

"We will ride with our father, Pine Leaf. Is that what you wish us to do?"

"It is what I wish," Pine Leaf answered. "If you have not returned to us by the time of falling leaves, then I will lead a war party against the Pawnee. You must tell them this when you meet with them. They will know that Pine Leaf means what she says. Then they will sell Benton the Yellowhair. But will she not run away from the Pawnee if she does not want to stay with them? Our women usually come back when they have been stolen by our enemies."

"Perhaps a white woman is too weak to do such a thing," Big Dog said.

"Even the Pawnee are better than the Long Knives," Two-tail Skunk laughed. "Charbonneau looks tired, Father," the young warrior added. "Do you wish to take a different horse with you? Pine Leaf will take care of your old mare until we return."

"Son," Benton grinned, "ye never did understand

65

about this horse. Old Charbonneau can still outrun any of your fancy spotted critters. Now if this thing's settled, let's head south. Pine Leaf, this coon thanks ye."

"You must tell my three wives that I will be back soon," Two-tail Skunk said, turning to Pine Leaf, "for otherwise they will begin to cry and pull out their hair and cut off their fingers."

"I will tell them . . . that they must seek consolation with the younger men," Pine Leaf replied, her dark eyes sparkling with mischief.

"We will return before the time of snowfall," Big Dog said. "And my father will have many gifts from the Long Knives. Then Two-tail Skunk and I will ride with Pine Leaf against the Blackfoot. We will harvest their horses and their scalps, for they have too many of both."

Chapter 4

Working with his father, Big Dog Benton, the tall
Crow warrior, had gained a reputation as trapper,
tracker and fighter in competition with the best of the
mountain men. At the final rendezvous, organized by
the Scotsman Stewart and Gabe Bridger for the summer of '43, Big Dog had gotten into an argument with
the notorious Tom Fallon. The argument had quickly
resolved itself into a matter of honor when Fallon
drew his Green River and offered to take Big Dog's
scalp. The two had circled each other while the gang of
drunken trappers screamed encouragement. Fallon's
blade came down across Big Dog's shoulder, and in
that moment the Crow's knife spun away into the
darkness. Fallon laughed and moved in for the kill. But
as he leaped forward, Big Dog miraculously grasped
his opponent's arm with both hands and brought it
down over his knee, snapping the arm midway between

wrist and elbow. In almost the same motion, Big Dog seized the fallen knife and ripped it up the length of Fallon's torso, completely disemboweling him. Yet another swift thrust, and the blade was plunged into Fallon's throat. Big Dog, himself bleeding profusely, calmly proceeded to take Fallon's scalp. He shouted the *hoo-ki-hi,* the war cry of his people, and flung the bloody scalp into the midst of the stunned mountain men. With blood streaming down his slashed leather shirt, Big Dog stood within the circle of mountain men and demanded the return of his own knife.

The weapon was returned within a matter of moments.

Aloysius Benton, who had stoically watched the entire proceeding, rushed forward to assist his son. Grinning broadly, Big Dog asked, "Father, can you sew me back together?"

The Bentons, father and son. They were known and respected throughout the mountains during the years they trapped together. When Big Dog returned to his people, Aloysius hired on with the wagon train. But the old scout always turned back when the settlers reached the point where the trails to Oregon and California branched off.

Now they were together again, and Benton's other "son," the redoubtable Two-tail Skunk, was with them. And they were moving south, the three of them, on a venture which, though lightly entered into, could well prove fatal for the two Crow warriors and the white mountain man. What could three men hope to accomplish by riding into the very teeth of the Pawnee power and demanding the return of a white girl? If Chastity were dead, the Pawnee would disclaim all knowledge of her. If she were alive and married to one of the warriors, she would be hidden away, with knowledge of her presence equally disclaimed.

Perhaps the Pawnee would indeed honor their word to Big Dog. But one who came to claim the wife of another would surely be seen as an enemy. There was also the highly unpredictable nature of the Pawnee, who might see betrayal of a trust in this demand for the return of the white girl. Then the three men would be turned coldly away and followed by a war party and killed. Even the promise of an attack by Pine Leaf and the Dog Soldiers would be mocked with ridicule. What might possibly happen at a future time as a consequence of some present action would carry no weight whatsoever.

But now that Benton and Big Dog and Two-tail Skunk were together once more, together and going somewhere, their spirits were extremely high. Danger was the wine they all loved, the wine they were addicted to.

The three rode steadily southward, Big Dog leading, and the pack horse trailing behind. They followed the Bighorn upstream to where it was known as the Wind River. Then, when the river swung westward, coming down from the Absaroka Range on one side and the Wind River Range on the other, the men crossed over to the Sweetwater, thirty miles from South Pass. Here, from a low rise, they watched a wagon train toiling slowly toward the pass, not Mormons this time, but a sturdy band of settlers bound for Oregon country, their Conestoga wagons drawn by oxen or huge Lancaster horses.

"Son," Benton said to Big Dog, "they's likely one of our old pals guidin' 'em. Maybe we should drift down and talk for a spell, see if they've got some decent tobacco with 'em."

"No," Big Dog answered. "Let them pass by, Father. We still have far to go, and the settlers would wish you to repair axles and harnesses for them. Or else they would see only that we are Indians and would decide to fire on us as we ride up."

"Perhaps they would give us presents?" Two-tail Skunk suggested. "The Long Knives know how much we like presents, and so they always bring something for us."

"The presents might be made of lead, my brother. Let us continue on this strange warpath of ours. Father, what do you think?"

"Figger you're right, I guess. It's sixty, seventy miles across the Great Divide Basin and another thirty over the Red Desert. Guess we'd best keep ridin'."

"Killer of Beavers is old and no longer wishes to receive presents," Two-tail Skunk complained.

"What would you do with these presents if you got them?" Big Dog asked.

"I would buy my brother a wife. It is not good for a warrior to sleep in an empty lodge, for then he is always having troubles beneath his breechcloth."

Benton chuckled as Big Dog scowled at his blood brother and urged his spotted pony forward.

The days drifted by and the three men rode from dawn until dusk. They crossed over the back of the mountains at Buffalo Pass and thence to the head-waters of the Laramie and down into the drainage of the South Platte. There was heavy frost at nights now as they moved southward along the foot of the Front Ranges, keeping well away from the Arapaho and Cheyenne villages and maintaining their distance from the occasional outpost of Long Knives.

It had crossed Benton's mind to enlist the as-sistance of a troop of bluecoats. But Big Dog had dis-suaded him, arguing that the bluecoats did not understand the mind of the Indian and could not be trusted to act reasonably in any case. One foolish as-sertion of military authority, and a small band of sol-diers and three Crow warriors could well end up with their scalps hanging from the roof pole of a Pawnee lodge.

"Trouble with Injuns is they don't respect author-ity," Benton lamented.

"Trouble with Long Knives is they don't listen to what the coyotes are saying, Father. If we ride in alone, just three of us, the Pawnee will offer us hospi-tality. They will think we are crazy, and so they will be good to us. Or they will think our medicine must be very powerful, and so they will not wish to offend us. If we had bluecoats with us, the Pawnee might just kill us all. Pawnee are not rational people. We all know that."

The day after they had passed by Pike's Peak, the great mountain still streaked with white in mid-Septem-ber, and had continued on toward the Arkansas River, the first storm of the season dropped down over them. Heavy rains persisted all through the morning so that

71

the horses barely crawled through heavy mud. By late afternoon the temperature had begun to drop. Darkness came early, and with it a thin, wet snowfall.

They made camp for the night at the head of a draw and took cover beneath a matted growth of scrub cedar up against some boulders. In deference to the weather, they built a good-sized fire and huddled about it, their leather shirts and leggings steaming as they roasted portions of a buffalo calf they had killed earlier in the day.

"My wives are lonely for their husband," Two-tail Skunk lamented. "Even though I am many miles away from our lodge, I still seem to hear them moaning and crying for their lost husband. They are certain they will never see him again, for the Killer of Beavers has lured him away to a place where his medicine will no longer protect him from his enemies."

"Skunk has weak medicine," Big Dog suggested.

"My medicine is strong, but when it must be used to protect my brother and my father, then it is too thin—and so it is weak."

"Weak in the head," Big Dog retorted.

"Well, that's a wonderment," Benton laughed. "We're gettin' close now, so maybe we'd better get us some stronger medicine."

"You think the Pawnee are on the Arkansas, Father? Perhaps they have moved farther south."

"Way them varmints like to move around, there's no tellin'. Could be one place, could be the other."

"Two-tail Skunk is hungry," Skunk complained. "We must not cook this buffalo meat too much. It grows weak if it is cooked too much."

"True," Big Dog agreed. "Let's eat and sleep if we can. Perhaps a medicine dream will come to one of us this night."

The three men ate quickly and washed their meal down with Benton's coffee and powdered willow-bark mixture. Then Two-tail Skunk withdrew his pipe, filled the bowl with shreds of native tobacco, and proposed a smoke. Big Dog held out a flaming twig, and the pipe was passed around the little circle several times.

"It is good that we three are together once more," Big Dog said. "Father, I would like you to return to the Many Lodges to live. The life that Old Man Coyote has given us is much better than what the Long Knives have. That is why they are never satisfied and are always seeking for something else—that is why they cross the mountains in their wagons. The whites believe that things will be better for them in the lands of California and Oregon, but that will not happen. They carry all of their troubles with them. Those people do not know how to be free."

"Big Dog," Benton drawled, "I expect you're right. Mebbe it's time for this old trapper to settle down, back with our people. Guess I've never really been happy anywhere else, anyhow. Sure would like to see California with my own eyes first, though. Big valley between mountains, son, and from what I've heard, it don't even snow in the winters. The cricks never freeze, and big, green rivers come down out of the mountains. Ever since Jed Smith came back the first time, I've been wantin' to do 'er. Kit Carson, Joe Meek and all the others, they been out there. And Medicine Calf, that's where he is. If it wasn't good land, he'd of

come back by now, and ye can lay to it. It's somethin'
I've promised Charbonneau, and I've gotta keep my
word to the old beast. She don't have all that much
time left, and me neither, mebbe. Then it'll be time to
come home for good."

Two-tail Skunk scoffed. "Our father suffers from
the white blood."

Big Dog snorted and passed the pipe.

"I think I wouldn't mind seeing it myself," he
said. "It is good to see new places, but then one must
return to the land of the Crow. There are already too
many white men, Father. We have always been friends
to the whites, but if these people kill our buffalo and
fence our lands, it is possible that we may have to fight
them, even though they are as many as the small birds
that eat the seeds of the grasses. Old Man Coyote gave
us this land and we must protect it. We would not
want California, for what we already have is much better."

"I reckon it is at that," Benton agreed. "But I
don't want to live in California, I just want to see 'er."

"Perhaps we could go when the sun is high in the
sky and the grass grows tall," Two-tail Skunk said.
"Perhaps we could find Medicine Calf and tell him that
Pine Leaf and Little Wife and the others are sad for
his absence. Then he would return, and once again our
enemies would flee from us. I saw this chief only a few
times, when I was yet a young boy, but Pine Leaf says
that no warrior could stand up to him."

"First we must find this white girl," Big Dog said.
"Later we will worry about making a long venture. We
must dream this night and hope that our medicine

grows strong. Without the help of Old Man Coyote, we will never live to see the time of tall grass. . . ."

The fire had died down, and the three men rolled into their robes. Already the air was cold so that their breath went up in trickles of steam. Big Dog lay awake, listening to his father's snoring and Skunk's occasional gruntings. He stared up at the Star People, so many of them, scattered like fiery dust across the blackness of the night. A single wolf howled twice and then was silent, and from off in the brush came the sound of a deer suddenly taking fear and bolting through the darkness. Big Dog breathed in the cold night air and exhaled slowly, wondering about the white girl. Why was his father so concerned for her? Benton was not thinking of taking another wife, whether red or white. Perhaps it was simply as he said, then. The Yellowhair had become his friend. If this were the case, then the Yellowhair must indeed be an unusual young woman and not like other white women at all. Perhaps the Pawnee had seen this too, and that was why they had kidnapped her?

But why would Benton want to return the girl to the Long Knives—and receive money for doing so? Big Dog had never known his father to be particularly concerned with the white man's money. The money, then, was not important. Apparently Benton feared for Yellowhair's life. Perhaps what he actually wanted was to bring this girl to live among the Sparrow Hawks, but for what purpose?

He remembered his father's words, "Son, ye've got to take a wife someday or other. . . ."

Had Benton chosen this white woman to be a wife to his son?

Big Dog snorted and then breathed in again. It was a mystery, a *wonderment*, as Benton sometimes said. But the wonderment could only make itself clear after the Yellowhair had been rescued, if indeed she was not already dead.

He slept, and in his sleeping a dream came to him.

Rumblings stirred deep within the earth. Grandmother Earth was crying, moaning. Then the rocks split open, and a flow of red water welled upward in bubbling fountains that screamed and hissed in the haze-filled air. The waters rose higher, mounting into great waves, and rushed toward the mountains.

He drummed his heels against the sides of his horse, urging the animal toward high ground, but the waters were gaining, and they closed about him. An unseen force lifted him, carried him high into the air and held him, suspended. Far below he could see the tides of bloody water rushing westward, overtopping all but the highest peaks of the great mountains, spilling down beyond, bearing with them a debris of sand and rock and tree and bush. Buffalo struggled against the flood, and elk, wolves and antelope were swept along. He heard the screams of the engulfed animals. . . .

Then came the dog-headed god, Old Man Coyote, man-bodied, painted in jagged stripes of red and white and black, the quivering muzzle, the mysterious amber eyes, the pointed ears.

When the voice came, it sounded like thunder or

*wailing or howling. The words were not decipherable,
and yet he could understand them quite well.*

Big Dog Benton, do you hear me?

I hear you, Old Man Coyote.

*What I am showing you now is what will happen.
This tide of blood is the tide of the Long Knives. They
will wash over our lands, and our people will not be
able to resist. The buffalo and the wolves will indeed
vanish for a long time. But the future is yours, Big
Dog, for your sons and daughters will be both red and
white. Many generations will pass, but your seed will
survive, will survive even the times of the sun fires
which will spot the land and destroy all that these Long
Knives will build. You will look back from the Spirit
World, and you will see the buffalo return from out of
the earth, you will see the ice come and go again, you
will see the plains and the mountains grow quiet and
empty once more. . . .*

*How is it that my sons and daughters will be both
red and white?*

*You will come to love a woman who is not of
your kind. There is no way to change what will happen, Big Dog. You will see this thing clearly in the
time of new grass. We must be patient, we must let
the generations of mankind pass. Then I will complete
the dream that the Creator gave me long ago. You will
watch me finish this dream, Big Dog. You will watch
from the Spirit World, and your true mother and father
and Benton, your white father, and your woman and
your sons and daughters and their sons and daughters
will watch with you. . . .*

You are fading, you are growing dim.

77

I cannot stay with you, Big Dog. I can only tell you that. . . .

The vision was gone, and Big Dog found himself once again on the earth. The stars blazed down from the heavens, and far off a coyote howled. A moment later, an answering cry came, and the twin cries echoed back and forth through the canyons. . . .

When Big Dog awoke, Benton was kneeling beside the coals of the campfire from the preceding evening. Twists of dry grass spurted up into yellow flame, and Benton was holding his hands over them. Benton looked across at his son. "It's time to be ridin', I expect. Thought I'd warm up this buffler meat a little, boys. When a man gets old, cold buffler don't set good on the meat bag." He looked at the sky, and shouted, "It's a *shinin'* day."

"A good day to die," Two-tail Skunk muttered, rising from his robes.

"We will not die on this warpath," Big Dog said. "In my sleep I have seen Old Man Coyote. He has made my medicine strong enough for all of us. Let us eat and then go to find the Pawnee."

Two days later, Big Dog, Benton and Two-tail Skunk approached the great encampment of the Pawnee Loups, adjacent villages with a total population of perhaps two thousand souls. The lodges were arranged into two large circles, and the cooking fires were burning. Oddly enough, the three men encountered no lookouts and were able to approach to the crest of a low ridge some three hundred yards from the camp. They stood their horses for several minutes and gazed down at the Pawnee who milled about below

them. Big Dog watched a group of boys who had taken
cover behind a patch of young cottonwoods. Close by
were some drying poles from which chunks of buffalo
meat hung and which were presided over by several
women. Big Dog gestured to Benton and pointed. Two
of the boys were sneaking up on the women, obviously
intent upon stealing portions of the meat. The women
seemed oblivious, as though purposefully pretending ignorance of the whereabouts of the young thieves. Suddenly the boys dashed for the meat, grabbed off
sections, and retreated toward the cover of the cottonwoods, the three women in half-hearted pursuit.

"These Pawnee are almost human," Two-tail
Skunk observed. "Their young boys play the same
games that Crow children play."

As the camp dogs began to bark, the women
caught sight of the three strange riders. The men fired
their rifles into the air and rode slowly down to the encampment. When a cluster of Pawnee warriors ad-
vanced toward them, weapons in hand, Big Dog
signaled a halt.

"Pawnee!" he shouted in the language of the
Loups. "This is Big Dog the Sparrow Hawk. I have
come to talk with White Bear and Antoine Behele. My
father and my brother are with me. Tell my two friends
that I have come to see them and that I wish them to
show me their hospitality!"

"What is he saying to the Pawnee?" Two-tail
Skunk asked Benton.

"Says we're coming in. That we want to see Behele and White Bear. Skunk, you need to learn some
more lingo, this coon's thinkin'."

"Why? I have learned the language of the Long Knives and also the words of the Cheyenne. Is this not enough?"

"Not if ye want to know what the Pawnee is sayin', I expect."

The Pawnee halted, consulted with one another and dispatched a runner back to the villages. The remainder came forward, their weapons at the ready. Big Dog, Benton, and Skunk were escorted, somewhat suspiciously, into the encampment. They were presented to Behele, who emerged from his lodge, arms folded.

"Big Dog the Crow," Behele greeted him. "It is five winters since you have come among us. Who are these two?"

"I come with Aloysius Benton, my white father, and Two-tail Skunk, my blood brother. It is good to see you, Behele. We have brought presents for you and White Bear—lead and powder and also some arwerdenty from the Long Knives."

"That is good," Behele replied. "White Bear is not here—he is leading a war party against the Ute, for we knew that the Ute had too many horses. You and your friends will be guests in my lodge."

"I am glad for your hospitality, Antoine Behele."

"My bird tells me you did not come so far without a reason, Big Dog. Why have you come?"

Big Dog looked aside at Benton, who nodded, indicating that it would be well to get right to the issue.

"We have come to buy back the white girl your warriors stole a moon ago. Have we come to the right place?"

Behele hesitated before answering, and when he spoke, it was in English.

"She is here, but she is married to Crooked Knife, and he will not be willing to part with her. You have ridden a long way for nothing, Big Dog. But you must stay in my lodge until you are ready to leave. Remember that I am not the only Loup who knows the English tongue. It would not be wise to speak further. Come—tether your horses and enter into the lodge. My wives have a pot of buffalo tongues cooking. We must share food and smoke the pipe of friendship."

They ate the buffalo tongues, which were spiced with dried plums and shreds of blackroot. Benton solemnly praised the food, and Behele's second wife, who had prepared the meal, was pleased, even though she made no outward sign. Behele spoke of white encroachments into Indian lands. Even the buffalo herds, he said, were smaller than in years past. This, he concluded, was the work of the Long Knives—and specifically of the trade in buffalo robes, even though most of the kills were made by the Indian peoples. More animals were being slain than was needful, with much meat being wasted.

"When the starvin' times come, then," Benton allowed, "it'll be partly our own fault."

"No," Behele returned. "It is the fault of the whites. We would never kill so many animals if the white traders did not pay us for the hides. And what do we get? Whiskey that dulls our brains and takes away our will to resist what is happening."

"There are still many elk and antelope," Two-tail Skunk interjected. "If the buffalo are few, we will kill

81

more of the elk and antelope people. That way we will not be hungry during the times of snowfall."

"If the buffalo are gone," Big Dog said, "even the elk and the antelope and the deer will not be enough."

Behele passed the pipe to Benton and nodded.

"About the Yellowhair," Big Dog interrupted the silence. "She is here?"

"It is as I told you," Behele replied.

"She must be returned to her people, the crazy ones who build their city on the Big Salty."

"Crooked Knife is a proud warrior, Big Dog. He wants to keep this woman, and he will not sell her to you, no matter what price you offer."

"This ol' hoss says she's got to come with us," Benton said, "or big troubles are comin'."

Behele laughed.

"What could happen?" he asked. "The blue soldiers? If they were to move against us, they would be like helpless children. Their guns are good, but they do not know how to fight. My Pawnee would kill them all."

"I will challenge Crooked Knife," Big Dog said slowly, "for that is my right. I am a Sparrow Hawk war chief, and I have taken many coups and many scalps. This Crooked Knife will have to fight me. If I am killed, then my father and Two-tail Skunk must be allowed to leave the encampment unharmed. If I kill Crooked Knife, then the Yellowhair is mine, and I will give her to Benton so that he can return her to her people. You must tell Crooked Knife so that he can consult his medicine. If he does not wish to fight, then we will pay him a marriage price."

"It is your right to challenge," Behele agreed, "but if you do, and if you win, you know that you may never again enter the lodges of the Pawnee. Though you once gave White Bear his life, if you take the life of Crooked Knife, then the bond between you and my people is severed forever. When you leave our camp, my braves will follow you and track you down. I will not be able to stop them, nor would I attempt to. Four new scalps will be raised during the scalp dance, for there is no way that you will be able to leave our lands without my warriors overtaking you and killing you. These are my words, Big Dog of the Sparrow Hawk Crows."

"I have already made the challenge, and I cannot withdraw my words. My medicine spirit has heard what I have said."

Behele stared at Big Dog, then at Benton and Two-tail Skunk. He studied their eyes. Finally, he shrugged, rose and left the lodge.

"This coon figgers the fat's in the fire," Benton said. "Son, I'm the one that should have risked his topknot. This whole thing's my doin', not yours."

"They would not accept your challenge, Father. They would take our weapons and horses and set us off on foot. And," he added, with a trace of a smile, "Charbonneau would never be happy here. She is old, and they would kill her and eat her. I could not let that happen."

"I tried to dream of Grandmother Moon," Two-tail Skunk interrupted, "but no vision came."

"My medicine is strong," Big Dog replied. "I will

kill Crooked Knife and then we will try to outrun the Pawnee."

Behele returned and told the men what had been decided. "It will happen tomorrow," he said. "The Yellowhair does not wish to stay with our people any longer. She asked who was challenging Crooked Knife. When she heard you were here, Benton, she said she wished to go with you. Crooked Knife has agreed to the fight and has now gone out into the darkness to consult his medicine. It is done, and it will happen, just as I told you."

One of Behele's wives put down buffalo robes for the three men, and soon the lodge was dark. For a time, Big Dog was unable to sleep—not from fear but from anticipation of what the next day would bring. When at last he closed his eyes, he became aware of a noise outside the lodge. Supposing Crooked Knife had come to murder him in his sleep, Big Dog drew his knife and slipped to the closed flap of the opening.

He could hear nothing now, but he remained certain that someone stood just outside the tepee, waiting. He slipped carefully outside the lodge and dropped to his hands and knees. In the thin moonlight, the Pawnee encampment was a world of shadows, but he saw nothing. Slowly he circled the tepee.

A figure loomed nearby, facing away from him. Golden hair gleamed in the moonlight and he knew who it was. Rising cautiously from all fours, he slid his hand over the girl's mouth and held her in a viselike grip.

"Why are you here?" he whispered in English.

"Do not scream when I remove my hand, or I will kill you."

"I have come to speak with Benton," the girl said quietly, her voice utterly calm. "He is in the lodge, and I wish to speak to him."

"You are the one my father calls Cozzie?"

The girl stiffened in his grasp and was silent for a moment.

"Big Dog? Benton's son? Yes, I'm Cozzie. Where is Benton?"

"He sleeps, Yellowhair. You must return to the lodge of Crooked Knife, for he will kill you if he discovers that you have run off. Tomorrow I will fight him, and then you will come with us. Go now." He nudged her gently forward.

Cozzie turned her face toward him and studied his features in the pale light of the waning moon. Then she was gone, gliding away as though she were not real at all.

Big Dog grinned in the darkness. Now he knew why Benton had befriended this one. Even in so short a time, she had learned much of the ways of the Pawnee. She was like Benton. Her skin might be white, but something inside her was not white. Benton had sensed something in her, and now Big Dog sensed it too. She was worth it, this one. Among the Crow, she would wish to imitate Pine Leaf, would want to be a woman warrior.

Only a few words had been exchanged, and yet Big Dog knew his thoughts were correct. He turned and slipped back into the dark lodge, where he lay back on the soft buffalo robes.

With his hand on his bowie knife, he finally fell asleep.

The morning dawned cold and clear. The cottonwoods and aspens had taken on a deeper hue of gold just overnight, and the yellow grasses were powdered with crystals of frost. Antoine Behele's three wives whispered among themselves as they lay twists of grass and dry twigs on the cooking fire and prepared the early morning meal. In keeping with the rites of hospitality, Behele ate with his guests. Big Dog, however, did not eat—not wishing, by means of some dietary lapse, to vitiate his medicine.

By mid-morning the circle had begun to form, and a subdued but excited crooning rose from the spectators. When the crowd had reached perhaps two hundred observers, Big Dog stripped to his breechcloth. Painted in red and white, after the fashion of the Crow, Big Dog strode to the middle of the circle and called out in Pawnee for Crooked Knife to meet him.

"I have heard that one among you lacks bravery!" Big Dog shouted. "This man is unwilling to pay a marriage price for a woman of his own people, and so he steals a woman from the Long Knives and holds her against her will. I have challenged this man to a battle to the death, and yet where is he? His name is Crooked Knife, and I think he is a coward! My name is Big Dog of the Crow. Long ago I gave White Bear his life, and now I challenge Crooked Knife, for that is a right I have earned from the Pawnee. Now I wait for this Crooked Knife to face me, though I think he hides in his lodge. I will wait. These are my words."

A murmur of disapproval rippled through the assembled Pawnee warriors. Big Dog's words were hurled not just against Crooked Knife but, by implication, against the honor of all.

Was this Crow a crazy man? Who else would affront so large a gathering, and in their own encampment? Perhaps he was a Crazy Dog, ready to die. Perhaps he had come to them so that they would have to kill him. Perhaps his medicine was very strong, so strong that he could not be harmed.

The Pawnee warriors stirred uneasily and waited for Crooked Knife to appear.

Then the lance was cast. It whirred through the air and buried itself in the earth not far from Big Dog. At the moment of impact, one eagle feather came loose from the plumed tuft and spun slowly in the air, carried by a sudden drift of wind. The feather settled to the ground, and Big Dog snatched it up, holding it before him in his clenched fist.

"Crooked Knife's medicine is weak," Big Dog said. "If he will give me the Yellowhair girl, I will give him his life. There is no honor in killing such a man, for he has no medicine and no strength."

Crooked Knife entered the circle. Like Big Dog, he was stripped to his breechcloth.

"I remember this, Big Dog," Crooked Knife called. "It was a dishonor to White Bear when the Crow carried him in with broken legs. I say it was an insult to the medicine of our people. Pawnee! Crooked Knife does not fear this man. Since he is a Crazy Dog and wishes to die, I will do him a favor and kill him while all of you watch. This man got his name from a rabid wolf that he killed. Now I will kill a rabid wolf of the Crow, and whatever strength he has will be mine. Crooked Knife has spoken!"

The circle of Pawnee warriors fell silent as Big Dog and Crooked Knife approached each other, their knives unsheathed and held out before them.

The two warriors moved together in a ritual dance, each man testing the other's movements, gauging, judging. As they circled inside the ring of warriors, Big Dog saw Benton and Skunk standing close by Antoine Behele. The latter was dressed in ceremonial fashion, complete with the trailing feathered headdress appropriate to his position within the Pawnee nation.

As the Pawnee warriors set up an anticipatory yipping sound, Crooked Knife suddenly lunged, his blade driving downward. Big Dog, surprised by the sudden move, stumbled backward, his left moccasin coming down hard on the honed rear edge of the implanted lance point. He fought to regain his balance, but fell instead, taking the impact with his right shoulder. The bowie knife skidded from his grip. He rolled over quickly, grasped the knife once more, and sprang to his feet just in time to deflect another thrust by Crooked Knife.

"The Crow's medicine grows weak?" the Pawnee taunted, his face twisted into a mask of pure hatred.

But Big Dog's knife leaped out, and a long red line appeared across the Pawnee's chest.

"Crow medicine does not grow weak, little man. Now I must kill you."

Crooked Knife whooped with rage and charged forward. Big Dog feinted, twisted to one side, and delivered a bone-rattling kick to Crooked Knife's rib

cage. The force of the blow sent the Pawnee sprawling
to the ground. In an instant Big Dog was upon him,
pinning his knife hand and drawing his own blade to
Crooked Knife's throat.

The Pawnee warriors howled in unison and then
were suddenly quiet.

"Behele!" Big Dog shouted. "Shall I kill this boy
who pretends to be a man?"

Behele replied, his voice heavy with authority:
"Spare his life, Big Dog. The Yellowhair is yours."

As Big Dog released the pressure from Crooked
Knife's arm, the Pawnee warrior spat viciously in his
face and twisted away. Blade in hand, he lunged once
more at his antagonist. The knife missed Big Dog's
throat, struck his collar bone and deflected away. Instantly, Big Dog thrust his own knife upward, and the
keen steel buried itself in the Pawnee's solar plexis.
Crooked Knife's mouth opened wide, as though in dis-
belief. For a moment he went rigid, motionless. Then,
with his remaining strength, he crumpled to Big Dog's
knees. The Pawnee slashed once more with his blade.
Gasping for breath, he pitched forward, mouth open,
his teeth gouging into the blood-pooled earth.

Shouts of anger rose from the Pawnee warriors,
and Big Dog spun about. He brandished his bowie
knife, and shouted the Crow war cry.

"It is finished!" Behele thundered. "The Crow
fought with honor. Crooked Knife is responsible for his
own death, for he could not accept his life in defeat.
He died as a Pawnee warrior must always die.
Pawnees! We will give these Crow safe passage from
our lands, but Big Dog of the Sparrow Hawks is no

longer our friend. If we meet him again in battle, we will kill him, for then the honor of Crooked Knife will be avenged. Now he must take the white woman and leave. I have given my word that these three will not be attacked until they are out of our lands. Nephews! Go to Crooked Knife's lodge and bring the Yellowhair. When the Crow are gone, we will bury our brother Crooked Knife. He died as a warrior!"

Big Dog walked with Benton and Two-tail Skunk to Behele's lodge. He dressed again in his leathers, untied his long hair and settled his own feathered headdress carefully into place.

Behele said nothing, but his eyes were cold—cold with a need for revenge.

"Son," Benton whispered, "for a minute I thought ye was a goner out there. Your left arm all right? Better we put some bear grease on the nick."

"I was very lucky," Big Dog said. "My medicine was strong, but I was careless. The Pawnee did not know how to use his knife. He was a brave man, but he was foolish. I did not wish to kill him."

"He could not live in shame," Two-tail Skunk said. "He had to do what he did."

"No way he could ever have made up for 'er," Benton agreed.

Abruptly, Behele left the lodge and the three men began to wonder whether they would in fact ever leave the Pawnee encampment alive.

When Behele returned, he spoke in English. "Your new wives and their horses are outside, Big Dog. Take what you have won and return to Crow lands. My warriors will follow you when you leave the villages. Do not stop to camp until the third night. I tell you this only because you are a brave man, even though you have brought grief to my people. Take the women and go."

Outside Behele's lodge, Cozzie Yellowhair was mounted. Astride the horse beside her was a beautiful young Pawnee woman. Her delicate features were marred only by her slightly crooked nose. Broken at some earlier time, the bone had not knitted straight.

"Benton!" Chastity asked, "What's going to happen now?"

"Guess that's up to the Pawnee and to Big Dog, gal. He won you fair and square. Ye belong to him, now, Cozzie. That's how the stick floats."

Chapter 5

October 1848

The aspens blazed their vibrating gold among the canyons and up over the lower slopes of the mountains, the yellow-leafed trees interspersed with the dark green of ponderosa pine and the blue spruce of the higher ridges. The little party proceeded at a breakneck pace from the Pawnee encampment. As Big Dog knew well enough, a band of warriors, hungry for revenge, could not be far behind. Upon leaving the camp, they rode hard across the plains for a few miles, and then turned directly westward toward the snow-dusted peaks that the trappers called Greenhorn Mountain and Deer Mountain. Coming to a well-worn horse trail, they followed it for some way until it crossed a shallow stream. They then waded their horses upstream for perhaps a mile before resuming their retreat toward the mountains.

For three days the little group pressed on, stop-

ping only long enough to tend to their animals and
their own needs and to eat scant meals of dried meat
and parched corn. Benton complained humorously
about what kind of a damned world it was where a
man couldn't even risk a fire to brew up a pot of willow bark and coffee, while Big Dog and Two-tail
Skunk insisted that the liquid was bad for the teeth of
old men in any case.

"Bad, hell," Benton snorted. "If ye've got a
toothache, the willow bark will fix 'er up, and the
coffee keeps ye goin'."

"Skunk, is this some story our father has heard
from old, toothless women?"

"Yes! That is who told him, I am sure of it."

"I hope Ephraim chews a leg off both of ye!"
Benton grumbled. "How'd I ever let you boys talk me
into this wild-goose chase, anyhow?"

"I must have dreamed it," Two-tail Skunk said.
"Big Dog, was this not Benton's idea all along?"

"It was your idea, Skunk, your idea. Benton and I
did our best to talk you out of it."

"If that is so, then why do both of the women belong to you, my brother?"

"More to the truth," Big Dog replied, "we belong
to them. Besides that, one of them is white and no
good to us. The other wishes Two-tail Skunk to be her
husband."

"Skunk has enough wives already," Two-tail
Skunk grumbled. "Anyway, it is not that you have captured these women in battle. Then you would not be
able to marry them but instead would have to give
them to other Sparrow Hawk warriors. No, these

women came to you as the result of a challenge. That is the same as paying the marriage price. These are your wives, Big Dog."

Two-tail Skunk called over his shoulder to Chastity. "Yellowhair, ask the Pawnee woman if she wishes to be Big Dog's wife. He has won her in a challenge, and so she must be his woman."

Chastity was near exhaustion and had been clinging desperately to her horse for the preceding several miles. She had been only half aware of the men's talk, though the general drift had registered upon her. The talk, she gathered, was only the sort of meaningless banter that all men seemed to engage in during times of danger or boredom. Nevertheless, she addressed the question to her companion, speaking in Pawnee.

The Indian girl, herself weary from the seemingly endless ride, nodded affirmation.

"Yes," she said to Chastity. "It is the way of things. Now we are both his wives."

"Two-tail Skunk!" Chastity called in English. "Tell Big Dog that Funny Nose will accept him as a husband, but I will not marry him, no matter what the custom is! Benton! You promised to take me to Salt Lake—or to St. Louis. I have been a wife to one Indian warrior, and that's enough. You must keep your word!"

"My father has given his word, and he will keep it," Big Dog said abruptly. "I do not wish to have a white woman for a wife. White women are helpless, like children. Who would wish to have a child for a wife?"

"We're in agreement, then," Chastity said coldly.

"No willer-bark coffee," Benton complained, "an' I still have to listen to a lot of squabblin'."

"Funny Nose wishes to be your wife, Big Dog. That is enough for you."

"Who says I want a wife, Yellowhair?"

"My name is Chastity Cosgrove."

"That used to be your name," Big Dog insisted. "Now it's Yellowhair. Tell the girl I will take her. But I don't like her name, and I'm changing it. Tell her I said her name will be Pawnee Woman."

Once again Chastity spoke to her friend, and then turned to Benton, her eyes questioning.

"I'll get ye on over to Salt Lake," Benton assured her. "I promised 'em I'd bring ye there. After that, Cozzie, I'll help ye get away if that's what ye want."

Chastity was too tired to argue further. She nodded and clung grimly to her horse.

They had left the first range of mountains behind them, and were at the Arkansas River. Gradually the going became easier. Now, the river flowed through an ever-widening valley until, near the end of the third day, they reached the Bayou Salid. They avoided a small encampment of whites living with some Ute who had apparently wandered far to the east of their own lands and had decided to settle in for the winter. The party rode onward toward a huge wall of mountains that thrust up like knives and were powdered with an early snow. The late afternoon sun dropped behind the peaks, and the sky slowly changed from intense blue to a thin, watery redness that hung on the horizon.

"Cold air is coming down from the high country," Big Dog observed. "This is a year when winter comes early, perhaps a long winter like the one we spent near the Tetons, Father. I think the storms will come soon. If that happens, how will we reach Big Salty and then cross back to our own lands? If the snow comes, we must go home to our people. We will have to pass back over the mountains and onto the high plains, through the lands of the Cheyenne and the Arapaho."

"We'll make 'er, Big Dog. We're out of range of the Pawnee now. Damnation! I'll have my coffee tonight, by the Great Blue Jesus! And things is goin' to get better all around, if this ol' hoss has still got his topknot."

"You wish to continue on to the Big Salty, then?" Big Dog asked Benton.

"I give my word, Son. Gotta get Cozzie back, if we can do 'er."

"Tonight we can build a big fire, like the Long Knives do," Two-tail Skunk laughed. "Tonight we will not only sleep well, but we will be warm also. Wherever the Pawnee are, we are beyond them now. They are looking for us among the great herds of buffalo, perhaps."

Chastity listened impatiently to the talk and at last interrupted. "Then we're not going to ride all the way to Salt Lake without stopping? Benton, I've never been so tired in my life," she protested.

"Well, tonight we'll sleep, Cozzie my gal. They was only one way not to get our hides stretched on beaver boards, and that was to keep on goin'. You goin' to make 'er?"

"Yes, yes. But how did you know where I was? I

97

was certain I'd spend the rest of my life as an Indian wife."

"Every varmint's got its own habits," Benton chuckled. "Only five, six places where the Pawnee Loups is likely to set up their villages for the winter, and it was time for that. Findin' ye wasn't the hard part, believe me. The problem was gettin' ye away from 'em. You saw how it was."

"Funny Nose explained what was happening, but we were not allowed to watch."

"None of the women could watch. Just the way it is, is all. Whites have got their ways, and the Indians got different."

"Behele came to our lodge and told us about the challenge. He asked me what I wished to do, and I said I wanted to go with you, Benton. Crooked Knife became very angry with me. He knocked me down and clubbed me with his quiver of arrows. Then Funny Nose made him stop, and he left the lodge for a long while."

"And that was when you came to Behele's lodge?" Big Dog asked.

"Yes. I thought Benton could protect me."

"If ye'd been gone when Crooked Knife had come back, Cozzie, he'd probably have killed ye on the spot soon's he got hold of ye."

"Funny Nose told me that, but I had to come. . . ."

They rode on, their talk distracting their minds from the numbing fatigue that was now overtaking all of them. Only Pawnee Woman did not speak but instead rode silently, never looking at her new husband.

Big Dog, however, had studied his new wife carefully
and had come to like what he saw. Why had Pawnee
Woman decided to come with the Yellowhair? Challenge or no, the Pawnee would not have forced one of
their own to leave the camp. She had chosen to link
her own fate to that of her friend. Obviously, the
women had talked often enough, for otherwise they
would not be friends. And the Yellowhair must have
expressed her intention, should the challenge prove
successful, of going with Benton, back to the Mormons. Was it possible that Pawnee Woman hoped to
accompany Yellowhair back to her people?

It could not be, Big Dog thought. *I know about
the crazy people. They are not like other whites. They
do not take Indian women as wives.*

A great deal of confusion swept through Big
Dog's mind. Perhaps it had been the terrible danger of
the challenge, or perhaps it was simply that he too was
bone weary from the long, sustained ride. But he was
attracted to both women, and perhaps even more
strongly to the Yellowhair. Yet she could never be his.
She was beautiful, and she was different, he was certain, from all other white women—but she was destined to return to her people.

Put her out of your mind, he counseled himself.
One woman is enough, is more than enough. . . .

How was it that he had somehow managed to
agree to take Pawnee Woman as a wife? On numerous
occasions, as the result of successful war parties, a female captive had been offered to him. But he had always rejected the women who were not of his people.
Of course, he had had numerous lovers, even upon oc-

casion the wives of other warriors, but he had never been tempted to marriage. And now, because of little more than a jesting conversation with Skunk, he had agreed to a marriage with Pawnee Woman. He could easily enough have rejected the idea. He could have insisted that both women were his captives, and therefore his to give away to whomever he wished.

But was there a connection, somehow, between his acquiescence to this totally unexpected marriage and his attraction to the white girl? It was true. Something about her caused him to feel sensations he had never before experienced. And he seemed to feel nearly the same stirrings toward Pawnee Woman, now his wife.

It had happened too quickly. If he had not been so tired, if his mind had functioned more quickly....

Don't think about the Yellowhair, he told himself once again.

He remembered that night outside Behele's lodge—Yellowhair in the moonlight, his hand suddenly over her mouth, her momentary attempt to wrench free from his grasp. What had happened in that moment? What fire had gotten loose under his skin? Big Dog thought of the Yellowhair going back to her people, of her marrying one of the crazy men. And he felt a sudden and intense sense of rage. Something was wrong with the essential fabric of the world he lived in and loved.

What did he feel toward Pawnee Woman? Because he wanted her too, wanted her in a way that he had never before wanted a woman—and none of it made sense, not the slightest.

It's simple, a voice back in his skull said. You want both of them.

He was weary; they all were. Big Dog knew that he would think more clearly later, that his strength would be fresh again and that his mind would speak with reason. At the same time he was amazed at the endurance of the two women. Perhaps an Indian woman would be able to make such a ride. Pine Leaf, for instance, had endurance that was not exceeded by any of the warriors. But this Cozzie Yellowhair. She was different. In a single moon with the Pawnee, she had seemingly become all but one of them.

Was this a woman, then, like Pine Leaf herself?

"Not possible. Don't think of her," he said under his breath.

"My brother is dreaming as he rides," Two-tail Skunk interrupted his reverie. "Look, we have found a place to stop. Now Benton will wish to cook up his muddy water."

"Aww hell," Benton exclaimed. "Ain't no time for stoppin' now. Boys, we was just gettin' a good start. I figger we should keep on goin' for another two, three days, anyhow."

"Do you wish to ride farther?" Big Dog asked.

"Guess not. I know how tired you red devils get after a little pony trot."

"Benton!" Chastity cried. "I can't go any farther. I don't care if the Pawnee are right behind us. I want to stop."

"This is a matter for the warriors to decide, Yellowhair," Big Dog snapped, suddenly and inexplicably angry. "We will say when to stop, not you."

"Damn all of you," Chastity retorted. "I'm stopping, and that's that. You do whatever you want, Big Dog."

"The child's got a mind of her own, just like I told ye," Benton drawled.

Big Dog glared at his father, who was grinning widely.

"I have not listened to the Yellowhair," Two-tail Skunk said. "All on my own I have decided to stop. We must eat and sleep. Then we can kill hundreds of Pawnee if we have to."

"Right!" Big Dog echoed. "I didn't hear the woman either. Let's camp!"

Benton laughed. "Damned if I don't agree with ye, Son."

"Jackasses!" Chastity grumbled. "I should have stayed with Crooked Knife."

At that moment Charbonneau lunged sideways, as though attempting to assist Benton from her back, and everyone laughed.

"God-cursed mule," Benton said. "Now I'm of a mind to ride another hundred miles or more!"

Chastity shook her head and slid from her horse. The others dismounted also. Two-tail Skunk led the horses to a nearby patch of grass, and Benton started a fire with flint and steel while Big Dog gathered dead twigs and branches from beneath a thicket of young pines. Yellowhair and Pawnee Woman withdrew the last of the remaining meat, more than a little stale but still edible, from the pack saddles. There remained also a small quantity of parched corn, enough to go around, but not more. The two women spit the meat on willow sticks and placed it over the flames, the fire's warmth more than welcome in the last thin, yellow-gray light of the day. For a few moments all five stood silently around the fire. Pawnee Woman hung back a step, behind but not touching her new husband.

Then, as though suddenly remembering, Big Dog turned to her and placed a hand on either cheek.

"You are my woman now," he said to her in the language of the Pawnee.

"It will be good," Pawnee Woman replied in English. "Yellowhair has taught me some words of the Long Knives. I will learn more. Then you do not have to speak the tongue of your enemies, my husband."

Big Dog was astounded by the speech. After a moment he realized that the girl had rehearsed the words, that at some point on the long trail they had ridden, Pawnee Woman had asked Yellowhair just how to say it so that it would be right.

He moved her gently in front of him, closer to the warmth of the flames, and said to her in English, "I am proud of my wife. Tomorrow you will ride with me, and I will begin to teach you the tongue of the Crow, for those are my people, and now they will be your people."

He was almost certain she had not understood everything he said, but she answered, "It was good."

Touching his lips to her hair, he smiled. He cupped her face in his hands once more and did not correct her.

Two-tail Skunk was clucking softly with his tongue, and Big Dog glanced at his blood brother. Then he noticed that Yellowhair was staring at him intently. What did the expression on her face mean? But he had no time to contemplate it, for in an instant she averted her eyes.

"By the whiskers of Old Man Coyote," Benton said, "this child believes it's time to brew a pot of coffee. I'd even be willin' to share it, but I know they's no one wants any but me."

"I'd like some, Benton, if you don't mind," Chastity said.

"Well now, I guess that'd be fittin'. It's a drink for white folks, not for heathen red devils."

Big Dog smiled and his eyes twinkled. "Wal, now, I figger we all ought to drink a speck of 'er," he said, mimicking Benton.

"Son," Benton returned, "you be talkin' more like your daddy every day. There's hope for ye yet."

"Stop talking and make the coffee," Chastity insisted. "You're the one who corrupted me, Benton, and I've been dying for some of that terrible stuff ever since I was kidnapped."

Benton grinned, fished into his possibles sack, and withdrew the metal can of coffee beans mixed with strips of willow bark. Then he raised one eyebrow, as though he had lost the forged iron pliers he used to crush the beans.

"The meat will be done in a moment," Big Dog stated. "Get on with it, Father. Pawnee Woman would also like to test your concoction."

Benton fetched water and brewed his coffee, and the little party consumed its first cooked food in three days. Benton tasted the coffee and squinted his eyes in pleasure. He passed the small, blue enameled pot to Two-tail Skunk, who sipped and then handed it to Yellowhair. The pot went the rounds, and even Pawnee Woman drank, grimacing as she swallowed the hot liquid.

With food in their stomachs, exhaustion overcame them quickly. Big Dog untied his robes and walked a few paces from the dying campfire. Pawnee Woman followed silently a step or two behind him. Big Dog had the sensation of eyes upon him, Yellowhair's eyes, but he did not glance at her. This would be his first time to sleep with Pawnee Woman, and he would not allow thoughts of any other woman to creep into his mind.

He dropped the robes on the ground beneath an overhang of young pines. Stooping over, Pawnee Woman spread the buffalo hides evenly. Then she lay back and lifted her eyes to Big Dog. He was filled with warmth toward her, despite his exhaustion. When he sank down by her side, she reached over and placed her hand upon his manhood.

Holding her in his arms, he pressed his forehead to hers. He felt the pressure returned. And suddenly she seemed very small to him, very fragile.

He had killed her husband, and yet now she lay in his arms, awaiting his pleasure, her hand squeezing him and drawing his member erect. And he wanted her terribly, although he did not understand why and could not comprehend his own feelings in the slightest. This woman was now to be his wife. He would couple with her. He would push his erect member into the dark, hot place between her legs, the hard and throbbing manhood that she herself had brought to life and had given a will of its own. He would take her. Their bodies would come together here in the darkness beneath the trees and amidst the rich odor of earth and pine needles. He would drive to a moment of flaming sensation that would course through his entire body. And she would cling to him. Then they would sleep, their bodies still close together, their arms entwined.

But did she want this? Or was this something she knew she was obliged to perform, something done out of fear of him, the man who had slain her husband?

That thought was intolerable.

The aching of his erect manhood was also intolerable, and now she had drawn it from beneath his breechcloth. She was touching him gently, tantalizing him with her fingers.

"Pawnee Woman," he murmured, "is this something you want? I will not force you to be my wife. I will give you your freedom if you wish, and I will take you back to your people. I don't. . . ."

"Big Dog," she whispered. "My name is now Pawnee Woman because that is what my husband wishes. I wanted you when I first saw you, and I prayed that you would kill Crooked Knife so that I would be free to go with you. I can only speak in Pawnee because I do not know enough words yet. But I will learn the language of our people, the Crow, because those are my husband's people. I want what you want, Big Dog, because I want you. You are my husband now."

106

She clutched him so tightly that he winced in pain.

"And I want you, Pawnee Woman," he breathed hoarsely, "but you must not castrate me."

Quickly she loosened her grasp and, releasing him, she drew her deerskin dress over her thighs.

"I wish my husband to enter me," she whispered in English.

His mind seemed to cease functioning, but his body knew exactly what to do. It knew in a way that he did not understand, could not even control. He slipped into her, felt her relax, felt her fingers digging into the flesh of his back, through his heavy leather shirt, the pressure certain, yearning, desperate, her whole being reaching out toward life.

When he awoke it was still not light. Pawnee Woman was curled within his embrace, her body melted to his own, taking his form. He breathed in the musky odor of her hair, the smell of bear grease and some herb he could not identify.

He could not remember having reached the point of release. Had exhaustion overcome him at the final moment? Had he dropped into the oblivion of sleep before his body had finished what it had begun? He tried hard to remember and finally the memory came.

He remembered the moment when the strength had left him, when he had collapsed over her and had struggled against sleep to roll to one side. He remembered how she had clung to him.

He could hear the creek, its water threading its way among the stones of its bed. He could feel the stinging cold air against his face, and he knew that ice was forming. By daylight he would see the fretworks of ice crystals, the hoar frost on the yellow grasses that would be weighted and bent along the edges of the running water.

He heard a coyote singing, perhaps a mile distant.

And then he slept once more, a greater darkness spilling over him and drawing him down into it.

When Big Dog awoke again, the sun was well up into the sky, and Pawnee Woman was not beside him. He rose from his robes, somewhat disoriented, and saw Two-tail Skunk standing by the rekindled fire.

Benton and the Yellowhair were also nowhere to be seen.

Big Dog walked to the fire, and Skunk properly interpreted the question in his eyes.

"Our father and the women have gone to find something to eat. He will be back soon, and then we will have a morning meal before we begin to ride once again. Did you make Pawnee Woman your wife last night?"

Big Dog shrugged, nodded.

"It is good for you to have a wife, my brother. She is good, that one. She will build a new lodge for you, a larger one. Our lodges will stand side by side, and we will grow old and fat together and never wish to ride the warpath again."

Big Dog poked nervously at the little fire. Had he been able to please Pawnee Woman? Never before after lovemaking had the thought seriously crossed his mind. If he had ever thought about what a marriage night should be, his vision was far different from what had transpired. Indeed, the events of the previous days all seemed now to blur together.

"It has been very strange," he said.

Within a short while, Benton and the two women returned, bringing a pair of cottontails and a ruffed grouse with them, Benton having taken the creatures with willow-stick and rawhide snares. The two women dressed out the game, working quickly, and within minutes the flesh was roasting over the flames.

When Pawnee Woman looked up at Big Dog, her eyes gleamed with life, and Big Dog's heart soared. Chastity glanced at him somewhat askance. Big Dog, his eyes upon his new wife, was unaware, but both Benton and Two-tail Skunk saw and took note.

Got me one daughter-in-law, Benton thought. Be nice to have Cozzie around during my old age, now that's sure. Well, who knows what'll happen?

As they finished their meal, Charbonneau began to whinny and frisk about.

"Your mare says it's time to go," Two-tail Skunk reminded Benton. "Now all she wants to do is follow the trail. Perhaps she is thinking of Bighorn River grass."

"That's not where we're going, is it, Benton?" Chastity asked.

"Nope, not for a while. Salt Lake, Cozzie. I give my word I'd bring ye back to 'em if I could, so we gotta do 'er."

"All right," she said, her voice resigned, "that's best. I've lived with the Pawnee, and the Crow wouldn't be any different. Maybe there's no place that's right for me. Some people are strangers in any land—and I guess that's how it's always been with me."

"We are Sparrow Hawk Crow," Big Dog said sharply. "We are not Pawnee. You have listened too much to your Pawnee friends."

Chastity put her hands on her hips and glared defiantly at the tall warrior. "Pawnee Woman was the only Indian friend I had, and now she is yours. Benton will take me to my own people, and I will forget what has happened."

"Yes," Big Dog said slowly, "I give you as a present to my father, and he will sell you to the crazy people at Big Salty. Then you will be wife to one of those men, if any of them will have you. Who would wish a woman who does not know how to act like a woman? Perhaps you are a man who wears the clothing of a woman. I do not know."

"No, and you're not going to find out, either." Her eyes blazed as she added, "Be glad that Pawnee Woman will have you. She's my friend, but she's always been too impressed by . . . strong . . . men."

"Oh, ho!" Two-tail Skunk laughed. "Now we will have another challenge fight!"

"Children," Benton drawled, "children. We don't need no squabblin' just now. Let's pay heed to old Charbonneau and hit the trail. We got a mountain or two to cross."

Big Dog and Chastity continued to glare at each other until Pawnee Woman walked slowly to her husband's side and stood close to him. Then he turned quickly and went to bring in the horses.

When the sun had reached mid-sky, the little

party was moving northward, along the drainage of the upper Arkansas. The great, snow-crested monolith of Antero Peak rose west of them, and a chill wind was blowing.

Chapter 6

October 1848

The travelers continued to move in a northerly direction. The lofty peaks of the Rockies nearly encircled them now as they approached the very source of the Arkansas. The mountains glittered white in a brilliant sun after what had been, for the riders, two days of mistlike rain. They crossed the divide through what the mountain men called Tennessee Pass, and as they moved down toward the Red Cliffs they rode through gusts of sunlight alternating with furious spates of hail that stung their faces and collected in the manes of their horses.

The days of travel drifted one into another, but for Chastity Cosgrove, each was an adventure of discovery. How vast the mountains were! A world of mountains and canyons, forests and sage-clotted basins, the aspens high up flaming their autumn gold, the days brisk, and the nights increasingly cold after the storms.

She rode next to Benton now, for Pawnee Woman stayed close by Big Dog. They camped earlier in the evenings, no longer fearing pursuit, and Big Dog, as Pawnee Woman told her, was teaching his wife the language of the Sparrow Hawks. Oddly enough, Chastity felt slighted, left out, while at the same time telling herself that her emotions were totally irrational. Nevertheless, after two more days had gone by, she asked Benton to teach her the Sparrow Hawk language also. When he began, she was amazed at its complexity—different words for almost every possible shading of meaning and a syntax that made her want to wring her hands.

While the language lessons proceeded, Two-tail Skunk grumbled to himself, told stories about Old Man Coyote and underground buffalo and Buffalo Skull and White Bear and Grandmother Moon—just loud enough so that everyone was aware that he felt left out. And when he could no longer amuse himself with the stories, he carved designs into sections of pine wood and placed these outside the circle of firelight as protective magic, or so Chastity supposed.

When the firelight died down at night, Chastity lay awake in spite of herself and listened to the faint whispers and moanings of Pawnee Woman and Big Dog as they made love.

Was it jealousy that she felt? No, for Pawnee Woman was her friend, the one friend she had had during her month of captivity.

Envy, then, that even here, in this strange situation, she was once again, as she had been all her life, the one who somehow didn't quite fit in?

She and Pawnee Woman had both been wives to Crooked Knife. Had the idea crossed her mind that they might now both be wives to Big Dog?

"No!" she cried out, burying her face into the reassuring warmth of her buffalo robe.

She lay still and heard repeated gaspings, the small sounds of sexual congress. It was not a new thing. She had lain with Crooked Knife and Pawnee Woman, had lain side by side with them as they coupled, had made love herself knowing that Pawnee Woman was beside her, awaiting her own turn.

But she could not tear her thoughts from the tall Crow warrior. *To live with the Sparrow Hawks, to be one of them, to be wife to Big Dog Benton. . . . The man who had risked his life for her, had killed the husband she never wanted and whom she feared. Big Dog, the man who had given her to Benton so that he might return her to her own people, the man who had taken her friend for his wife, the man who seemed to dislike her for no reason that she could comprehend. . . .*

The journey continued, and they made better time now. They passed on to the main branch of the Colorado River, and a day's further riding brought them upstream to grassy meadows and some sulphur springs. Benton concluded it would be a good idea to rest the animals here for a day or so and allow them to have their fill of grass. He wanted to do some hunting as well, take a couple of wapiti if possible and dress out the meat and green-cure the hides.

"Another week's ridin'," Benton told Chastity, "and we'll be back on the Sweetwater, whar all this began. A few days after that, an' we'll be over to

Bridger's Fort—just straight down the Sandy to Seedskeedee and across to Black's Fork. Cozzie, my gal, we'll have ye over to civilization in no time. After that, she's up to you."

"You're bound to take me back, Benton?"

"Give my word, gal. But if St. Louis is on yore mind, why you come winter with us up on the Absaroka Range, an' when the first thaw hits, we'll head to Fort Union and book us a riverboat down the Muddy. One way or other, I'm bound to hang with ye as long as ye need me. Old mountain trappers ain't no good for nothin' else."

"You're not old," she remonstrated. "Why do you keep saying that?"

"Nothin' wrong with being old, gal. Old is what a man gets to be if he's lucky and he keeps hold of his ha'r. I spent my whole life tryin' to get old, and now that I'm just about there, I sure ain't goin' to let go of 'er. You're just a kid still—you'll understand 'er some day."

"One of us is a kid, anyway. I think I learned it from you, Benton."

"Hard tellin'. You still remember how to shoot the Hawken?"

"Of course. I had an old sourdough for a teacher."

Benton laughed and removed his two rifles from their sheaths. He called to Two-tail Skunk, asking if he wanted to do some shooting with the Kentucky long rifle the young Indian prized so much.

"They's no reasonin' with an Injun," Benton confided to Chastity. "That weapon's as worthless as tits

116

on a boar hog when ye get down to it. Clumsy to handle. If a man knows how to shoot, what he wants is a short barrel. Even them U.S.-issue Whitneys that the bluecoats use ain't no good, and a coon'd have to be a genuine damn fool to haul a cap an' baller around with him. Nope, flint 'n powder's the only way to go. Come on, gal, let's go kill somethin'."

Hunter's luck was with them that afternoon, and despite what Benton had said, Two-tail Skunk was the first to bag meat, a fat deer at two hundred yards. Benton shrugged, and he and Chastity continued up the little canyon on foot, leaving Skunk to dress out his kill.

As they crested a low rise, Benton pushed Chastity down and pointed. Just below them, peacefully grazing on the lush late grass, was a group of six elk, a buck with a magnificent spread of antlers and the rest does.

"We'll take the does. Better meat, an' they're closer anyhow. You remember what I taught ye, now. Cradle that Hawken good, an' squeeze 'er off gentle."

Chastity fired first, and Benton's shot sounded the moment after. Those elk not hit bounded frantically away, but both shots had been true—Chastity's through the neck and Benton's to the heart.

They were gutting the animals when Chastity looked up and saw a single gray wolf and four coyotes. The animals were sitting a few yards distant, patiently, like house dogs at a dinner table. She nudged Benton and pointed.

"Just want what we're leavin', is all. Nothin' to get riled about, gal."

The mountain man rose, flung a fist-full of intes-
tines in the general direction of the animals. A coyote
darted forward, mouthed the guts, and carried them
back, dropping them. The wolf ate, and the coyotes
continued to wait.

"It's a deal they've got worked out," Benton
grinned. "The song dogs know they's more. Takes the
edge off true dog's hunger, and then they'll all have a
go at what we leave. I told some St. Louis greenhorns
about what you just saw, and they wouldn't listen to
this ol' man. Folks don't believe nobody no more."

Chastity watched in fascination as the wolf ate
and the coyotes waited. She could almost believe their
tails were wagging, but she could detect nothing.

Soon Two-tail Skunk arrived with the pack horse.
Together they finished the task and, loading the meat,
started back up over the rise.

A pair of coyotes had hold of a string of intestine
and were tugging on either end. They seemed to be
playing.

As they arrived back at the camp, Chastity heard
Pawnee Woman laughing delightedly.

"Yellowhair!" she cried. "Come and see!"

Chastity walked quickly to the thicket whence the
voice had issued. On a spread buffalo robe were
Pawnee Woman and Big Dog, both naked. Big Dog lay
back with his hands under his head, a foolish grin on
his face. Pawnee Woman was tapping Big Dog's erect
member back and forth, stroking it with her fingers as
she did so.

"See what I have found?" Pawnee Woman

giggled. "A mushroom is growing between my husband's legs!"

Chastity felt her face flush crimson. She turned
away immediately and, stumbling over some dead
branches that lay nearby, fell to her hands and knees.
She rose and ran back toward Benton and Two-tail
Skunk, Pawnee Woman's laughter ringing in her ears.

Benton looked up from his task.

"Them two at 'er again?" he asked noncommittally.

"Yes," Chastity managed.

She knew that her face was still red, but she
hoped that Benton and Skunk wouldn't notice.

Benton stretched out the hides, and the three of
them set about dressing them. After a time, Pawnee
Woman and Big Dog joined them, and all but Skunk
worked silently. Sensing the tension without understanding it at all, Skunk rattled on and on about the
first buffalo he had ever killed, a hunt when he was
only twelve years old and already beginning to think of
himself as a man. His real father, not Benton, had
made him a present of a new bow, and, on foot in the
company of a group of seasoned hunters, he approached the standing beasts, who had been herded
into a surround. He had carefully singled out a bull
calf, and his arrow flew true to its target.

No one commented on the young warrior's tale
but simply bent their backs to the chore. When the
task was finished, Chastity walked apart with Pawnee
Woman.

"Why did you call me to see that, my sister?" she
asked.

"I thought you would think it funny, Yellowhair.

I did not mean to offend you. I forget sometimes that you are a white woman. Many times our minds are the same, but sometimes they are not. Are you angry with me?"

"No, it's not that. . . ."

"Do you also wish to be Big Dog's woman? If that is what it is, I would like it very much. We both had the same bad husband, and now we could have the same good one. We would always be together."

At first Chastity hesitated. She could think of no words with which to answer Pawnee Woman. Finally she said, with a touch of sadness, "No, no. I must return to my own people. I will miss you terribly when the time comes, Pawnee Woman. Do you know that I love you? I have never had such a friend before."

"Then we should not be apart."

The two women clasped each other's hands and then, after a moment, embraced openly.

"I do not understand what it means to be a white woman," Pawnee Woman said plaintively. "It must be very different. . . ."

By evening the tension had resolved itself, but Big Dog remained puzzled. He sat next to Benton and rubbed bear grease over the stock of his rifle. At length he spoke to his father: "The Yellowhair does not like me."

Benton whistled softly, rose and walked to the stream to get water for another pot of coffee. He would be glad to get over to Bridger's Fort, he thought, if for no other reason than to purchase a new supply of coffee beans.

Benton returned to the fire and eased down beside

his son. "Ain't that at all, Big Dog," he mused. "Women are strange people. My guess is she likes ye more than be good for 'er. Get right down to it, Son, ye've been kind of hard on 'er—your words have been sharp and without patience."

"Often she does not act as a woman is supposed to act, Father."

Using his pliers, Benton crushed up a handful of coffee beans.

"Among the bufflers," he said, "the herd follows the lead cows."

"That is true, but. . . ."

"And come to think on 'er, Pine Leaf don't act like your normal female either, now do she?"

"No, but that is different."

"This ol' coot guesses that Cozzie's like 'er in some ways. If she'd lived with us all her life, mebbe she'd be riding on war parties too."

Big Dog was silent for a time.

"Perhaps it is as you say, Benton. But it makes no difference, for she must return to the crazy people. It is sad, for Pawnee Woman loves her, I think. My wife will be lonely for her friend."

"I don't suppose you'd be missin' 'er too, now would ye?"

"Perhaps that is true, Father. This Cozzie Yellowhair is indeed different from other women."

"Mebbe not as different as we think. Ye want a snort of coffee?"

"I'll have some, Father. Is there enough for everyone?"

"Everyone as wants some."

121

"The wind is cold tonight. Perhaps your coffee will do us all some good."

It was cold, bitter cold. A north wind had begun blowing shortly before sundown, and frost had already formed on the grass away from the campfire. The horses stamped about uneasily, and Two-tail Skunk went to calm them down, to convince them that the mountain lions were far away and were not hungry for horse meat in any case. When he came back in, assuring Benton that Charbonneau had listened to his words and had been comforted, the five wanderers began their evening meal—choice cuts from the deer that Two-tail Skunk had shot.

The wind continued, whipping at the flames of the campfire as the evening meal hissed and dripped its melted fat into the fire. The coals turned incandescent and transparent, and sparks swirled up and flew with the rushing currents of air.

"Don't look good," Benton said between mouthfuls of roast deer.

Big Dog agreed. "The wind will shift soon, and clouds will be over us. Look eastward—there are no stars in the lower part of the sky."

"Not clouds," Chastity insisted. "It's just the shadow of the big mountains."

"They have grown taller then," Big Dog replied flatly.

"Figger it's clouds, all right, Cozzie—just like Big Dog says. Like I said, it don't look good."

"Already it grows warmer," Two-tail Skunk said. "It will rain, maybe."

"Snow," Big Dog said, licking at his fingers. "If it

does not snow here, it will snow over the mountains we must cross."

Pawnee Woman nodded agreement and edged closer to her husband.

They finished their meal and retired to their robes, still hoping to get an early start in the morning. With luck they would be over the pass and down into the drainage of the North Platte by sunset—providing only that the trail remained firm enough for the horses to keep their footing. But it was not to be. The wind shifted, just as Big Dog had guessed, and the temperature continued to rise. Past midnight a soft rain began to fall, and the wind finally stopped blowing. Big Dog awoke, pulled the robes more tightly around Pawnee Woman, got up, and walked out into the darkness where the horses were nickering and stamping their feet nervously. He called to Charbonneau and the others, sang to them a few lines from a Crow chant of the time of green grass, and promised the animals that all would be well. Charbonneau nibbled at Big Dog's fingers, as though asking why it was that Benton had not come out to her. Big Dog laughed, scratched her behind the ears, and assured her that the party would soon be on the trail once more.

As Big Dog turned to walk back to his robes, the first snow began to fall. Within moments, large flakes were showering down, and the darkness turned to gray-black. He returned to his wife and slid in beside her.

"My husband does not sleep?"

"I went to check the horses. The snow is falling

now. If it continues, we will not be able to cross the pass tomorrow."

"Then we must stay here close to the bad-smelling water," she murmured, "for here there is warmth. The weather will change soon, and then we can ride on to where your people—our people—are camped. Then I will build you a new lodge, and it will not matter if the snow falls from the sky."

They fell asleep in each other's arms. Yet, just in that moment before sleep, Big Dog was startled to realize that his mind had created the illusion of Yellowhair beside him. At first he attempted to chase the image from his thoughts, but then he gave in to it. Both women were with him, under the enveloping warmth of the robes, one on either side.

Two wives, he thought. Why should a warrior not have as many wives as he wishes to have? It would be good if she chose that. Then Pawnee Woman would not lose her friend. . . .

Morning came, and the world was gray-white, the snow nearly a foot deep and still falling heavily. The blanket of whiteness would lie twice as deep across the pass. They rose, shaking out their robes, and huddled around the fire that Benton had rekindled. The two women sliced strips of meat and suet into a pot of boiling water, and waited for the broth to form. They ate without speaking. To continue their journey now would be not impossible, but simply unwise.

"Best I go tend to the bad-natured mule," Benton chuckled finally, shaking the snow from his beaver hat. He walked toward the horses, which stood huddled together, and began to whistle to himself.

"Poor damn time for the white stuff," he mused aloud, "but she's pretty, though. Be a lot prettier if we was up on the Bighorn an' all settled in for the season. Mebbe I'll set me some traps again this year—no sense lettin' good steel rust. . . ."

A form loomed before him in the thick downfall.

Ephraim!

The grizzly was close, curious about the horses, and hadn't seen him yet. Benton drew his Texas Paterson, a poor weapon for confronting a white bear, but all he had other than his bowie knife.

Aware of the bear's presence now, the horses became frantic, splitting the air with sharp screams of fear. The grizzly rose to its hind legs, its great head wagging from side to side, its dim eyes searching through the snowfall.

It's done smelt me, Benton thought.

He fired one shot into the air, both to alert the others and in the vague hope of frightening the huge beast. But the pistol report did not intimidate the grizzly. It staggered forward on its hind legs like some monstrous creature from the prehistoric past. Benton leveled the Paterson, aimed for the heart, and fired, fired again, and fired yet a third time.

Then the bear had him. The terrible force of a huge, clawed paw spun him backward, head over heels, into the snow. His head was nearly torn from his body.

He was still alive, but his gun was gone. He knew that part of his face had been torn away, but he could feel nothing. His right side was paralyzed. He couldn't move his hand.

Knife, he thought quickly and rolled over. Reaching for the blade with his left hand, he grasped the handle and pulled the knife from its thong-bound sheath.

The blurred outline of the monster towered over him, but Benton forced himself to his knees. The grizzly roared with pain, and for a frantic moment Benton was afraid the animal would fall on him, crushing him in its death throes. With his right arm hanging useless at his side, Benton forced himself upright. As the bear lunged for him, he plunged the knife deep into the animal's belly.

Benton was off the ground. He was being shaken. Ephraim had him by the shoulder, the great jaws clamping down on his collarbone. He could feel the teeth grating against his bones and, still flailing with his knife, he screamed, a long, inhuman cry.

He was suddenly aware that the shaking had stopped. He was no longer being flung about—he was falling. Then darkness came. He couldn't see.

This ol' trapper's gone under . . . he thought and passed into unconsciousness. There was nothing but blackness, pitch blackness. Next came brief moments of consciousness alternating with periods of grayness, of dreams, distortions. He was a young man, trapping with Jim Bridger and Davy Jackson over on the Seedskeedee, up on the Snake. He and Bridger were pinned down by the Piegans. Powder and lead were running low, but the two of them slipped away, right out through the Piegans, moving as silently as cougars. Now the face of Sweetgrass floated before him, no body, just the face, the kind, sensual eyes of his wife, then the two of them together and the boy with them, their son now. He saw the wagon trains, the flood of the Long

Knives, westward, always westward, and one of them, a girl named Cozzie, stolen, he had to find her. . . .

Where was he?

"Big Dog? Is that ye, Boy?"

"I am here, Father. You will live, you will live. . . ."

But the grayness enveloped him once more, and a great bear reared up and called his name. He struggled, tried to reach for his knife but could not find it, where was it?

One eye would not open, and he squinted with the other. Things came slowly into focus, and his field of vision grew wider.

Skunk was lying naked in the snow, not moving, as if sleeping.

Come to find me, Benton thought. Come to bring this old man back. . . .

He sank back into the beckoning haze.

On the fourth day he awoke and his mind became clear. His first movements brought pain, and the grayness swirled about him, then receded.

"He's awake," he heard an anxious voice say. It was Cozzie.

Then Big Dog was next to him, the strong hands pressing him down, gently, firmly. Benton relaxed.

"Father?"

"I'm back, damn it all! Ye kill that goddamn white bear, Big Dog?"

"You killed it, Aloysius," Chastity said softly.

"She speaks the truth, Father. The bear was dead when we reached you. We thought you were dead, too. The Yellowhair has cared for you, and Two-tail Skunk

127

dreamed to bring you back from the Spirit World. You will live now."

"I'm goin' to make 'er?"

"Long Knife blood is stubborn," Skunk grinned. "It does not know when the time has come to die."

"Meat don't spile in the mountains," Benton muttered, closing his eyes against the heavy flashing of pain in his face and shoulder. "How bad be I chewed up?"

"Broken arm and broken shoulder and your face. . . ."

"Ephraim gnawed me a bit, did he? How'd ye get me sewed back up?"

"Charbonneau," Skunk said, "she gave us a portion of her tail. And Yellowhair and Pawnee Woman laced you up, Benton."

"Damn this coon's eyes, Cozzie. I knew there was a reason for lookin' out for ye. Charbonneau's still findin' something to eat?"

"As mean as ever," Big Dog said. "She's been mooning about, but her spirits will return now. Should I lead her in to see you?"

"Be good, be good. Blue Jesus, Son, this old-timer's finally got the ha'r of the b'ar in 'im, after all these years. Come to think of it, I figger it was a debt I owed to the mountains. A man's not more than a greenhorn until he's got the ha'r of the b'ar."

"Rest now," Chastity said gently.

"Hellfire, gal, that's all I been doin' of late. How long I been lyin' here, anyhow?"

"Four days, a little more," Big Dog told him. "And the snow has been falling. It's up to my waist all around us, but Skunk and I have shot several deer that foundered in the snow. We have plenty to eat, but we will not be able to move again for some time. Then we will rig a travois for Charbonneau and attempt to cross over the mountains and on to the Bighorn."

"Too damned early for this much snow," Benton growled. "Our medicine's gone bad. Got to get over to Bridger's Fort and on to Salt Lake. I give my word, Son."

"No," Big Dog said. "We have spoken among ourselves, and all agree. We must take you to the encampment of the Many Lodges and the Kicked-in-their-Bellies. There you will heal and regain your strength. Later Two-tail Skunk and I will take the Yellowhair to her people, if she wishes to go there."

Benton looked up at Chastity and she nodded to him.

"Guess I ain't been much help to ye after all, Cozzie. But old coons like me heal quick. Give me a little time, and I reckon I'll be as good as new—specially with this fancy stitch job on my ugly puss. Figger ye can take livin' in another Injun village for a spell?"

"Aloysius, I think you've worked out an elaborate plot for no other reason than to get me to the Crow people—so I could see that all those stories you used to tell me were actually true."

"Ye figgered me out, gal." Benton winced with pain as he attempted to smile.

"He is the same as always," Two-tail Skunk observed. "Nothing can change him, not even white bears."

"I actually kilt old Ephraim?" Benton asked.

"Three shots to the heart, and then you disemboweled him, Father. There was nothing left for us to do but skin him."

"Meat any good?"

"Very good, but the Yellowhair will not eat it."

"Cozzie, ye got to try some. Nothin' beats good bear meat but buffler hump-rib and doe venison. What ye think I kilt it for?"

"Incorrigible," Chastity said, shaking her head.

"Now don't go talkin' no French on me. Never could understand them frog-eatin' Frenchies. Ain't no civilized way to talk, no sir."

Benton closed his eyes, very tired once more, and began to drift into sleep. Suddenly, his eyes snapped open.

"Where's my damned bear robe?" he demanded. "I kilt him, and the least ye can do is let me have the hide."

Chapter 7

November 1848

A week later, the warm rains began to fall. At first there was no apparent effect upon the snowpack. Gradually, however, the white blanket became sodden, and a run-off began. After a night of heavy winds, with rain pouring from a thick sky, the Colorado River was a raging brown torrent, broken free from its banks. The willows and cottonwoods along its margins were now like two parallel lines of all but leafless gray branches curving well out into the flood of the river. The ridges were free of snow, and water tumbled down from everywhere.

When the weather turned, Big Dog and Pawnee Woman constructed a travois and attached it to Charbonneau. The mare objected at first, and then, seeming to understand the purpose, she shook her head and stared about curiously.

The bear robe was doubled over and fixed to the

travois with deerhide thongs. Benton was bundled in his buffalo robe and securely tied down to avoid any bumpings that might damage his knitting bones. Charbonneau neighed several times and pointed her long nose up into the rain. She knew what would happen next. She would be moving once again, heading northward, toward the Absaroka Range. She stamped her feet restlessly and fluttered her breath through her nostrils.

With Big Dog and Pawnee Woman leading the way, the travelers toiled upward, leaving the rain behind and entering the realm of the great snow-covered peaks, now locked in winter. As they approached the pass called Willow Creek, the horses were struggling through the deep snow. But they crested the summit before nightfall and began the descent. Once out of the zone of whiteness, their spirits lifted. The rain had stopped and moonlight broke through the ragged trailings of cloud, lighting their way into a valley.

Here they camped and built a blazing fire against the deepening cold. They were over the mountains, back into country they considered an extension of their own, and there was even a thick, hardy growth of late grass for the horses.

Benton lay propped before the fire, surrounded by his friends, and complained heartily that the venison was not sufficiently cooked.

"Big Dog, how am I ever goin' to get ye civilized? Raw meat's fine, but not when ye've got a chance to roast 'er good."

"Our father is feeling better this night," Two-tail Skunk concluded.

"Aloysius is right," Chastity asserted. "I'm going to put this back into the fire."

"That's my gal. Let the red devils eat 'er raw if they want. You and me, Cozzie, we know how she tastes best. We could have some coffee, but they've drunk 'er all up."

"No coffee until we reach home, Father," said Big Dog. "Then perhaps the white trader will sell you some."

"Who's the damn thief ye've got livin' with ye now? Buttermilk Thompson still there?"

"He'll be there until the mountains wash to the sea, I'm afraid. Perhaps he'll sell you some coffee for the bear robe."

"Like hell. I paid high for that bearskin, and I ain't lettin' go of 'er."

"You could sell Charbonneau," Two-tail Skunk suggested.

"Heathen red devils, ain't they, Cozzie?"

"I'll stay out of this discussion," Chastity answered.

With their robes spread around the dwindling fire, the party slept. At the first light they were up. They swallowed a quick meal and set out along the trail once again. It was cold, and the ground was frozen hard, but they were making good time. A week's more riding brought them to the confluence of the Sweetwater and the North Platte, where the main migration trail turned westward toward South Pass.

"Another day and we'll come full circle, Cozzie. I'm still half of a mind to push on to Salt Lake. . . ."

"We will do what Big Dog says, Aloysius. I'm not

133

ready to go back yet, anyway, and you need some time to get well. In any case, I want to see these amazing Crow you've told me so much about. You wouldn't deny me that?"

"Gal, I wouldn't deny ye anything. But damn, I hate to be a burden this way. I get well again, I'm goin' on a warpath against the damned white bears. I'll darken my lodge with their goddamn scalps, I tell ye."

"Maybe you should avoid bears now," Two-tail Skunk called out. "They have very strong medicine, the bear people. You must remember that, Benton."

"Brother Hawken's got medicine too," Benton snorted.

The days drifted by, cold and clear, the temperature dropping below zero at times. They followed the wagon trail to within fifty miles of South Pass and then moved northward to the Wind River, as the upper reaches of the Bighorn are called.

During the days Benton grouched constantly, more from boredom than anything else. He complained that he was well enough to ride with the best of them, and accused Charbonneau of attempting to drop turds on him. Chastity hovered over him, and at night, after the evening meal, Benton and Two-tail Skunk conspired to teach the girl the rudiments of the complicated Crow language.

Big Dog and Pawnee Woman slept apart, for, as Benton told his son, Cozzie felt better about things that way.

"I think she will wish to come and live with us one day," Pawnee Woman told Big Dog. "She acts distant toward you, my husband, but that is a woman's way."

"This woman's way, anyhow," Big Dog replied. "In any case, you're the only wife I want. A man would be a fool to have more than one wife."

"My husband does not speak the truth. I can tell that you wish to make love to the Yellowhair, but I do not mind that. She is my friend, my sister. It would be good for all three of us to be together in a lodge of our own."

"Maybe that's why Crooked Knife accepted my challenge. He was a Crazy Dog Who Wished to Die. The two of you would drive any man to it."

"I do not understand your words, Big Dog."

"Nor do I, Pawnee Woman. This is a world in which everyone walks backwards and talks in riddles."

They were approaching the lands of the Sparrow Hawks now, the upper end of the Bighorn Basin. The Owl Creek Mountains rose to the west, and the southerly ridges of the Bighorn Range towered some fifty or sixty miles to the east. The party had just passed the extensive hot springs near the Bighorn and had reached the crest of a low ridge when Big Dog sighted a small herd of buffalo off to the north. He signaled to Skunk, who rode up to join him.

"Shall we take some meat and hides?" Big Dog asked.

"Yes. We can use the robes to buy coffee for Benton when we reach the Many Lodges. That will put him in a better mood."

Big Dog and Two-tail Skunk explained their plan to the others and, leaving Benton and the two women behind, proceeded toward the grazing buffalo. They circled around from below, then left their mounts and continued on foot to get within firing range of the big animals without being detected. Moving up under the cover of brush and young cottonwoods along a small stream, Two-tail Skunk suddenly reached out and gestured for Big Dog to drop to all fours.

"What is it, Skunk?"

"By the standing rocks, my brother. Do you see what I see?"

There were half a dozen Indians, Cheyenne, apparently also of a mind to take some buffalo robes.

"We will get more than meat, perhaps," Big Dog grinned. "Our friends the Cheyenne are not expecting competition. Do you think there are more of them?"

Two-tail Skunk and Big Dog remained hidden as they studied the situation with extreme care. Then the two warriors moved on upstream, slipping along silently and cautiously. They scrambled up the slope of the ravine and emerged on high ground, above both the buffalo and their Cheyenne hunters. There, grazing contentedly, were a dozen horses, several of them the coveted spotted mounts bred by the Nez Perce. The animals were unattended, pack horses and war ponies alike.

"We are within the boundaries of our lands," Big Dog smiled. "These Cheyenne are hunting on our ground. We must not allow such a thing."

"That is true. Besides, my brother, those are beautiful horses, and each of us would like to have a new war pony. The others we may give away to our friends, who will be very grateful."

136

"Do you think the Cheyenne will kill our buffalo for us if we give them time?"

"I think they will."

"Then we must wait for them to put aside their rifles and butcher the animals they will kill."

"That is a good idea, Big Dog. But the Cheyenne are always hungry, and they will eat the livers of the animals they kill. There will be none left for us. . . ."

"That is true. So we must take revenge upon them, for they are not generous."

"Yes, and we will take their horses and their meat and robes. We will take their scalps also."

"Cheyenne must not be allowed to hunt upon the lands of the Crow," Big Dog repeated.

As the two men worked their way down toward the standing rocks, the first Cheyenne rifle blazed. A fat cow staggered forward and collapsed. Then more rifle fire sounded. Within moments the remainder of the small herd was charging toward the river, and the Cheyenne warriors let up the fierce yells of successful hunters. Big Dog and Two-tail Skunk, now within a hundred yards or less, counted four downed buffalo, all cows. They watched the Cheyenne begin the skinning and butchering, first stacking their rifles together.

"No one has bothered to reload," Big Dog whispered. "That is surely a mistake. One must always reload immediately."

"One of the rifles has two barrels," Skunk added. "I watched the Cheyenne fire it. I will take that weapon for my own."

"Is your pistol ready, the one Benton gave you?"

"Of course it is. We will each kill one Cheyenne

with our rifles, and then we will rush at them. They will think we are crazy or that our medicine is very strong. The Cheyenne are always thrown into confusion when we rush at them. They do not think quickly, these Cheyenne."

"Yes," Big Dog agreed. "They must plan things carefully in advance, for otherwise they do not know what to do."

"After we run at them, we must take cover."

"They will flee toward the brush along the creek, and we can take cover behind the carcasses of the dead buffalo. Are you ready, Two-tail Skunk?"

"My medicine is very strong today. I can hardly control it."

Big Dog and Two-tail Skunk approached yet closer, drew dead aim, and fired, the reports of their rifles sounding almost as one.

One Cheyenne fell as though he had suddenly fallen asleep on his feet. The second twisted about, attempted to crawl, and then lay still. Another ran toward the stacked rifles, and Big Dog brought him down with a single shot from his pistol. Then the two Crow rose to their feet, and screaming their *hoo-ki-hi!*, charged toward the remaining three Cheyenne. The warriors fled toward the brush along the creek.

"They have only their knives with them!" Big Dog shouted. "We must catch them!"

The desperate foot race toward the river was on as the long-legged Big Dog slowly drew up on his prey. One Cheyenne swerved to the south, and Two-tail Skunk followed.

When the nearest Cheyenne stumbled, Big Dog

fired, missed, and fired a second time. The Cheyenne, attempting to regain his footing, spun about, his arms flailing the air. A dark hole appeared suddenly at the base of the warrior's throat. His voice failed him, and the blood welled out.

Big Dog dashed past the fallen man, continuing his pursuit. The Cheyenne plunged into the river and knifed through the cold water. Taking the current, he stayed with it as the river swept him downstream. Big Dog stood at the edge of the water, panting from the frenzied run to the river, and watched the Cheyenne bob to the surface. The warrior sucked for air, and then disappeared once more beneath the surface of the fast-moving, green-brown water.

"You have run well, Cheyenne," Big Dog said. "I will give you your life, if you do not lose it to the river. But you will have a long walk home. . . ."

He turned then and strode back toward Two-tail Skunk. Emerging from the brush along the river, he heard a pistol report. A shiver went through him as he realized that Skunk could be the victim. Big Dog broke into an easy run, rapid and long-striding.

But Skunk was gleefully scalping a dead Cheyenne. He looked up at Big Dog, grinned, and ripped the scalp loose, flourishing it in the air.

"Two-tail Skunk and Big Dog are powerful warriors," the burly warrior said matter of factly. "We will paint our faces the black of victory before we enter the great encampment. Even Pine Leaf will envy us. Did you not kill the other Cheyenne, my brother?"

"He leaped into the river, Skunk, and I did not wish to go into the cold water. He was a good runner, and now he will have to run all the way back to the Cheyenne villages."

"Perhaps we should leave one of the horses for this man."

"The run will be good for him. But his chief, Leg in the Water, may not like his story when he tells it. When the Cheyenne dries off, he may wish to lead a party against us."

"Yes, that is true. Now let us scalp the other Cheyenne. After that we must inspect the horses and look into the bundles on the pack animals. No doubt they hold many presents for us."

Big Dog and Two-tail Skunk finished the grim business of taking the scalps and then scrambled up to the grazing horses, who pulled at the grass as though nothing at all had happened.

"Three Nez Perce animals," Big Dog exulted. "All of them fine horses."

"One for each of us and one for Benton also," Two-tail Skunk agreed.

"Our father will not want it—or he will use it to buy coffee from Buttermilk Thompson. No, we will give it to Pine Leaf. She knows how to appreciate a fine horse. She will not trade it away."

"We must hurry, Big Dog. Our father and the women have surely heard the gunshots. They will worry that we are dead."

"Benton will calm the women," Big Dog replied.

Upon their return, Two-tail Skunk waved the string of five bloody scalps, and Benton let out a whoop, grimacing with pain even as he did so. Pawnee Woman, though obviously pleased with her husband's success, said nothing, but ran to Big Dog's side and leaped upon him before he had dismounted.

Chastity was horrified at the casually described violence. She stared at the string of scalps and a wave of nausea flooded over her. She turned and took a few steps away, then stopped. Her vision blurred.

She had learned to accept much, but why not this? Now, suddenly, she felt herself naked and alone in a world of incredible violence and death.

Her head whirled. Benton, who seemed to understand her, who had singled her out, who had rescued her, was now grinning like an untamed savage at the bloody tropies. Pawnee Woman, her friend, her sister, leapt joyfully at the sight of her husband's grisly triumph. And Big Dog Benton, who once lived in the white man's world, but was never a part of it. Big Dog, now gleeful at the horrible deaths of others of his own kind.

A voice broke into her churning thoughts. *Control yourself, gal, an' learn to accept 'er. Stop actin' like a damn white woman. Ye ain't, not any more . . .*

It was Benton's voice, but he was not speaking. He lay on his travois, his face beaming with pride. She fixed her gaze on Two-tail Skunk, still holding aloft the string of scalps.

"How . . . many?" she asked, her voice faltering.

Big Dog stared at her. He was standing beside Pawnee Woman, and his eyes were full upon her, as though he could see through her clothing, through flesh and bones as well, could see into the most secret part of her. Or perhaps that wasn't it at all. Perhaps he too was not certain how to cross the gulf. Perhaps he knew there was an undefinable space that separated them.

"The Cheyenne are our enemies, Yellowhair," he answered, his voice possibly more gentle toward her than ever before. "It has always been this way. You come from the Long Knives, you are still new to these lands. It is not easy for you to understand our way. In your world, this would be murder! I have lived with the Long Knives of the mountains, and I know that is how they think, and yet I have seen them kill Indians without thinking, and I have seen them kill each other as well. In the ways of our world, Skunk and I have won a great victory, and when we approach the Many Lodges, we will paint our faces with the black of victory, and we will be honored. Can you understand this thing?"

Had he been reading her thoughts? Or did her face express that clearly what lay hidden within?

Somehow he knows, Chastity thought. His compassion for her elicited a similar compassion within her, and she knew she would never feel the same toward him again. It would be different now.

"May I . . . touch them?" she asked, reaching out tentatively.

Benton broke out laughing, but Big Dog was solemn. He took the scalps from Two-tail Skunk and handed them to Chastity.

"There is medicine in them," he said. "Can you feel it?"

She felt strangely inhuman, as though in touching she had somehow stepped across an invisible line. The twin sensations of horror and fascination rose up and competed within her being.

"Damn fools, both of ye!" Benton complained. "Two of ye, an' five of them. Why not just let 'em take a couple of bufflers and be on their way? Suppose ye'd got kilt? Two women here, an' what happens to them?"

"There were six of the Cheyenne," Two-tail Skunk said. "Big Dog let one get away because he did not wish to swim across the river after the man. Big Dog does not like cold water!"

"Well," Benton chuckled, "two Sparrow Hawks against six Cheyenne. I guess that's about even odds at that. But unless you boys expect to rest on your laurels a spell, I figger we better get to movin'."

Charbonneau whinnied and rolled her lips as Big Dog took the scalps from Chastity and held them in front of the mare.

"Benton is right," Two-tail Skunk agreed. "It is possible there are other Cheyenne close by, even though we are now in our own lands. Already the sun is dropping from the sky."

"Ride!" Big Dog ordered, and the little party mounted up and continued on its way northward, the long venture now drawing to its close.

On the second day after the skirmish with the Cheyenne hunters, Two-tail Skunk galloped on ahead. He returned late in the afternoon with the assurance that the Crow encampment was still there.

"Sometimes the women take it into their heads to move the villages, even though the men may be out hunting or stealing horses," Benton explained to

Chastity. "That's why Skunk went on ahead to check 'er out for us."

Chastity was puzzled. As far as she had been able to determine during the month of her captivity, Pawnee women did not exercise such power. Perhaps things were different among the Crow.

With Two-tail Skunk once more riding with the party, Big Dog led on. Close to sundown, he indicated that they should make camp for the night, even though they were apparently no more than a few miles from the villages.

"We will enter the encampment by morning light," Big Dog said. "It is better that way."

Once darkness had fallen, Pawnee Woman and Cozzie built a small fire, and the party cooked generous portions of the buffalo meat they had taken from the ill-fated Cheyenne hunters.

"Hump-rib, Father," Big Dog grinned. "We're home again! Ears-of-the-Wolf, the ancient one, will cast out whatever demons he can so that you will mend more quickly, and we'll trade that bearskin to Buttermilk Thompson for some coffee beans. Between the two things, you should be up and about in no time."

"Not this ol' hoss' bearskin, ye won't! What kind of fate is it for a man to be in the hands of red devils? That meat done yet? I've got a powerful hunger."

"We must be certain the meat is well burned," Two-tail Skunk said solemnly. "If the meat is not spoiled with fire, Benton does not like it."

"This once I'll put up with 'er half raw," Benton conceded. "An' afterwards we'll pass the pipe around. Think there's a couple of plugs of good downriver tobaccy in my possibles sack. A fine time to smoke some of 'er, all things considered."

Chastity removed the steaming meat from the flames, placed it on an elkhide mat, and began cutting off portions.

"Perhaps I will smoke also," she said.

Benton chuckled, but Two-tail Skunk and Big Dog glanced nervously at each other.

Then Big Dog spoke. "The Yellowhair will not smoke. It is not right for women to smoke the pipe with their men—it will weaken the medicine."

"That's foolish, Big Dog," Chastity insisted. "I've never smoked before, and I want to try it."

"No. It is not permitted."

"Damn your stupid traditions," Chastity persisted. "I will smoke if Benton will let me!"

The old mountain man stared at the girl, then at Pawnee Woman and his two sons.

"Cozzie, my gal, I'm afeard Big Dog's right on this one. We're close to the Sparrow Hawk villages, an' we've got to follow their ways. Besides, what's a young lady want with smokin'? Just make ye sick, gal."

Chastity looked from one man to another. She spat out the words, "Damn all of you, then!" Rising abruptly, she took a portion of meat, and stalked away to eat by herself.

Pawnee Woman stared after her friend, then looked questioningly at Big Dog. He nodded, telling her it was all right to go. Pawnee Woman took her portion of meat and hurried off after Chastity.

The three men chewed in silence.

"Pine Leaf smokes the tobacco," Two-tail Skunk offered.

Benton made no comment.

"This one is not Pine Leaf," Big Dog replied.

"Not Injun, either," Benton suggested.

"Even white women do not smoke the pipe," Big Dog said. "A few smoke the little cigars or the cigarettes, though. Have I said the wrong thing again, Father?"

"I don't expect so. Some things Cozzie's just goin' to have to learn to accept. Besides, none of her own people smoke at all, and they don't drink whiskey neither. God-fearing folks with not a vice in the world."

"I have heard that some of the men have more than one wife, though. Is that not a vice?"

"Don't guess it is. Now Skunk here, he's got three wives—an' look at the troubles he's got."

"It is a great responsibility," Two-tail Skunk agreed. "That is why I must go on so many horse raids."

Out under the junipers at the edge of the clearing, Pawnee Woman and Chastity sat together, eating. Chastity was still angry, but she appreciated her friend's presence.

"It is true, what they say, my sister," Pawnee Woman said finally.

"About their medicine?"

"Yes, about that. It was that way with the Pawnee, and it must be the same with the Crow. You know that I speak truth."

"We're not with the Crow yet," Chastity protested.

146

"Big Dog and Two-tail Skunk are Crow, and Benton is a Long Knife who has become a Crow. We are with them."

"Your husband has no right to forbid me to do whatever I wish."

"If we were in the Crow villages, even their women would not wish us to do this thing."

"Maybe that's what should change."

"We must follow the traditions, my sister. Is it not this way among the whites, among your people?"

"Who are my people? So much has happened that I do not know any more."

Pawnee Woman was silent for a time. Coyotes yipped across the flats on the far side of the Bighorn River, and Pawnee Woman waited until they had ceased their serenade before she spoke again.

"Only you can know that. You were forced to live with a people who were not your own. I am also going to live with a people who will be strange to me for a time. I came because I wished to be with you for as long as I could and also because I might not be able to find another husband among the Pawnee. The braves would all fear that I would bring them bad medicine. I did not know at the time that I would love Big Dog or that he would love me. Now I am his wife, and I must learn the ways of his people. See? Right now we are speaking in their language, and yet it is new to both of us."

"Why do you love him, Pawnee Woman?"

"He is a brave warrior, and he will paint my face when he returns from battle with coups. Also he is gentle with me when we make love. I did not know it

147

would be that way, though I hoped it would be. I love it when we lie together, my sister. I think you would love it too. He looks at you often, and you could be his wife if you wished it to be that way. It would please me if you did this."

Chastity embraced the Indian woman—or was it the Yellowhair who embraced Pawnee Woman? Chastity could not have said at this moment as she ran her fingers over her friend's long, braided hair, so black, so different from her own, her pale hair that would forever mark her as an outsider if she should finally choose to stay with Big Dog's . . . with Benton's people.

"I have never had such a friend before," she confided to Pawnee Woman.

"Nor I either, my sister. In many ways our minds are alike, and yet in other ways we are very different."

"Why would you want me to be Big Dog's wife?"

Pawnee Woman was silently thoughtful for a moment before she answered.

"Because both of you wish it," she replied.

At length they returned to the fire. Pawnee Woman stood beside her husband and did not speak. He placed his hand upon her moccasined foot and rubbed softly. Then he stood up, and the two of them moved away from the fire and put down their robes upon a mattress of juniper boughs that Big Dog cut from the thicket.

"I will be glad to see my wives once again," Two-tail Skunk sighed, and then he too slipped into his robes and seemed to fall immediately asleep.

"Are you comfortable, Aloysius?" Chastity asked.

148

"Help the old coon up, Cozzie. He's got to hobble out to take care of the body's needs. It's a turrible thing, havin' an arm an' shoulder that ain't no good for nothin' except gettin' in the way. I'll be back in a minute or two. Maybeso you should get some sleep?"

"In a little while," she said, helping Benton to his feet.

She stared into the dying flames, and when Benton returned, she asked, "I always speak the wrong words, don't I?"

"Ye've got a bit of a temper, Cozzie. Most of the time, that's good—it makes ye what ye are."

"What am I, Aloysius?" she asked, easing him onto his robe.

"Can't answer that," he replied. "But this ol' trapper loves ye, I expect. Ye really want to smoke the pipe, gal?"

She felt the blood come to her face, and she did not answer right away. Then she said, "Yes, I do."

"Guess I could stand another puff or two myself," Benton said.

He dug out the pipe, put a pinch of tobacco into the bowl, and Chastity lit it with a flaming twig. Benton sucked on the pipe, savored the taste, and blew out a thin stream of blue-gray smoke. Then he handed the pipe to Chastity, cautioning her about the dangers of inhaling the smoke. The girl nodded, placed the pipe to her lips, and puffed. She tried to stifle her coughing, and handed the pipe back.

"Smoking is dangerous," Two-tail Skunk murmured from his pile of robes and then fell silent.

Benton grinned and glanced off in the direction of Big Dog and Pawnee Woman.

Chastity smiled, and once again could feel her face flush. There were tears in her eyes, and she blinked several times.

"The smoke got in my eyes," she said, rubbing them with her knuckles.

"Guess so," Benton said, puffing once again and once more offering the pipe to Chastity.

She shook her head.

"Well," he said, "let's sleep a mite, then. Tomorrow's homecoming, and I'll find out if Ears-of-the-Wolf can get the Big Coyote in the Sky to rub the bear's medicine off me. If the old bastard ain't dead yet, that is. He must be a hundred or so. I swear, the man's nothing but wrinkles and bones—can hardly see, and I don't figger he hears much at all. Probably he's damned near as old as this ol' coot, when ye get right down to 'er."

Chapter 8

November 1848

When morning came, the two Crow warriors splashed the black paint of victory across their faces. Benton was also up and about, moving with difficulty but also with grim determination. He called Chastity to him and asked her to daub his face.

"I don't understand, Aloysius," she questioned.

"Ye don't think this ol' trapper's goin' to get dragged back to the Many Lodges, do ye? I'll ride in the way I rode out if it kills me. I been hauled around long enough. And now my boys has got them a fine string of scalps an' some horses an' meat. That's good, no two ways about 'er. But I killed me a grizzly b'ar and took coup on 'im hand to hand. Big medicine, gal, an' I got a right to it. Now paint me up black, like I tell ye."

Two hours later, flanked by his sons, with the two women behind, Benton rode proudly into the adjoined

Crow villages. The party was hailed with gleeful cheering and whooping. Benton's bearskin was drawn up over his shoulders, and Big Dog and Two-tail Skunk displayed their string of scalps and the Cheyenne horses. The people thronged about them in admiration, young braves and woman and children, all babbling excitedly, while the camp dogs set off a continuous, frenzied barking and yapping.

Chastity and Pawnee Woman, staying close together, watched as Two-tail Skunk's three wives elbowed their way through the crowd to greet their husband. The warrior leaped from his horse and greeted the women warmly.

Yellow Belly, the head chief, and the old warriors Coyote Running and Red Eyes, along with Pine Leaf and High Bull, approached the party and greeted their return.

Big Dog raised his Hawken in salute.

"The Killer of Beavers and his two sons, Big Dog and Two-tail Skunk, have decided to return to their people," Yellow Belly called, barely able to conceal his delight. "You have brought us a white bear and some scalps and horses, but where is the white girl you set out to capture?"

"That's her, ye damned old fool!" Benton answered in English. "Can't ye tell a yeller-haired female when ye see her?"

"Oh!" the chief exclaimed. "She looks so much like a Sparrow Hawk that I did not notice her hair."

"We thought she was one of our own," Coyote Running added.

"And her hair had turned pale from listening to

152

your stories of the times we have fought the Blackfoot," Pine Leaf laughed, continuing the pretense of ignorance.

"We are glad for your return, Benton," Yellow Belly said. "Are you injured? Big Dog, what has happened?"

"Our father killed the white bear with his pistol and knife, Yellow Belly, but the bear nearly killed him also. His arm and shoulder are broken, though we have set them as well as we could and have bound them with deerhide. Then Skunk and I met some Cheyenne hunters, and so we hunted them and took their scalps and their horses. We have much meat in the pack bundles also."

"And the two women," Pine Leaf inquired, "where did you find them?"

Two-tail Skunk took it upon himself to explain how the women had been taken from the Pawnee. His story was accepted with smiles and words of admiration.

"Will your wives nurse Benton back to health?" Coyote Running asked, looking at Skunk.

"Yes, of course. Our lodge is large and warm. We will all take care of our father."

"We must go to Ears-of-the-Wolf now," Big Dog said. "There is great medicine in the killing of a white bear, and we must take no chances. My father is regaining his strength, but Ears-of-the-Wolf must help."

"I will send for him," Yellow Belly agreed. "Now we must prepare for the scalp dance and tomorrow a bear dance as well. One Who Strikes Three, the medicine woman, must preside for that. Pine Leaf, will you speak with her? She is your sister, and so that is proper."

"I will do it," replied the warrior woman. Then, turning to Big Dog, she smiled warmly, "It is good that you have returned, Big Dog. Soon we will ride the warpath together, as we have done before."

"We will go to my lodge now and make a place for Killer of Beavers," Two-tail Skunk interjected.

"Buffler dung!" Benton retorted. "This coon don't need no pamperin', and ye all know it, too."

"That is true," Big Dog agreed. "But we must bring in the medicine man. Later we will count our coups."

A great fire was lighted that night, and the dancing continued for many hours. Big Dog, Two-tail Skunk, and Killer of Beavers all recounted their coups to an enthusiastic audience of Sparrow Hawk warriors. When Big Dog spoke of allowing the one Cheyenne to escape, there was some heated discussion. Red Eyes asserted that the Cheyenne had done nothing to deserve his life, whereas Pine Leaf believed that Big Dog had done the correct thing.

The dance was still in progress when Pine Leaf left. She sought out Benton, who had retired earlier. Entering Skunk's lodge, she greeted the mountain man and the two captive women. She was surprised to discover that Pawnee Woman was in fact Big Dog's wife. But if that was the case, why was it that the white woman was not also the wife of the Sparrow Hawk warrior? Was something possibly the matter with her?

"Among our people," Pine Leaf explained to Pawnee Woman, "when a woman is taken captive in battle, she becomes the sister of the one who captures her and must be given in marriage to someone else. After that she becomes as one of us and is accepted as a Sparrow Hawk."

"I do not know your ways yet," Pawnee Woman said softly. She was uncertain how she should converse with the legendary Sparrow Hawk warrior woman, whose reputation was well known even among the Pawnee. Did one speak as to another woman, or as to a war chief?

"Not the same with a challenge fight," Benton insisted. "Since Big Dog killed Crooked Knife, both of the Pawnee's wives were forfeit to the winner. Pawnee Woman wanted to be Big Dog's wife."

"Then why is the Yellowhair not also his wife, Killer of Beavers?"

"Because I do not wish to be his wife," Chastity replied, carefully choosing the correct words, "and because he does not wish me to be his wife."

Pine Leaf stared at the white woman and raised one eyebrow.

"Is it both things, perhaps? Or is it that you wish to return to your own people?"

"It ain't that, Pine Leaf," Benton explained. "Whatever Cozzie wants to do is up to her. I had to go bring her back 'cause she's my friend, and life among the Pawnee ain't all it might be, not for a woman, anyhow."

"She looks more Indian to me than white, Benton. If she should wish to stay with us, then she must either marry Big Dog, or else both she and Pawnee Woman must be given in marriage to others. It cannot be both ways at the same time."

"Big Dog is my husband," Pawnee Woman said solemnly. "I do not wish any other."

"He is a brave man, a war leader with many coups to his credit. I am sure that he is a fine husband to you. Now you must convince your friend, Yellowhair, to be Big Dog's wife also."

"It's different with whites," Benton said, speaking now in the tongue of the Sparrow Hawks. "I have given my word that I would return her to her own people. I will break my word to them only if that is what Yellowhair wishes, for the bond of friendship is greater than the giving of words to the Long Knives."

Pine Leaf smiled, for it amused her to toy with the matter of tradition and custom.

"It is always confusing when we attempt to deal with the Long Knives," she said, "for their thoughts often do not make sense. Killer of Beavers, even you could not think very well until you came to live among our people. After that you got better."

"Are you truly a leader of the warriors?" Chastity asked suddenly.

"Yes, that is true. Long ago my brother was killed in battle with the Blackfoot, and I vowed to take vengeance upon them. Medicine Calf, who was later to be my husband, took me with him and showed me how to fight, even though I was only a young girl. After that my revenge-taking was strengthened, for I could not shame the great warrior who had made me his student."

"He is dead now?" Chastity inquired.

156

"No, Yellowhair, he is not dead. He went back to live with the Long Knives, for he was one of them. When he lived with us, he learned our ways and became our great leader. Even though he is back among the Long Knives now, and far away, he is the only warrior I will ever love in the way of a man and a woman. When he had to leave us, he promised to return, and I know that he will keep his word. The fate that Old Man Coyote imposes upon us is often strange. But I have learned patience, and I must be patient for a while longer. Those were good days, when Medicine Calf led us. If you had been among the people then, Yellowhair, you would never have thought of returning to the world of the white men."

"Where is . . . Medicine Calf?" Chastity asked, hesitantly.

"To the west, near the great flowing water. Once I went with him to the far lands, and we saw the great fish that swim along the coast."

"California," Benton added. "Gabe Bridger told me a year back. Others have told us also."

"Pawnee Woman, you must now build a lodge for Big Dog. Then you are truly one of us. Will you then allow the Yellowhair to live with you until she is ready to return to her own people?"

"Yes," Pawnee Woman answered. "Yellowhair is my sister, for we were both wife to the same man."

"Did you like that man as well as you like Big Dog?"

"No. That is why I wished to leave the Pawnee."

"Perhaps Yellowhair wishes to be Two-tail

157

Skunk's wife? Or will Killer of Beavers take a new wife now?"

"Pine Leaf, ye carry on like a damn raccoon once ye get an idea into your head."

"You must speak in the language of the Crow, Killer of Beavers. I have never been able to understand the language of the Long Knives."

"Ye understood it well enough not more than five minutes ago. This coon figgers you're just tryin' to stir things up a mite."

"I cannot understand your words," Pine Leaf laughed and then switched to English. "Soon you will wish to put fences on the land, like the other whites, and you will ask the buffalo if they will please stay inside so that it will be easier for you to find them when you wish to kill one. Yellowhair is more one of us than you are, it is possible."

"When that happens, Pine Leaf, it will be the end for all of us," Benton answered in Crow. "My skin is white, but inside I am a Sparrow Hawk."

"I know that is true," Pine Leaf said. "I have spoken only in jest. Tomorrow I will help you construct a lodge, Pawnee Woman, and I will bring others to help also. You must be shown how to build a proper Crow lodge. We will even instruct Yellowhair, for she will need to know this thing when she is also Big Dog's wife. . . ."

"I will not marry him!" Chastity blurted out.

Pine Leaf laughed, placed her fingers momentarily upon Benton's forehead, and left the lodge. She had been gone only moments, when Ears-of-the-Wolf, the medicine man who was older than anyone knew, entered the lodge. He held before him an amulet adorned with the claws and teeth of a bear. The ancient one gesticulated and then broke into a mumble of words that Chastity could not recognize.

Benton stared directly into the lodge fire, his face utterly immobile. The medicine man, oblivious to the women, danced about the mountain man as though half-asleep. His eyes were wide and seemed to focus at various points far outside the lodge. At length he ceased his ritual, called Benton by his Crow name, Killer of Beavers, and then popped the amulet into his mouth. He closed his eyes and wagged his head back and forth. When finally Ears-of-the-Wolf opened his mouth wide, for all to see, the amulet was gone.

"You will grow well now, Killer of Beavers," the medicine man intoned. "I have purified this lodge and have shown the spirits that the bear teeth that tore your flesh have been taken from within you and into me, whence they have passed back into you in a way that can no longer harm you."

"I give my thanks to Ears-of-the-Wolf," Benton said. "Do you wish to have two fine horses for payment?"

"Yes, that will be good. I am old and can no longer ride, but still horses are beautiful to look at."

"Big Dog has said that you are to have one Nez Perce horse and another of your own choosing from among those he and Skunk won in battle."

"Thank you, Aloysius Benton. One Who Strikes Three will preside at the Bear Song Dance tomorrow. You will be well enough to watch, but you must not participate, for then my medicine will be spoiled."

The shaman slipped from the lodge as quickly as he had entered.

Chastity in particular had been fascinated by the entire performance, even more so since it was obvious that Benton himself accorded it great significance.

"What good did that do?" she asked.

"Helps this old-timer's bones to knit," Benton said gravely.

"And the Bear Song Dance, what is that?"

"Cozzie, I wouldn't spoil it for ye for the world itself," and then in Crow, he spoke the word *bat-sir-a-pe*, "the tail-within."

"Aloysius, that doesn't make any sense. . . ."

"Not to white folks," Benton replied in English.

At first light, Pine Leaf appeared in the company of One Who Strikes Three. With them were the two wives of Coyote Running and a group of young boys, who carried bundles of poles and stacks of tanned hides. Pine Leaf pointed out where the lodge should be constructed and, under the direction of One Who Strikes Three, the building was begun. Both Pawnee Woman and Chastity paid close attention to all that Pine Leaf said, and within the space of three hours the lodge was completed.

"You must ask Big Dog to tell you of his victories in battle, all his coups, so that you will be able to record these on the central panel of the lodge, Pawnee Woman," Pine Leaf directed her, "for this is what a good wife must do. I will show you how it is done when you are ready."

"Are your coups painted on a panel in your lodge?" Chastity asked.

Pine Leaf laughed.

"Yellowhair, I have no wife, so how could my victories be signified on the lodge skin? One Who Strikes Three and I are both wives to Medicine Calf. We live in his lodge with Still Water and Cheyenne's Sister and Medicine Calf's son, Black Panther, and his wife. Our tepee is large, and the elkhide is filled with Medicine Calf's victories. Soon Black Panther and his wife will build their own lodge, and then she will do for him as I have told Pawnee Woman to do for Big Dog."

"But you are also a famous warrior. Benton has told me that."

Pine Leaf smiled and touched her fingers tentatively to Chastity's hair.

"You are a very pretty woman, even if you are white. Do you not understand, Yellowhair? I am wife to Medicine Calf. Now I must go, for it may be that my sister will need my help."

When the warrior woman had left, Pawnee Woman said, "My sister, this Pine Leaf is a very strange person. How could she be a great warrior? She does not look any stronger than other women."

"Perhaps not," Chastity replied, "but I can feel the strength of her mind when she speaks. I know already that she is stronger than Chief Yellow Belly, stronger in all the ways that matter."

"I feel it too," Pawnee Woman agreed.

The lodge fire was built early that evening, and the new home was honored with several guests, including Two-tail Skunk and his wives, Benton, Pine Leaf, and Coyote Running and his wives. Pawnee Woman and Chastity had spent several hours preparing the choicest portions of buffalo meat as well as a soup of buffalo tongue spiced with roots and berries and wild onions. The two women together served the guests, just as they had when among the Pawnee.

Big Dog showed evident pride in his new wife, but glanced at Yellowhair hardly at all.

The trader Buttermilk Thompson arrived with a bag of coffee beans and a can of smoking tobacco. Grinning broadly Benton shook hands with the trader as well as he was able.

"Figured these things might be welcome to you, Aloysius. Is there room for another hungry Long Knife?"

Following the meal, One Who Strikes Three announced the commencement of the Bear Song Dance, in honor of Killer of Beavers.

"Few men," she said solemnly, "have ever killed a white bear in single combat. Now our medicine will grow strong, and our hunters will succeed, and our warriors will be victorious against our enemies!"

That evening, a great fire was lighted, and the spectators gathered around in anticipation. As they watched, two young girls glided into the circle, and began to dance slowly around the leaping flames. Their bodies glistened with perspiration as they gyrated in rhythm to the steady cadence of the drums. Suddenly, One Who Strikes Three emerged from the shadows. Crouching low, the medicine woman swayed toward one of the dancers. With one swift gesture, she reached out and scooped a handful of white clay and owl feathers from the girl's abdomen. She held them high for all to see and then quickly pressed them back into the girl's flesh. The dancer groaned and fell heavily to the ground, rolling wildly about. A fume of red dust poured from her mouth. Then she lay still as the medicine woman stood over her, gesturing with her braceleted arms, seeming to ward off some unseen force.

All the while, the second girl continued to twist and turn in the firelight. As the first regained her senses, her companion danced to her side. Reaching toward the fallen girl, she withdrew two eggs from between her lips. Raising them triumphantly aloft, she then returned them to the girl's gaping mouth.

Her arms outstretched, One Who Strikes Three slowly danced toward Benton while his two sons, one on either side, lifted the huge grizzly skin over the trapper's head.

The spectators applauded loudly.

Several warriors, eager to assist, jumped up and carried the bearskin to the center of the circle where they fastened it to a cottonwood post. Next, the people brought out pouches filled with pemmican and larded meatballs, as well as containers of freshly harvested nuts and berries.

One Who Strikes Three danced toward the bearskin. Others fell in behind her, the column snaking back and forth, in and out. Still others surged toward the pole, and the medicine woman's voice sang out. "See the skin of the bear that Killer of Beavers has slain. Who has ever seen a larger bear, and yet Killer of Beavers was able to take its life! Look, all of you! The bear cub is there, its parent is here! The enemies of the Sparrow Hawks will hear our song and tremble, for our medicine grows strong!"

At length, exhausted from their efforts and sated with food, the crowd began to disperse.

Pawnee Woman and Yellowhair, accompanied by Big Dog, returned to the new lodge. The young warrior's eyes glittered with excitement.

"My father has been well honored!" he repeated several times. "Old Man Coyote has heard, and our medicine is indeed strong!"

Chastity had placed her sleeping robes on the far side of the lodge, and she slipped wearily into their warmth. She was desperately tired. Her mind and spirit seemed almost to have deserted her during the continual motion of the preceding two days. She had seen much that was either beyond her capacity to grasp or which made no sense at all. What of Ears-of-the-Wolf and his mysterious medicine that Benton accepted without question? How could she account for the amazing magic of One Who Strikes Three? Pine Leaf, the warrior woman, so different from any other woman she had ever known, strong and powerful in ways that defied understanding. And what was she to make of Big Dog, the fearless young warrior who now slept in the same lodge as she but whose arms encircled another woman?

Chastity stared at the sputtering fire and her eyes grew heavy. She slept deeply and dreamed of a great white bear. He loomed before her and spoke, calling her sister. He told her not to be afraid and to journey on until she found the sacred spring in which she must study her own reflection. His words said she would know what to do then.

She awoke, fighting for breath. The cold of the night had found its way into the new lodge, and only a faint red glow from the coals of the fire remained. Chastity shivered and pulled the buffalo robe tightly around her.

The days drifted by, and soon the last of the leaves had disappeared from cottonwood, aspen, and willow alike. Several light snows fell, and life in the Crow encampment was busy and purposeful. Benton improved with each day, and Chastity (who now had begun to think of herself as Cozzie Yellowhair) looked forward keenly to her occasional talks with Pine Leaf. Indeed, she wondered if she were not in some way hypnotized by the aura that seemed to radiate from the older woman.

How old was Pine Leaf? Her mid-thirties perhaps, but she had lost none of her beauty. Chastity wondered too why it was that such a woman would choose to wait for the return of a husband who had been gone for more than ten years now.

Throughout the autumn days, Chastity worked with the other women at their chores. They prepared pemmican from the meat brought in by the hunters, scraped and cured hides, gathered wood and carried water from the river. The cold grew ever more intense, and the ground was now hard underfoot. During most nights, it was necessary to awaken at intervals and stoke the lodge fires.

By late November a freezing rainstorm had unaccountably been followed by a thin, night-long snowfall that blanketed the Bighorn Basin. Several inches of cold, dusty white powder swirled and blew with each gust of wind. Sometimes the flakes spun in white funnel forms, and sometimes, if the wind was strong, the snow became a horizontal blizzard, like a prairie dust storm, even though the sky was clear and blue overhead.

Big Dog and Two-tail Skunk, unable now even to trap for beaver in the frozen streams, busied themselves fashioning harnesses, carving new designs on the stocks of their rifles, and making love to their wives.

On the afternoon that the gusting winds had finally cleared the encampment of snow, a band of Blackfoot descended on the villages. The attack came without warning, since Wolves—the warriors who acted as sentries—had not been posted in their usual outlying positions. But in this time of severe cold, no raid could have been anticipated.

Despite the suddenness of the attack, the Crow braves kept their heads, and were quickly astride their war ponies. With Pine Leaf and Big Dog leading the counterattack, they surged repeatedly toward the band of Blackfoot, whose relatively small war party was ineffectual against the combined strength of the Many Lodges and the Kicked-in-their-Bellies.

As the Blackfoot turned to retreat, Pine Leaf and Big Dog bore down on the hindmost. Big Dog clubbed one of the enemy from his horse with a blow from his Hawken's butt, and Pine Leaf's lance, famous for its deadly accuracy, leaped from her hand. The lethal shaft floated through the air and imbedded itself in a warrior's back, the razor-sharp tip emerging through his chest. He slumped forward, dead on his horse, and rode some thirty yards before leaning sideways and slipping to the ground.

Leaping from his pony, Big Dog fired his pistol into the throat of the stunned Blackfoot whom he had knocked from his mount.

The scalps were taken, but the Blackfoot did not return. The sally at the villages was nothing more than a diversionary attack. The real goal had been the theft of Sparrow Hawk horses, and the deed had been accomplished with dispatch. When the counting was finished, some three hundred horses were found to be missing.

Pine Leaf was in no mood for a celebratory scalp dance, even though Yellow Belly counseled patience.

"Warrior Woman, the Blackfoot have only borrowed these horses, and they have paid for their act by the death of two of their warriors. Our pastures will be thin soon, for the winter is truly upon us, and our herds have grown so large that many of our animals would go hungry. Let the Blackfoot take care of our horses for us, and when the grass grows once more, I will lead a war party against them. We will redeem our animals and many more beside. The Blackfoot are not so strong as they were years ago, before the white man's disease took so many of them. With a large party we will be able to ride through the lands of the Blackfoot without fear, and we will take whatever we wish. These are my words, Pine Leaf."

But Pine Leaf was not to be placated. The matter was one of principle, and she would take her revenge—even though no Sparrow Hawk had been killed and the pastures were indeed sparse, just as the head chief said.

"Yellow Belly, you are not now so eager for the warpath as when you were younger, for then you and I and Medicine Calf and Gray Bull and Red Eyes all rode together, and none could stand before us. It is true that we do not need these horses that have been stolen. But the Blackfoot must never again come to believe they can ride into our lands and escape with only two of their number left behind to be scalped. To believe such a thing would only make them strong again. No, my medicine for war is strong now, and I wish to take the Dog Soldiers with me and to ride until we have caught up with these thieves. Then we will bring back our horses and the scalps of the Blackfoot as well."

Yellow Belly knew well enough that it would do little good to argue with the indomitable warrior woman, for the fire shone in her dark eyes and her blood was up. He himself had courted her years before, only to see her choose Medicine Calf, his friend, his fellow Dog Soldier. Then Medicine Calf had wandered away from his adopted people, had gone back down the Big River to fight for the Long Knives, and Yellow Belly had become head chief of the Crow.

Head chief or not, however, his words were futile in dealing with Pine Leaf.

"My sister," he said finally, "if your medicine demon tells you to go, then that is what you must do. But I am not so old as you pretend, and so I think it is best that I ride with you and the Dog Soldiers. What other warriors do you wish to take with us?"

"Big Dog has already struck coup on these Black-foot, and so he will also wish to add to his revenge. High Bull of the Lumpwood clan is brave, and he has ridden with me many times, even though he is not a Dog Soldier. He will bring some of his Lumpwood warriors. Two-tail Skunk should not go, for he and Big Dog are blood brothers, and one of them must care for Killer of Beavers until he is completely well. Black Panther, the son of Medicine Calf and One Who Strikes Three, will wish to go. Dog Soldiers!" she called, turning to the eager warriors who had clustered about her. "Are there others among you who wish to ride with Pine Leaf? Are there others among you whose war medicine is strong and sings in your ears, sings the name Blackfoot?"

Scores of braves cheered and brandished their weapons. Pine Leaf embraced Yellow Belly lightly, and the chief held her for a long moment. Then he broke away and walked briskly toward his lodge.

When Big Dog told Pawnee Woman that he intended to ride against the Blackfoot she accepted the news without comment, and proceeded to ready his war implements.

As Chastity assisted her friend, she questioned her. "Why do you not object, Pawnee Woman? What if your man is killed in battle? Then you will be a stranger among these people. I think you should tell Big Dog that he must not go on this warpath, that you wish him to stay with you."

"Yellowhair," Pawnee Woman replied, "you know very well that would do no good. Big Dog is a great warrior among these people, who are now my

people, and his medicine is strong. He will return unharmed, so there is no danger to me. Can you doubt
his medicine, my sister? Do you not remember how he
challenged and killed Crooked Knife, one man against
the entire village of Pawnee warriors? That is why I
wished him to be my husband. Should I now grow
fearful for his life and humiliate him? He would
despise me then, and he would be right. A woman
must always respect her husband's medicine. Then, if
some time his medicine is not strong, she will see it in
his eyes. Then she should beg him to stay with her in
the lodge and wait until his medicine has grown strong
once again. That is what I think."

Chastity worked a new leather thong through the
loops of Big Dog's possibles sack and said nothing.
Then she nodded.

"My sister is wise," she said. "I still have much to
learn."

But that night, after the lodge fire had died down
and Chastity had listened to the sounds of Pawnee
Woman and Big Dog making love in the darkness,
even then she could not sleep. She shifted restlessly
beneath her robes.

Was it simply that she was fearful for the safety
of this man who had rescued her from the Pawnee?
Was his medicine truly as strong as others believed?

Call it what they will, she thought, some men and
some women have a power that cannot be accounted
for. Pine Leaf has such power, and Big Dog has it
also. . . .

In slaying Crooked Knife, had Big Dog in some
way actually come to own her, so that there was a

bond between them? And was it for that reason she did not want him to be injured or even killed in battle? She scoffed at the idea. It was foolish to suppose that in some way she was indeed owned by this taciturn, bull-headed young warrior.

But was it possible that she had, in the space of three months, begun to think like an Indian? Once, back on the prairies, Benton had said to her, "Cozzie, ye think like an Injun," and she had seen immediately that the mountain man had meant the words as a high compliment. If it really was true, then she was far more suggestible, far more impressionable than she had ever imagined herself to be. In the days following her abduction by the Pawnee, and after she had been given to Crooked Knife as his woman, she had vowed that she would never surrender her identity. She would do what she had to do, but she would never truly become *one of them*. But, after all, had it happened anyway?

"Do I love him, and that is why I am fearful for him to go?" she murmured to herself.

No inner voice denied the thought. She shivered under the buffalo robes, but it was not the cold that made her shudder. She asked herself the question again.

Big Dog Benton, she thought as she drifted into sleep, it's true—I love you, even though you despise me, and even though I despise myself for admitting it. But I will never tell you, Big Dog. We live in the same lodge together but there is a distance between us that neither of us could overcome even if we wanted to, and you don't, and neither do I. . . .

Rising early, Chastity built up the fire and helped

171

Pawnee Woman to tend to last-minute matters. When Pawnee Woman walked out with her husband to the spotted war pony, and Big Dog embraced his wife, Chastity stood watching at the entrance to the lodge. She wrapped her arms about her sides and squeezed hard until she became aware of the pressure. Suddenly she straightened her arms and held them to her sides, as though she were bound.

Big Dog mounted the Nez Perce horse and rode toward the center of the village where Pine Leaf and the other warriors were prancing their horses around the gray-black scar of the main fire-spot. They all circled for several minutes and then, with Yellow Belly and Pine Leaf in the lead, the war party slowly trotted from the encampment.

Pawnee Woman returned to the lodge, and she and Chastity embraced in an exchange of feelings that both knew and neither uttered.

Chapter 9

December 1848

The war party moved northward, across the Yellow-stone River, and into the lands of their enemies. Nearly two hundred warriors in all—they represented the fierce cunning and pride of the Crow, a people constantly at war with all about them and mightily feared by their enemies.

Big Dog listened as Pine Leaf bantered with High Bull about who would take the greater number of horses or the greater number of scalps. Even the po-nies sensed the excitement and moved along quickly. The miles melted away beneath their hooves.

Big Dog listened and felt the deep joy of the chase, the anticipation of danger, the possibility of his own death even.

It is a good day to die, he thought. It is a good time to die.

For the world was changing. The prophetic

dreams of Ears-of-the-Wolf that Big Dog remembered hearing as a boy were rapidly becoming fact. Even now the lands of the Crow were not entirely their own—not with steamboats operating on the Big River, the one the white men called Missouri, not with Long Knives settling near the rivers and spreading out away from the great arterial streams, not with plots of land being fenced and cattle grazing in places where only a few years past the mighty herds of buffalo moved unimpeded. And the endless flow of wagon trains, with each year bringing greater numbers of the lumbering carts moving ever westward.

Still, Big Dog felt the joy of his people, the Crow on the warpath, as it had been for many years. There were earlier times, he knew, before his people had horses, before they had formed an alliance with the Buffalo People and had become almost exclusively hunters. Before that there were no horses, so the stories went. And there had been an earlier time as well, before the Long Knives came from across the ocean to the east, from a land called Europe. In those days, so the stories said, the Crow had not yet found their own lands here in the Shining Mountains. They had lived far away to the south, where the winters were not so cold and where there were no mountains at all. But that was a long time ago. Only the stories remained, and not even many of those.

The white men recorded their stories in books and could trace their wanderings back to the times of the beginnings of things. The Crow also had their tales of how things began. Their legends told of a time when great waters came out of the north and the south and stood as tall as the Shining Mountains themselves, covering almost all of the land. One story told of four ducks who dived down and found the land, and after that Old Man Coyote hurled the mountains into place and set the stars into the sky so that they appeared as they still did in the present. And he chose the Crow as his own people and gave them these lands. He showed First Man and First Woman how to make fire and how to make weapons so that they could bring down the animal people and have them for food. Grandmother Moon, White Bear and all the others had helped the Crow. And then had come the time of horses—the Magic Dogs that had come first from the Spanish people who lived away to the south, near the Kiowa, the Apache, and the Navaho.

Big Dog knew the stories of the beginnings of the white men, for Benton had read them to him as a boy. His adopted father had taught him not only the language of the white men but how to read as well. Benton had always been concerned about his books and had invested them with great medicine. When Big Dog learned how to read, he too realized the strength of the medicine. He had considered how good it would be if the Crow could also have a way of writing their words into books so that the words would never be lost, just as the Cherokee people on the other side of the Father River had learned to do. Perhaps if things did not change too rapidly, the Crow would learn this magic and would be able to keep their own stories in books.

There would be time, Big Dog concluded.

The Sparrow Hawks, years since, had envisioned something of the white man's quest for western land

and had realized that in the times to come an alliance with the Long Knives would be good. While the Sioux and the Cheyenne and the Blackfoot fought the whites, the Crow were friends to them and were able to buy weapons to fight off their enemies. And yet, if it were not for the white men moving ever westward, and pushing the Sioux and the Cheyenne and others before them, would the Crow ever have needed to be friends with the Long Knives?

His thoughts turned to Chastity. Cozzie Yellowhair would go to her people on the Big Salty—she would become one of *them* again. And he would not see her anymore, for their worlds would be too different. She would bear the children of a white man, and no doubt she would be happy. That was the world she came from, after all.

He, Big Dog, was a Sparrow Hawk. But he was part white man too, although not in his blood but because he was the son of Aloysius Benton. Two worlds, Big Dog thought, and both of these worlds pull at me. I am Crow, and yet I am also Benton's son. I have hunted and trapped and fought and lived with the Long Knives. I have sung and danced with them at the times of rendezvous. I was one of them, and they accepted me and respected me, knew my medicine was strong.

Big Dog grinned as he remembered the mountain men, his old companions. They were different from the St. Louis people or the settlement people or the traders or the wagon people. "Nuther Long Knife nor Injun. Both, mebbe," Benton had said.

And he, Big Dog, was one of them. The innocence of Pine Leaf or Yellow Belly, for instance, was not his innocence.

"Better if it were," he mused.

Even Benton was innocent in the same fashion. He knew what was happening and yet he refused to give heed to it. Perhaps, after all, that way was better. Certainly nothing could be done. What was happening could not be stopped, and, as Big Dog knew, the wild and free ways of his people were doomed, whether in a few years or in many. The winters continued to pass, and each time the new grass came the world was different in small ways, just as the rivers coming down from the snow-covered Shining Mountains dug their canyons deeper, cut back at the earth itself, sweeping all before them into the swollen, brown flood of the Big River, and down to the Father River itself.

We do not see it, Big Dog thought, because it is gradual—and yet it continues to happen. Ears-of-the-Wolf saw these things many years ago, and he told us how it would be. Our old chiefs also saw, and they agreed with Ears-of-the-Wolf. And now it has come. If we bend as the willows do when the great winds blow, then we will not break, we will survive. But what kind of world will we survive in?

Time and again Big Dog's thoughts returned to Pawnee Woman. In his mind he lay with her once more in the dim warmth of their lodge. He thought also of Cozzie Yellowhair, perhaps lying awake in the darkness beyond the lodge fire, listening to them, thinking about them, passing judgment on them for being Crow instead of white.

The war party had encountered heavy snow in

crossing the mountains beyond the Yellowstone, and the short days of late December limited the number of hours they could travel each day. But now the party moved down into country free of snow and into the lands of the Blackfoot. Wolves went ahead to try to discover the whereabouts of the Blackfoot camp. The scouts returned with word that two villages were assembled below what the mountain men called Gallatin Gateway, upstream from the confluence of the three forks of the Missouri.

With the enemy now in prospect, Pine Leaf insisted upon an enactment of the War Path Secret, a detail not attended to earlier. Pine Leaf herself, with Black Panther, rode out to find a buffalo. With the onset of winter, however, the great beasts had all disappeared. After a full day of luckless hunting, Pine Leaf decided on a new approach.

"We might have to kill an elk. But the medicine of the elk is not as strong as that of the buffalo. Black Panther and I will ride into the mountains once more, for there we saw the white buffalo of the mountains. It is winter now, so the white buffalo will be right for the War Path Secret. While we are gone, I want someone to shoot an elk anyway, for we may have to make its medicine work. We should hunt now anyway, for later we will have to ride long and hard, and we will not want to kill our horses for food."

Pine Leaf and Black Panther rode off in the direction of Gallatin Mountain. Big Dog and High Bull and a few others went in search of game. When they rode in a few hours later, the westward sky blazed a deep red above the mountains. The dark, angry redness often meant a storm was coming on. Pine Leaf and Black Panther had already returned and had indeed been able to kill a mountain goat. Big Dog's party had also been successful, and slabs of meat hung high in the spruce branches above the four campfires.

The Crow filled themselves with roasted venison, elk, and moose as well as small portions of the mountain goat. Rising from their meal, they formed a circle around the largest of the fires. Each warrior grasped the long loop of white-buffalo intestine that was drawn about the circle.

"Now the War Path Secret will begin," Yellow Belly declared. "Old Man Coyote will strengthen our medicine, and we will defeat the Blackfoot and take their horses, even those they stole from us. Now each warrior must tell all that he has done with the women of the village since the last time he was part of the Secret. All must speak, even if they have lain with the wives of other warriors who are present. In this way we will sever the feminine bonds of weakness, and we will all share in the knowledge. Warrior Woman too will speak, for she is the only woman who is allowed to participate in the War Path Secret. We must all speak truthfully, for in that way we are drawn together and made stronger. Now let it begin. These are my words, Sparrow Hawks!"

And so each spoke in turn, revealing details and actions, who used their mouths and who was taken in the manner of dogs, who cried, and who giggled and laughed. Only the details of what was done with one's own wife or wives might be spared. Even when a warrior spoke of making love to another warrior's wife, the

179

faces in the firelight remained like stone. Pine Leaf avowed that she had made love with no one and that she was resolved to await the return of Medicine Calf. Her words were almost identical with others she had spoken at other War Path Secrets for the preceding twelve years. Some hoped that she might speak of going to the willows with Yellow Belly. The head chief's long-time infatuation with her was well known, but always the warrior woman's story was the same.

This night, however, further anticipation shimmered in the darkness, for many of the warriors wondered how it was between Big Dog and the Yellowhair. The woman was very beautiful, beautiful and exciting with her long pale hair. Many of the braves were attracted to the white woman and secretly wished to make love to her, deferring their attentions only because they knew that the situation had something to do with the odd ways of the Long Knives. Some even spoke the idea that white women had devils in them, and that was why Big Dog did not take her for his wife, even though he kept her in his lodge. Others thought that Benton himself intended to marry her, and that the son was keeping watch over her until her Long Knife strangeness had vanished.

But when Big Dog's turn to speak came, he said only that he made love each night to his new wife, Pawnee Woman. Of the Yellowhair he made no mention.

Black Panther surprised many, for he spoke of meeting with Noisy Gray Squirrel and of making love to her numerous times. Noisy Gray Squirrel, as all knew, was being courted by a warrior named Elk

Watcher, who had already discussed the marriage price with the girl's parents.

Neither Elk Watcher nor Noisy Gray Squirrel's father was present on this war party, and neither would be told. The things spoken of at the War Path Secret might not be repeated by anyone, on pain of death. Only the medicine men would be told when the warriors returned to their lodges. Those who had already heard, however, would watch the situation with some interest upon their return. Several young men began to consider that they, too, might attempt to interest Noisy Gray Squirrel in going to the willows, for the girl was tall and striking. Now it was seen that she was not interested in Elk Watcher's suit and was in fact looking for someone else. Black Panther would soon have competition.

When the ritual was completed, the Sparrow Hawks retired immediately, and all were up and ready to go before the full dawn had come. Only one day's ride remained between them and the camp of their enemies. The approach would have to be made with great care, for the Blackfoot might well be expecting a mission of reprisal and would probably have Wolves posted to keep surveillance over the likely paths of approach.

To counter this possibility, Big Dog counseled Pine Leaf and Yellow Belly to swing wide to the east of the villages and approach from the south, through the broad meadows where a good number of horses would no doubt be pastured.

"I had thought of the same thing," Yellow Belly

grinned, mimicking Pine Leaf, who had been about to suggest the procedure.

"It is a good idea," Pine Leaf agreed. "Yellow Belly himself would have thought of it, but he has nearly forgotten what to do on the warpath. He spends too much time at home, filling his lodge with tobacco smoke and counting the scalps he took years ago. Perhaps he does not like the odor of fresh ones."

"Yellow Belly has many scalps," the head chief said, "and some of them still drip the blood of Blackfoot and Assiniboin."

Big Dog nodded, agreeing with Yellow Belly and Pine Leaf at the same time.

"Now we must ride," he said. "The Dog Soldiers and the Lumpwoods are thirsty for the blood of Blackfoot and the smell of new horses."

The warriors moved up a lateral canyon, crossed the low ridge, and rode southward, circling back from below the Blackfoot villages. Taking cover, they waited for an hour or two past sundown and the light of the waning half-moon. In the clear, cold air of winter, the land shimmered before them, a world of shadows and outlines, but all quite visible.

"It is a good night for stealing horses," Black Panther said.

"It is always a good night for stealing the horses of the Blackfoot," Big Dog replied.

The Sparrow Hawks tethered their own horses in a secluded draw and crossed over the last ridge on foot. Like shadows themselves, they slipped down among the Blackfoot herd. Pine Leaf found two guards, both asleep. She and Big Dog crawled toward the men. Pine Leaf threw herself over the face of one and thrust her knife into the man's throat. His body convulsed for a moment, as though stunned by lightning, and then lay still. In almost the same instant, Big Dog slammed the butt of his pistol down between the other Blackfoot's eyes. He raised his arm to strike once more, and then held the blow in mid-swing. The guard was already limp, his forehead split open.

The two warriors deftly scalped their victims, snatched up the weapons, and then leaped up to participate in singling out the most desirable horses.

One animal, near the center of the area, was picketed in full war trappings, as though as a challenge to anyone who might wish to take it.

"It is yours, Big Dog," Pine Leaf whispered, her smile glinting in the moonlight. "I have too many war ponies already."

Three other guards were slain by the Sparrow Hawks, and only the final one woke in time to see his fate. His scream was cut off as his throat was slashed by Yellow Belly. The old chief was thoroughly enjoying this night's work, for, in the moonlight and the chill air and the frenzy of fast and careful movements, he was a young warrior once more. He was singling out his first stolen horse from a Cheyenne herd, slipping a noose around its neck, swiftly leading it away. For this moment, time had ceased to exist, and Yellow Belly rejoiced. Was it not for such times that a man was given life and strength? To steal the enemy's horses. To strike coup in battle. To kill the buffalo. To take the scalps of the enemy. To ride through wind and sun and heat and darkness, to be alive. . . .

For some time the work continued, until the Sparrow Hawks had drawn away perhaps a thousand horses, nearly a third of the Blackfoot herds. Assembling the horses beyond the low ridge, the Sparrow Hawks were quickly mounted and ready to ride. They would proceed in the direction of the Yellowstone, by way of the easy northern pass. There, with luck, the snow cover would be light and no great impediment to moving so large a number of horses.

They rode at a forced march through the remaining hours of darkness, not stopping with dawn but continuing until noon of the following day. The snow across the pass was deeper than expected, and the going was slow indeed. The half moon hung low in the sky. The air was frigid and the snow crusted hard. As the light returned with the thin gray of false dawn, the war party dropped down toward the river and passed out of the snow zone.

The Blackfoot would follow soon and would move more easily across the mountains, the trail well-prepared for them. Pine Leaf and Yellow Belly concluded that it would be best to remain on the north bank of the Yellowstone, crossing the smaller Shields River instead, and resting the animals on the far side of the tributary stream.

The horses milled about on the half-frozen grassy areas near the river. They shivered and snorted from the cold water of the crossing and pulled in a desultory fashion at the broken yellow grass. The Sparrow Hawk warriors downed a quick meal of cold meat and resumed their hurried downstream trek.

Another brilliantly crimson sunset was flaming behind them when a trailing Wolf, pushing his mount to the utmost, pounded up to the main group. The Blackfoot were indeed following and were no more than an hour's ride behind.

"How many are there?" Pine Leaf demanded.

"Two hundred and fifty, maybe three hundred warriors," the Wolf reported.

"Then we cannot rest this night," Yellow Belly concluded. "The Blackfoot slept last night, and their horses are fresher than ours. We can change horses, but with so large a herd, we cannot move as fast or as well as our enemies. They will certainly ride all night in the attempt to overtake us."

"Maybe we should double back and ambush them," Pine Leaf suggested. "The Blackfoot are brave, but they are also stupid. They never use caution, and that is why we are able to defeat them."

"They are not stupid at all, my sister," Yellow Belly contradicted. "We have fought these people many times, and it is only since the white man's disease, smallpox, destroyed their numbers that we have always won. And they are fierce fighters."

"They will not be expecting an ambush," Pine Leaf insisted. "They will think we are trying to get away from them, and so they will not expect us to come back at them."

"We would have to leave the horses, and it would take days to round them up again. Even if we are able to surprise the Blackfoot, we will lose our horses. It is better to escape, for we have not lost any of our warriors. If we can return to our villages with so many horses and yet not lose any of our young men, the victory will be far greater. If we fight, some will be lost, even though we defeat the Blackfoot. Then the families of the dead will have to mourn, and we will have to go out once again in order to take our revenge."

"That is true, Yellow Belly," Pine Leaf agreed. "But our animals are tired. Even if we ride all night, the Blackfoot will still catch up with us, and then we will have to fight anyway." And she added, "My way is better."

Big Dog listened with interest as the two leaders argued, and then he spoke.

"There is a box canyon a short way ahead. A creek flows through it and forms a waterfall at the upper end. There is one trail out, but only men on foot can make it. The Blackfoot will not know of this trail, I think. We can fortify the entrance to the canyon, and inside we will find room for our horses. If the Blackfoot attempt to follow us this night, we will be able to shoot down at them from the canyon sides."

"What if they too know this place, Big Dog? Then they will hold us in the canyon, while some of them come around from behind. They will attack us from both directions."

"Benton and I spent most of one winter in the canyon and were never bothered. All things are possible, but this way we may save our horses and use Mother Earth to protect us at the same time."

"What is your counsel, Pine Leaf?" Yellow Belly asked.

"I speak with Big Dog. I think it will work."

"High Bull, how do you speak?"

"With Big Dog. He knows this place, and the rest of us do not. I would follow his words."

"Long Bow?"

Long Bow stared off at the sunset and shook his head.

"I believe we should keep riding this night," he said. "If the Blackfoot know about the trail down from the cliffs, they will sneak in upon us in the middle of the night, and then the others will charge up from below."

"We can post guards up on the trail," Big Dog insisted. "If they come down the trail, we will be able to kill them, and they will not be able to protect themselves—the trail is narrow and comes down against sheer rock."

Long Bow thought a moment, then agreed with Big Dog.

"It will work, then. Yellow Belly and Pine Leaf, I speak with Big Dog. Let us move into the canyon with no outlet."

Big Dog led them forward through the waning light, hoping that his memory of seven years past was accurate. Suddenly, with the shadows blurring the details of the land, things had begun to look different. But when he reached the stream and saw the old scarface pillar of stone, he knew he had remembered well. He signaled to the others, and the herd of horses were driven up through the narrow corridor between twisted spires of rock, the warriors urging them along from behind. The crooked defile was only a quarter of a mile in length. After that, the stream opened out into large meadows surrounded by further walls of rock.

When the horses were moved up into the meadows, the Sparrow Hawks placed a number of riflemen along either side of the defile. Big Dog led half a dozen others to the brush-overgrown entrance to the rear trail, placing them in positions from which they would have Blackfoot targets, should any attempt to venture down. When the moon rose, anyone on the trail would be clearly revealed, whereas the Sparrow Hawk guards were protected behind boulders and ragged brush.

The Sparrow Hawk warriors ate a hurried meal of half-dried meat and waited silently. Crouched in the boulders above the defile with Pine Leaf beside him, Big Dog thought about Benton and his perpetual pot of coffee. The old man would trap half a winter just to buy his brew.

Damn, Big Dog thought, it would certainly taste good about now, even if he'd mixed it up with barley and willow bark all at the same time. . . .

"They will come soon," Pine Leaf said softly. "Blackfoot and Crow will both be firing at the darkness. We will be able to see only the explosions of the rifles. Then they will pull back and wait for morning."

"If they take their time, the moon will be up. Then the advantage will be ours. Moonlight should pour right into the canyon."

"Grandmother Moon glows beyond the horizon. I can see her. But I think the Blackfoot will be here before her light is able to help us."

Big Dog nodded in the darkness and grunted softly.

Suddenly, Pine Leaf touched his arm. "They are near, Big Dog. Do you hear them? They are by the river. They realize we have turned away from the main trail. Now they are puzzled and will talk for a time while they decide what to do. Perhaps they will wait until morning before following up the narrow canyon."

"Do they know that we are aware of them, Pine Leaf?"

"No. I do not think they know that. I think they will talk for a time and then keep coming. If they do, that means they are not familiar with your canyon, Big Dog. If they do not come, then they know we cannot get out, and probably they also know about the trail down from the back of the canyon. We will see what they do."

They heard the sound of horses moving up through the defile. "We have them now," Pine Leaf exulted. "They are as innocent as children, these Blackfoot. It is a shame that we must kill them."

Big Dog grinned as he leveled his rifle over the sandstone rim. The Sparrow Hawk rifles exploded, and a great commotion ensued in the narrow gorge below. Horses screamed, and Blackfoot warriors shouted. Again and again the Sparrow Hawks fired a withering rain of lead into the darkness. Then the Blackfoot began firing back, and thin blue-red lines of light filled the air. The hot odor of gunpowder drifted through the night, and wounded men cried out.

"That voice!" Pine Leaf shouted over the din. "It is a voice I recognize. Heavy Shield himself is with them! The old chief has led this pursuit. I did not know he was still alive. . . ."

189

"Heavy Shield, the Blackfoot head chief?" Big Dog asked, incredulously.

"He is the one. Once on the Yellowstone, a great battle occurred, and Medicine Calf and I both challenged him to fight, and yet he would not. He said he would not fight a woman. He wanted to fight Rotten Belly. Then he signaled for the Blackfoot to withdraw, Big Dog, and as he did so, Two Bears charged across the river, and all of us followed. We threw them into panic and chased them for a long way."

"Heavy Shield must be more than sixty winters," Big Dog replied, firing another blast from his Hawken. "It is strange that he has led the warriors. Perhaps he has chosen this time to die."

"I have an idea, Big Dog. Once he would not fight me, but now my medicine is known everywhere. I am still a woman, but our enemies fear me—and perhaps they even fear my medicine more because I am a woman. When they fight against me, these men do foolish things, and so I am able to kill them. Will Heavy Shield fight me now? Will he be willing to risk death beneath Pine Leaf's lance? He is a great warrior, and he has slain many of our brothers in battle, but now he has grown old, and I am still young. His medicine grows weak, while the strength of mine is well known. Big Dog, this chief will have to fight me now. In the morning we will see."

Big Dog grunted.

"Uhh!" Pine Leaf returned, mimicking him. "You growl as your father does instead of the way the Sparrow Hawks do it. Will your skin also turn white now?

You must not let it happen until we have defeated these Blackfoot. Will you promise me that?"

"My skin will never turn white, Pine Leaf, an' ye can lay to that!"

"Your father has corrupted you!" Pine Leaf laughed and loosed a shot into the darkness.

The Blackfoot had managed to turn about and were retreating back toward the Yellowstone.

Chapter 10

January 1849

The day dawned red, with long bands of crimson smeared above the eastern canyon wall. It was warmer now, and the sky was rapidly becoming overcast.

"Snowstorm coming," Big Dog remarked as he ate his morning meal of stale meat.

"It is a good day to die, this," Two Bears mused. "The Blackfoot and the Crow will all die in the falling of snow."

"Perhaps they will choose not to fight," Pine Leaf mused. "Already a number of bodies lie along the canyon trail."

"More likely they'll try to wait us out," Big Dog grunted. "They must have sent scouts to look over the land by now. If so, they know we can't get out anymore than they can get in."

"We will stay here all winter, with the Blackfoot for neighbors," Two Bears laughed.

193

Black Panther rubbed bear grease over the stock of his rifle, an old Hawken given to him by his father, Medicine Calf, years before. Now he looked up and squinted at the fading redness in the eastern sky. "Perhaps we could take a party out over the trail Big Dog has told us of. Then we could come at the Blackfoot from both sides."

"Not a bad idea at that," Big Dog replied. "Except they've probably got a couple of Wolves up on the top. If they didn't know about this canyon before, they do now."

Yellow Belly scrambled up beside the others and rubbed at his nose.

"Warrior Woman," he asked anxiously, "what is your counsel?"

"We should ride out to face them, Great Chief. Heavy Shield leads these warriors, and I will challenge him to single combat. Once, long ago, he refused to fight me. Now he will have no choice. The years are upon him, and he will not want anyone to say that he feared to fight with Pine Leaf of the Sparrow Hawks. He will not wish to admit that his medicine is not as strong as mine. Then I will kill him, and the others will flee before us."

"They will not retreat, even then," Big Dog disagreed. "They will want their chief's body. We would do exactly the same thing if Yellow Belly were to fall in battle, for the chief's bones must rest in the sacred place."

"I will give them the body," Pine Leaf declared. "I will not even scalp Heavy Shield."

"Big Dog is right," Yellow Belly said. "To kill

their great chief will make them fight like twice their number."

"No," Pine Leaf persisted, "my plan is the only one that will work. When we chose to keep the herd of stolen horses and came into this canyon, the fate was determined. There is no other way now."

Big Dog nodded.

"Yellow Belly, we must do as Pine Leaf says," agreed Black Panther. "We all have strong medicine. In this thing, Old Man Coyote tests us all. But let us allow them to retreat with their war chief still alive. He will step on a porcupine soon and die anyway."

"They will not give up while we are still in their lands and have their horses," Big Dog said. "We must fight them. It is the only way."

"I am ready to fight," said Black Panther. "Yellow Belly, you are the chief. What shall we do?"

"We will fight. Make yourselves ready. I will speak to High Bull and Long Bow and the others."

The Sparrow Hawks assembled at the foot of the meadow, and Yellow Belly harangued the warriors. He reminded them of their honor and of how the Sparrow Hawks had defeated the Blackfoot many times before. The warriors raised high their lances and rode proudly through the defile, grim-faced and ready for battle.

The Blackfoot were waiting.

Heavy Shield drew his war pony a few paces in front of his warriors and called across in English.

"Where is the leader of this band of Crow? Ride forward and we will speak."

Without waiting for word from Yellow Belly, Pine Leaf clapped her legs to her horse's sides and trotted out until she stood twenty yards from the Blackfoot chief.

"Do you remember me, Heavy Shield? I am Pine Leaf, and the strength of my medicine is known to all."

"I know you, Warrior Woman. Many of my braves have wished to take your long hair from you, but always they have lost their own. It is many winters since that day on the Yellowstone. This time Beckwourth is not with you."

"The spirit of Medicine Calf is with his people. He is gone, but we still hold his medicine."

"Much has happened to both our peoples, Warrior Woman, and our numbers have grown fewer. Now we must not fight but speak in peace. Return our horses, and we will depart."

"We have no horses of yours, Heavy Shield, but only a small band of our own."

"Warrior Woman does not speak truth. You have stolen many horses from our herds."

"We took only those horses your warriors stole from us—and also other horses they had made friends with. You would not wish our horses to be lonely for their friends? You should have thought of this before you allowed your warriors to raid our village, Heavy Shield."

"There is no way to control the young men. You know that as well as I do. But now you have taken your revenge, for many Blackfoot lie dead in the canyon above. I say again, take with you the number of horses we took from you and depart in peace."

"No, Heavy Shield. Once you refused to fight me because I was only a woman. Now my medicine is known to all, and even the great chief of the Blackfoot must recognize it. I say that we must fight. If you kill me, then my warriors will take my body and depart in peace. But if I slay you, we will keep these horses, and your warriors must take up your body and return to their villages and so begin the time of mourning for their chief. Do you refuse battle once more, Heavy Shield?"

"You will have what you wish, Warrior Woman. Go back now and speak to the Crow warriors, and I will speak to my people. Then we will ride out to where we now stand, and I will send you to the Spirit World. These are my words."

Pine Leaf and Heavy Shield reined their war ponies about and returned to their people to rehearse what was about to happen.

"Pine Leaf," Big Dog urged, "this is not a good thing. Heavy Shield is the head chief of his people, and all fear him. I will fight in your place, for if I am lost, the people will not mourn so long. My medicine is strong, and I will fight this chief."

Pine Leaf reached across and touched Big Dog's face with the tips of her fingers.

"You are loyal to me, just as you have always been, Big Dog. But Old Man Coyote has determined that this must be. If I fall in battle, then you must protect me. I do not want my scalp to adorn a Blackfoot lodge when Medicine Calf returns to me. I wish him to be proud of me and to know that I died in battle, that I was honored by our people. Will you do this?"

"If that happens, we will not let them touch you, Pine Leaf."

All this time Yellow Belly had been staring at the ground. His eyes were distant and withdrawn and full of a terrible sadness. Pine Leaf urged her pony close to his and embraced her chief—and suitor of days long past.

"Yellow Belly, the head chief of the Mountain People acts as though Pine Leaf were already dead, even though she is touching you. What is it that you fear, my friend?"

"Once against the Assiniboin," Yellow Belly replied, "your medicine was not strong, and you were nearly killed. Medicine Calf, Two Bears and I thought you were dying. Only Ears-of-the-Wolf was able to bring you back from the Spirit World."

"It is true," Pine Leaf sighed. "And my friends saved my life. Two Bears! Many times we have ridden together. Are you also afraid my medicine has grown weak?"

Two Bears stared solemnly at Pine Leaf, and then, to the surprise of all, he began to laugh.

"It is a good day to die!" he retorted. "See, the snow is beginning to fall even as we speak. Pine Leaf—go kill this great chief of the Blackfoot, for then we can keep the horses we have harvested and ride home."

Pine Leaf smiled radiantly but was annoyed that tears had started to her eyes. She brandished her lance high, turned her mount and urged the animal toward Heavy Shield.

The Sparrow Hawks sat motionless, silent, while across the meadow the Blackfoot whooped wildly.

Onward the Warrior Woman charged, her lance

held ready to strike. Then, as the Sparrow Hawks watched in horror, Heavy Shield slowly raised his rifle and took aim.

"Damn fool!" Big Dog moaned. "She's going to try to take him with her lance!"

"A good day to live!" her strong voice echoed back from the rock faces behind which the Sparrow Hawks had taken position.

Then came the blue puff of Heavy Shield's rifle, and Pine Leaf was nearly spun from her horse by the impact. The sound of the shot drifted out across the river, muffled now by the increasing fall of snow. But the Warrior Woman, clinging to her mount, bore down upon Heavy Shield and struck him a blow across the face with the shaft of her lance. The rifle flew from his hands, and he quickly drew his knife as Pine Leaf turned about and came back at him.

Then it was finished.

The owl-feathered lance took Heavy Shield full in the chest, its point thrusting completely through his body. For an instant, the chief sat motionless, his eyes wide, his mouth gaping. Then he pitched forward and tumbled face downward onto the gray-brown winter grass. Pine Leaf slipped from her pony and, staggering from her wound, approached the inert body, already being covered by a mantle of falling snow. With all the strength left in her, she withdrew the imbedded lance and waved it high in a gesture of victory.

The Blackfoot warriors screamed in anger and charged toward her, intent upon revenge. The Sparrow Hawks broke forward at the same instant, and within moments the battle was joined. Big Dog, Yellow Belly, and Two Bears as well as Black Panther and High Bull dashed immediately to Pine Leaf and formed a protective circle around her. Black Panther hauled the warrior woman up onto his own horse, turned abruptly, and retreated to the rear of the Crow forces.

Big Dog's pistol snapped until it was empty, and then, battle axe in hand, he drove into the Blackfoot. The battle raged on, the meadow echoed with war cries and the screams of the wounded and dying, with pistol fire and rifle fire at close quarters. A group of Blackfoot had converged about the body of Heavy Shield, forming a circle for its defense. Yellow Belly ordered his warriors to pull back so that the Blackfoot might take up their slain chief, and the Sparrow Hawks and the Blackfoot drew apart while Heavy Shield was carried to the rear.

Suddenly a voice boomed out over the tumult.

"Benton! Is that you? *Sacre bleu*, friend of me! This is Fontaine!"

Big Dog stared in amazement toward the Blackfoot.

"Pierre Fontaine?" he called. "What are you doing with the Blackfoot?"

"*Enfant de grâce*, I live with these people now. *Mon copain*, there is now blood on both sides! Let us put down our weapons so that no more go to the Spirit World, *mort*! The warriors, they will follow me. We wish now to return to our villages so we may mourn for our leader. It is better this way, *a vrai dire*!"

"This Blackfoot is a friend of yours, Big Dog?" Yellow Belly asked.

"He is not Blackfoot. He is a French trapper,

from the old days. My father and I both know him well."

"And now he is Blackfoot?"

"Apparently."

"If they will do as he says, it will be good. This man's name is Fontaine?"

"Yes, yes."

"Fontaine!" Yellow Belly shouted across the distance separating the two war parties. "I am Yellow Belly, chief of the Crow. I like your words. If you are friend to Big Dog, then I will trust you. Take your warriors and ride back the way you came. We will do the same thing. Take up your wounded and dead, and we will do likewise. These are the words of Yellow Belly!"

"It is settled!" Fontaine called back in Crow. "This warpath is over. Big Dog Benton! Ride with the Great Coyote. When our paths cross next, we'll eat hump-rib together, *sacré*!"

The taking up of the dead and wounded was accomplished quickly, and the Blackfoot disappeared into the thickening snowfall, leaving the Sparrow Hawks to gather up their own wounded and dead. Three young warriors had fallen and had been scalped, and a dozen suffered minor wounds.

Black Panther attended to Pine Leaf, whose left shoulder had been pierced by Heavy Shield's rifle ball. The warrior woman, although in discomfort, made little of the wound, calling it just a scratch.

"I am not hurt," she protested, "but I am sad that we have lost those young men. They were new to the warpath and did not know how to protect themselves."

"All would have been well if the Blackfoot had kept the word of their chief," Big Dog argued. "Pine Leaf, why did you not use your rifle? Or the pistol in any case? Did you wish to die here?"

"No, son of the Killer of Beavers, Warrior Woman did not wish to die. But the rifle and pistol are the weapons of the Long Knives. Heavy Shield was a great chief, and such a man should die by the arrow or lance. I did not wish him to go the Spirit World with the white man's lead in him. Besides, Old Man Coyote has controlled this thing. Heavy Shield was fated to die by my hand. There was nothing either of us could do to prevent it. Now my medicine is complete. I have taken coup upon the one who refused to fight me long ago, and I have slain him. My vow to Old Man Coyote is complete."

Big Dog stared at Pine Leaf and then at Black Panther, but said nothing.

"Now it will never be the same again," Pine Leaf sighed.

There was sadness in her eyes.

Big Dog turned away, confused. He mounted his pony and joined the others to gather the herd of horses they had sheltered in the box canyon.

Soon the Sparrow Hawks were on the move once more, downriver, into a world that was blindingly white at times. Gusts of snow alternating with periods of calm, when only a few flakes trickled down from the heavy grayness above them. They pushed on for two days until the continued snowfall forced a stop.

During the days of the long trek home, Big Dog's thoughts turned more and more to Cozzie Yellowhair.

Why could he not keep her from his mind? Why did this woman of all women have power over him? He could feel her medicine. It was almost tangible, like spider webs that blew in the autumn air, clinging to him, catching at his face and shoulders and hands.

But she does not want me, he thought, and this angers me. To her I am a savage. My world is ending, and hers goes on and on . . .

And so the days continued, through wind and snow and freezing cold. The Crow crossed the Yellowstone, losing only two animals that foundered in quicksand and were caught by the current and drawn under the water. From here the party, driving its herd of horses before it, passed overland to the head of the Absaroka Range. Anticipation drove them onward now, and one last full day of riding brought them to the encampment of the Many Lodges and the Kicked-in-their-Bellies.

Sending a pair of Wolves before them, they rode in just at sunset and were greeted by hundreds of their cheering fellows—warriors, women, children and a horde of yapping dogs.

A great fire was kindled in the middle of the village, and the odor of roasting elk flesh assailed the warriors as they entered the camp.

Their faces were painted the black of victory.

A scalp dance would be held this night, and there would be the public counting of coups. Only the families of the three who had fallen in battle would be forbidden to participate. They would put on mourning paint and call upon Pine Leaf or Yellow Belly or High Bull or Coyote Running or Big Dog to lead out another party for a revenge-taking, for only after that could their faces be washed.

And so it would go on, as it always had, each war party calling in turn for yet another war party. The perpetual wars of the Crow nation.

Pawnee Woman and Yellowhair, as well as Two-tail Skunk and Benton, stood outside Big Dog's lodge, familiar shadows in the growing darkness. Pawnee Woman threw herself into her husband's arms, and he embraced her tightly. Chastity stood by, her emotions controlled, and yet in her features revealed partially by the firelight from within the lodge, Big Dog thought he detected—what? Relief that he had returned unharmed? Or something more than that?

"You have brought us many horses," Two-tail Skunk laughed, "many more than the Blackfoot stole from us."

Then he too embraced his brother, while Benton, getting about quite well now, clapped his son repeatedly and hard upon the back.

"Father," Big Dog managed, "you'll break my ribs!"

"Ye heathen red devil, ye went an' done 'er! Swiped 'em back slicker'n fresh buffler dung!"

"Not exactly," Big Dog said. "We lost three of the young warriors. Heavy Shield followed us with a large party, and we fought at the box canyon where you and I camped that winter."

"Old Rock Face hisself? Ye was lucky to get away at all, then."

"Pine Leaf killed him in single combat, Benton.

204

Heavy Shield is in the Spirit World now, if that is where Blackfoot go when they are dead."

"Kilt 'em? My Gawd Almighty, that woman's somethin' now. Took 'im with her lance, didn't she?"

"Yes. How did you know that?"

"Just seemed like her way, is all. How many wounded, then?"

"A dozen, including Pine Leaf. She took a rifle ball through the shoulder."

"Damn! This coon wishes he'd been with ye. . . ."

"We met an old friend of ours, Father. Pierre Fontaine—he was riding with the Blackfoot war party. I spoke with him when the two sides parted. He says we'll have to get together to roast hump-rib."

"That lard-eatin' Frenchy! What's things comin' to, anyhow? Ridin' with the damned Blackfoot."

"Welcome home, Big Dog Benton," Chastity greeted him softly. "Or aren't you speaking to the woman you rescued?"

Big Dog stared at the Yellowhair and mastered an impulse to take her in his arms.

"Hello, Yellowhair. Are you glad to see me also?"

"Of course I am, you heathen red devil."

Her words froze in the air.

Then Two-tail Skunk began shouting and laughing all at once, and within moments everyone was laughing. Big Dog's spirits soared in a way that had not happened since the excitement of the battle. He stepped forward, reached out, and swung the white girl high over his head, hooting at her. She struggled wildly and attempted to hit him with her fists. Pawnee

Woman danced about excitedly, and Benton let out a coyote howl authentic enough that the camp dogs joined in with a spontaneous chorus.

"You must put her down and paint my face now!" Pawnee Woman insisted. "You can paint her face some other time, after she is your wife."

Big Dog and the white girl both ignored Pawnee Woman's remark, and Big Dog placed Chastity back on her feet.

"If I were a man, you'd not get away with that," she protested.

"If you were a man, I wouldn't have wanted to pick you up."

"Red devil," Chastity repeated, turning quickly away. But her step was light as she disappeared within the lodge.

"Absence makes a varmint's heart grow fonder," Benton grinned.

"For someone else, Father, for someone else. You've told me that many times."

"A coon can be wrong, can't he?"

"Big Dog, come paint my face for the dancing!" Pawnee Woman implored. "One Who Strikes Three says you know how to do it, and now you must."

The dancing continued through the night. And the warriors recited their coups—capturing a picketed horse, striking the enemy with a coup stick, lifting scalps. Pine Leaf was not among the warriors. She rested in her lodge with One Who Strikes Three who attended to her wound. All expected the warrior woman to join them after a time, but she did not.

Finally Black Panther went to summon her, but

she would not come. The young warrior returned with a gesture that signified he did not understand. Had Pine Leaf not slain the great chief of the Blackfoot? Why would she not wish to come out and speak of her victory?

"Is something wrong with Pine Leaf?" Long Bow inquired.

"She is one of your mothers," Two Bears said to Black Panther. "You must tell her that the people wish to hear of the death of Heavy Shield. No one can truly tell this story except her."

Big Dog nodded, but said nothing.

He knew why Pine Leaf would not leave her lodge, the lodge of Medicine Calf and Still Water and One Who Strikes Three. He had suspected all along, and now he was certain.

"I have already said these things to Pine Leaf," Black Panther explained, "and yet she still declines to witness the dancing. She says she will speak tomorrow, for she has asked Yellow Belly to call a war council."

"Then we must ask Yellow Belly to speak for her," Big Dog said. "All my life I have heard of the great Heavy Shield, and now he is dead. Pine Leaf has killed him, and it will be different now between the Crow and the Blackfoot."

"Yes," Two-tail Skunk said. "They will have a re-venge-taking against us and will try to kill Yellow Belly. But we are too many for them, and we will drive them off, just as we have done before."

"I do not think that will happen," Big Dog replied. "This thing will destroy their will to fight, perhaps."

"Where is Yellow Belly?" Two Bears called. "We must have the story of Warrior Woman and Heavy Shield!"

The head chief entered into the center of the circle, and, miming the actions of the two combatants, held them all breathless with the story. He was obliged to tell it a second and even a third time. After this he raised his hands and signaled that the scalp dance was finished.

"Tomorrow I will meet with my counselors and all others who wish to come," he declared. "We will meet in the medicine lodge which was erected when we made our winter encampment. This is the way I speak, warriors!"

Benton and his sons walked quietly back to their lodges.

Finally Benton said, "This ol' coot figgers somethin's up. Ye know what it be, Son?"

"I think so."

"Ye goin' to tell me about 'er?"

"It may be that I only think I know, Father. If I said, I might speak the wrong thing. We must wait for tomorrow. But is it true that all things end?"

"Sure as hobnails. Ye figger she's done with 'er?"

"We will know tomorrow. . . ."

The men parted and Big Dog hurried to his lodge where Pawnee Woman was waiting. Cozzie Yellowhair also waited. For a time the three of them talked together, and Big Dog and Chastity felt more at ease with each other than ever before. When it was time to sleep, Pawnee Woman invited Chastity to lie with her and Big Dog.

"No, no. . . ," Chastity said quickly, as though she had actually anticipated the question. "You and Big Dog have been apart. You will wish to make love. . . . I will be fine. It is warm in the lodge."

For a moment the two women gazed at each other, and Big Dog turned away uneasily. This bond between them was close, so close that he felt almost a stranger in his own lodge. Why had Pawnee Woman asked that? What had the women spoken of in the time that he had been gone? Was it possible. . . .

Then he and Pawnee Woman were together, under the secure warmth of the buffalo robes, and his wife gently placed her hands on his loins. Big Dog felt all the excitement and danger and fatigue of the long war party flow from him. He felt the strength of his sinews rising, the blood of passion beginning to ache in his manhood. His suddenly erect member felt oddly disconnected from his body, alive with some strange, mysterious life of its own, a life that was brought into being only by the close presence of his woman.

"My husband has been away from his woman for too long, he needs to be satisfied," Pawnee Woman whispered. "Lie still, Big Dog, and do not move. There is something I must do to you. After that I will let you make love to me. It has been too long for both of us. . . ."

She slipped down beneath the buffalo robes, and he felt the tip of her tongue moving around in little circles, small rings that seemed to touch him with flame. Then she took him into her mouth, and he groaned softly.

Morning came, but Chasity had risen even before

dawn and rekindled the lodge fire. Adding a bit of water to the leftover venison stew, she set the pot to bubbling beside the flames. Then Pawnee Woman was up also, but Big Dog continued to sleep.

"He looks . . . almost small when he's sleeping," Chasity said.

"He is not small," Pawnee Woman chuckled wickedly.

"I didn't mean that, you goose. I meant. . . ."

"I know, my sister. I only spoke those words because it is so good to have him back once more. Our other husband was much different."

Chastity laughed also, shaking her head as she did so. She turned and stepped out into the thin light of dawn. Noticing one of the dogs sleeping by the edge of the lodge, she placed a portion of the deer meat she had been chewing on next to the animal's nose. She watched as the dog's whiskers twitched, as the paws paddled, as though the creature were running in its sleep, running in at feeding time.

The dog blinked, awoke, discovered the morsel and devoured it immediately. The tail wagged, and the dog sighed happily. It looked up questioningly, and then closed its eyes and slept once more. Chastity shook her head and laughed softly.

At midday Yellow Belly met with his council, and once again he recited the story of the warpath just completed. He told also how Pine Leaf slew Heavy Shield with her lance and how she had been wounded. Then he turned to Pine Leaf. The warriors fully expected that Pine Leaf would now tell the story herself, acting it out at the same time.

Pine Leaf rose, her left arm bandaged and scarcely mobile at all.

"Sparrow Hawks!" she began. "For many years now I have ridden with you on the warpath, ever since the time Rotten Belly was chief, and after that Medicine Calf, and after that Yellow Belly. Long Hair himself told the Sparrow Hawks that I should be allowed into the war council and that I should be allowed to participate in the War Path Secret, even though I was a woman, for all acknowledged that my medicine was strong and that I was equal to any man in battle. Before that, when my twin brother was slain by the Blackfoot, I vowed to Old Man Coyote that I would take revenge upon our enemies. Medicine Calf and Yellow Belly taught me how to fight, even though I was a woman, because they knew that Old Man Coyote had heard my vow and that it was sacred. The winters went by, and I fulfilled my vow. And yet, because I had become counselor to the chief, I continued as a warrior, for I wished to protect our people from their enemies. Now I have slain Heavy Shield, who was chief of the Blackfoot even when my twin brother was killed. Now I must resign from the council, and Yellow Belly must pick another in my place—for I am finished with the warpath. There are many brave warriors who will take my place, and you will find that you do not need to have me ride with you. I will miss the fighting, for that has been my life for many years. Now I will begin to live a different life, for One Who Strikes Three has said that she will instruct me in the arts of healing and prophecy, so that I may become a medicine woman like her. Soon I will enter into the medicine lodge as a virtuous woman, and I know there are none who will speak against me. On this day I leave the warpath, for Old Man Coyote has told me that it is time to do so. Never again will I speak the name of my dead brother, for he is in the Spirit World and knows well that I have avenged his death and that I have attempted to be the warrior he might have been. Nor will I ever again speak the name of the Blackfoot chief who fell before my lance, for that way I will honor him. I leave you, Sparrow Hawk warriors! Choose a new counselor for Yellow Belly, and ride to victories still. But if a young woman ever tells you that she desires to ride the warpath with you, you must listen to her. These are my words, Sparrow Hawks, brothers!"

With that, Pine Leaf turned and strode quickly from the lodge. Yellow Belly and his council and his warriors sat in stunned silence.

Chapter 11

March 1849

Days on end passed without sunlight as occasional bursts of snow alternated with rain, downpours, mists, steadily falling rain. Each day the waters of the Gray Bull, a branch of the Bighorn, and the Bighorn itself rose, until the bankside willows and cottonwoods were engulfed and the brown water spilled out, finally all but doubling the width of the Bighorn. It was now a muddy giant flowing northward toward its eventual confluence with the Yellowstone. Viewed from an adjacent ridge-crest the Bighorn was a flood with twin lines of tree-tops curving parallel down its center.

Twenty or thirty of the Crow lodges had to be re-located to higher ground. Everywhere the earth underfoot was sodden, with tiny pools appearing almost immediately in each footprint. The Sparrow Hawks had no difficulty in finding sufficient game to keep the cooking pots full, but burnable firewood was another matter, for all downed logs were soaked through. Parties constantly went out in search of standing snags. But even with the good, metal-bladed axes from Buttermilk Thompson's trading post, the task was nearly impossible. Travois rigs were constructed, and large bundles of branches, driftwood, and green sections were drawn in from great distances and stored within the lodges to dry. Separate family lodges, including that of Big Dog, were temporarily abandoned, given over to storage, and relatives huddled together, drawing sufficient warmth from the closeness of human flesh.

When the rains diminished for one week and the rivers inched back toward their banks, the ragged willowbrush emerging once again from the water, it was time for rejoicing. And a single full day of sunlight was seen as time for a feast of elk meat, complete with a great fire at the center of the camp.

Then the rains returned, and once again the river spilled over its banks.

The temperature dropped, and a heavy snow began falling. The Bighorn basin was transformed into a featureless world of white. For five days the snow drifted down, and when the clouds broke and the cold air poured over the villages, the camp was a huge maze of footpaths, each packed into the snow between walls more than three feet high. At night the stars burned down in the thin, sheer blackness, and the wind drove waves of snow particles against the lodges and over the footpaths. Trees burst in the intensely cold nights, exploding like the discharges of rifles.

By day, the splintery fragments of branches were collected and dragged down to the villages. Dogs replaced the horses as beasts of burden, each dragging a small travois and struggling through the drifts of powder or sliding precariously over portions of hard-frozen crust.

Benton and Buttermilk Thompson shared coffee and tobacco in the trader's big lodge. The small cast-iron stove with its disconnected sections of pipe puffed and groaned and exhausted its smoke upward to the vent hole around the joined lodge poles above.

"Coon," Benton complained, "I don't figger this stuff's ever goin' to stop. Mebbe there be no summer this year."

"Three seasons," Thompson agreed, "July, August, and Winter."

"Just think, Buttermilk. These two ol' trappers could be fat, stupid and happy down in St. Louis, swillin' whiskey an' screwin' little red-haired prostitutes. What we doin' here, anyhow?"

"Aloysius, with men our age, it's either drinking or screwing. Can't have both of 'em."

"Maybeso that's how it is with ye, Thompson, but this ol' codger's as horny as when he was a kid of thirty. Figger I'll be drinkin' an' screwin' when I'm a hundred or more."

"Talk, Benton, just talk. You ain't even got you a woman. What you been doin', then, stump-breaking female elk?"

"Two-tail Skunk's ladies, they take care of me from time to time, don't ye be worryin' yourself about 'er."

"Strength coming back to that arm, Aloysius?"

"Damn right. This coon'll be good as new before

215

long. That white bear just had to make certain he'd give me the whole dose of his medicine, is all."

Thompson grinned, put a couple more chunks of wood into the stove, and clamped the door shut.

"Long Bow thinks maybe you're planning to hitch up with that Cosgrove girl. That true, Aloysius?"

"Cozzie? Hell, man, I be old enough to be her daddy."

"What difference does that make?"

"Nothin' ye'd understand, coon. With Injun gals it's different. I'll tell ye what, though. I figger she's going to hitch with Big Dog. Wait an' see. I'm goin' to have a genuine yellow-haired daughter-in-law."

"Father and daughter, ehh? Well, there's something to be said for it."

"Damn right, coon. That's how the stick floats, an' I wouldn't want it no other way. Gal like that, she needs a strong young warrior."

"Not going to take her back to the Mormons, then?"

"Just tellin' ye what I think is all. Can ye be serious, coon? I'll tell ye. I do love that little gal, an' that's a fact, but not the way you're thinkin'. Whatever she wants to do, why I'll do 'er. When the weather breaks, I'll take 'er wherever she wants to go. Just that I figger she's goin' to want to lodge up with Big Dog. She's a strange one, not like a white woman at all, to tell the truth. Whatever it was that brought us to the mountains, Thompson, she's seen it too. This old-timer don't figger Cozzie could ever be happy among the whites again, an' mebbe she never was in the first place. Comin' upcountry with Brigham Young and his saints,

I could tell she wasn't really one of 'em. Guess that's how we made friends."

"Never did understand you, Benton. Ten years and I don't know you any better than I did the day we met. . . ."

Benton relit his pipe, rose and poured another cup of coffee from the blackened tin pot steaming on the stove.

Then Two-tail Skunk was standing in the entranceway to the lodge.

"I have smelled the muddy poison," he said, briskly rubbing his hands together to warm them.

And so the days drifted on, wet alternating with cold, until the March moon had come and waxed and grown full and waned once more. The first of the spring grass had not yet appeared, but the snows on the mountains were beginning to recede, drawing back to the higher ridges and the great peaks of the Shining Mountains.

Big Dog, Pawnee Woman and Chastity had just moved back into their own lodge, all of them relieved to be released from the close quarters. They moved the remaining wood to the outside, all but the quantity they would need for cooking and heating purposes, straightened up the tepee, and rearranged the sleeping accommodations. The two women prepared a feast of beaver tails, for Big Dog and Two-tail Skunk had been setting traps for the taking of plew to fashion clothing and sleeping gear.

The relationship between the two women had remained extremely close, and, with the tension between Big Dog and Chastity essentially vanished, the three had formed a close-knit family unit. Still, Chastity continued to sleep apart from her friends, now once again taking her previous spot across the lodge.

Wolves howled in the night, and Chastity once more found it difficult to sleep, a problem that had vanished during the time of their residence in Two-tail Skunk's tepee. Now she lay awake and listened to the muted sounds of lovemaking from across the nearly dark lodge. Shifting about, she stared at the dwindling lodge fire and then across into the shadowed area where the sleeping robes moved as if with a life of their own. She could feel her pulse increasing. She bit at her lips and turned over and stared at the stretched elk hides of the lodge. But even when the lodge was completely quiet, still she could not sleep.

Coyotes answered the songs of the wolves, and for a few moments the night was filled with wailings and howlings as the camp dogs joined in with the music of their wild brothers and sisters.

Chastity had given much thought to Pawnee Woman's repeated suggestion, and the idea had become ever more appealing. Was there, indeed, any reason for returning to the Mormons? For returning to a world in which she had always been an outsider? Earlier dreams of places like St. Louis, New Orleans, Philadelphia and New York had now vanished. She had found among the Sparrow Hawks something she had never before in her life known—a sense of belonging, a sense of identity and sympathy with the purposes and needs of the people as a whole.

If not Big Dog, she knew there were numerous other young men who were attracted to her. Was it possible that she might simply become a Sparrow Hawk and live out her life with these people?

But it was Big Dog who excited her.

Why, then, the resistance that she continued to feel—some invisible obstacle, like a sheet of thin river ice that, broken loose and held up to the sun, permitted only dim light and vague outlines to pass through? The hesitance lay not only in her alone, but in Big Dog also. They were friends now, but still, when occasionally they touched, always they moved away, as if in recognition of the boundary that neither could see but both knew to exist.

Yet each had lived something of the life of the other, each had known and had moved within the other culture. Was this not sufficient to overcome the distance between them? Then what remained?

The night suddenly grew quiet, and the silence was almost audible. Chastity waited for the howling to resume. She was still waiting when sleep overtook her.

With the morning came some amazing news, brought in by a French Canadian scout named Jean LeClaire. Half a day's ride down the Bighorn, he told Yellow Belly, was a troop of bluecoats, led by a Lieutenant Edgeworth. And with them rode an Indian Agent named Madden, someone sent out straight from Washington. This Madden wished to speak with Yellow Belly concerning the possibility of a treaty of allegiance between the federal government and the Crow nation. He was also looking for Aloysius Benton and a Mormon girl who had been kidnapped from a wagon train the preceding fall.

Yellow Belly accepted the news without comment

and offered LeClaire some soup from the pot over the lodge fire. Then he gave one of his wives a message to deliver to Benton. Within a few moments the woman slipped away and walked quickly to the lodge of Two-tail Skunk. Skunk passed the information on, first to Big Dog and then to Pine Leaf and to Coyote Running and a number of others. Within minutes the news had spread throughout the villages of the Many Lodges and the Kicked-in-their-Bellies.

"I will go to hunt now," Big Dog told the women. Then he turned to his wife, "Your friend will wish to go with these white men. My father will wish to go also, now that he is able to ride once more. And you should go too, Pawnee Woman. In this way, you can stay with your sister until she has once more reached her people."

Pawnee Woman nodded, but looked quickly from her husband to Chastity.

"Big Dog. . . ," Chastity began, her voice betraying her confusion.

"No, my sister," he interrupted, "you must listen to me now. If it is time for you to return to your people, then that is what you must do. I cannot go with you on this journey, for my medicine tells me that I must ride out to hunt. I will ride slowly up the Gray Bull and listen to the songs of birds, for the birds will tell me where to find game. Pawnee Woman and Yellowhair, I must go now. You will know best what to do next. It has been good these past two moons, even when we were all crowded together in Skunk's lodge. I will not forget the things we have said to one another. Even years from now I will remember, and Pawnee

Woman and I will speak of you. Perhaps you will remember us also."

Big Dog turned abruptly and left the lodge, possibles sack in one hand and Hawken in the other. He mounted quickly and rode westward from the camp.

The birds were indeed singing in the thin warmth of early spring sunlight. Big Dog rode easily, his eyes and ears trained intently upon his surroundings. Inside, however, he felt the fist of loss forming. He was overcome by a sense of heaviness.

With each mile he covered, the distance between himself and something he knew had been valuable and beautiful became more final. He tried to resist the thoughts of Yellowhair and his wife and the closeness of the bond among them. He had begun to think of the white woman as a second wife, a wife who shared his lodge but with whom he did not make love.

Damn her, anyway, Big Dog thought. Now she's with the bluecoats. Now she's getting ready to ride away, and all this time since the falling leaves will vanish, pass into nothingness, just as though it had never been. . . .

He drew up sharply on the reins. He thought about turning around, about going back to the encampment. He decided against it.

The trouble is, he thought, I love her, just as I love Pawnee Woman. They are sisters, and I am their brother—and their lover. But I have loved only one in the way of a man and a woman. The other one's skin is the wrong color, her hair is the wrong color. . . .

Big Dog made early camp and built a fire, but he was not hungry. He stared into the flames and listened to the sounds of flowing water and the wind in the cottonwoods. Was he listening for something else as well? Was he listening for the sounds of a rider along the trail? Was he insanely hoping she might have followed him?

That was why he had said he would ride slowly up the Gray Bull, so she would know that truly he was not attempting to leave her, only allowing her to make her own decision.

Owls called and coyotes yelped, but no rider came up the river. At last, Big Dog pulled his robes about him and, his hand on his rifle, fell asleep with his back against the trunk of a scrub cedar.

By morning his hunger could not be ignored, and he cooked some stale deer meat. After that he found reasons to explore the area about his campsite until, no longer able to hide from himself the reason for his malingering, he mounted his pony and rode on up the Gray Bull, still moving slowly.

Clouds dropped down over the mountains, and the sky became heavy and leaden. Late in the afternoon a thin, warm rain began to fall, soaking his buckskin leggings and shirt. Part way up on the ridge ahead stood a ragged outcropping of boulders, dark at the base. It was a cave apparently, a shelter from the wetness. Big Dog dismounted and led his horse up the slope along a shallow ravine where the spring grass was actually up and where a few young aspens grew. Below the boulders lay a small opening, tufted with grass and spotted with rocks fallen from above. Big Dog removed the pack bags from his pony and turned the animal loose to graze.

There was an opening quite large enough to provide shelter, and wedged between the rocks was a segment of dry, pitchy pine log that had somehow slipped down from above and had become stuck in a vertical seam in the stone.

The little cave at least was friendly, the coarse sand on its floor hardly moist at all. He built a small fire at the entrance, a foolish thing to do perhaps anywhere else, but certainly safe enough here within the lands controlled by the Crow. And after dark it was a beacon to anyone who might be riding up the river. . . .

A wisp of smoke coiled into the air, and sometimes a sudden breath of wind blew it back into the cave, into his eyes, so that he had to move around to avoid it. But the warmth from the flames was doing its work, and his clothing gradually began to dry out.

Near sundown, the rain stopped, and Big Dog took his Hawken and set out on foot to find fresh meat. He moved through the dusk, close by the river, hoping to discover a deer that had come down to chew at the willow buds and to drink.

There it was. A single antelope. Big Dog dropped to all fours, took quick aim and fired. The animal leaped once, twice, and then collapsed.

Suddenly, a horse whinnied. Someone was close by.

Big Dog left the antelope for later and slipped immediately through the low brush, crouching and running toward the sound of the horse. He took cover in a vine thicket and waited. Then he saw the rider, a rifle in the crook of the arm, not in the manner of an Indian, but the posture of a mountain man. It was indeed someone who had learned from Aloysius Benton.

"Cozzie Yellowhair!" Big Dog called out. "Is that you?"

"Big Dog? Your shot a moment ago? Where are you?" came the answer.

Big Dog stepped from the cover of the vine tangle and stood in front of Yellowhair, who had reined in her horse.

Big Dog stared at Chastity. "You did not wish to go with the bluecoats, then?" he asked.

"They are not my people. What did you shoot at, Big Dog?"

"An antelope came to drink. Will you help me to skin and butcher it?"

Yellowhair dismounted and stood next to Big Dog. Even now they did not embrace, each perhaps waiting for a gesture from the other. Then Big Dog turned and began to walk back to the fallen antelope. Leading her horse, Chastity walked behind him. Working together, they quickly skinned and cut up the animal, moving about in the dull orange-yellow of the day's end. They put the sections of meat into a bundle, wrapped it in the hide, and slung it over Chastity's horse.

Together they led the horse up the steep, grassy ravine in the nearly complete darkness, toward the glimmering light of the cave fire. As Big Dog placed fresh sections of wood over the coals, Chastity spit sections of sirloin onto a hazel whip and set their meal to cooking.

"Why did you come?" Big Dog asked.

"Because . . . I wished to be with you."

"You do not wish to go back to your people?"

"Not . . . now. I could not let you ride off that way. You have saved my life and given me shelter and made me a part of your lodge. I. . . ."

She was crying. Astounded, Big Dog reached out toward her. He touched his fingers to her eyes and felt the tears on her face.

"Tell me if I am wrong," he whispered. "Do you wish to make love?"

"No, I . . . yes. Yes, I want that. Will you hold me, Big Dog? I'm sorry. I should not have come, but. . . . I will go back tomorrow, if you wish it. I feel so foolish, so alone. . . ."

"Then I am glad you have come," he murmured. "It was very hard for me to ride away from you, Yellowhair. Several times I started to turn around, but I did not think. . . ."

Then she was in his arms and he was holding her. He lifted her up and held her to him. She wrapped her legs about him and then was immediately afraid she had done the wrong thing. But she had seen Pawnee Woman do it. He did not object, only held her more tightly, kissed her hair, touched his mouth to her forehead. Would he kiss her, kiss her the way the whites kissed, or would she have to show him how to do that? He would not know how little she knew of such matters. They would have to learn together. . . .

Then his tongue was inside her mouth.

The bastard! she thought. Downriver. St. Louis. He went to the prostitutes. . . .

225

Suddenly there was the smell of burning meat. . . .

She pulled away from him, gasping, "Our meal!"

Big Dog laughed and put her down. He grabbed the hazel wand and snatched it from the flames. The tip was burning and flames showered off the fatty portions of the meat.

"We will make love in a little while," he said. "But first we must eat."

As they ate, the rain began to fall once more, but it was dry and warm and secure under the overhanging lip of granite.

Her eyes moved over her lover's face, over the wide cheekbones and the thin scar along the jawbone. She drank in the other scar over his left eye, the even, white teeth that pulled at the fibrous meat, the ooze of fat glistening about his mouth.

Then they were lying together on his sleeping robes, and he unfastened her clothing, removing it slowly until she was lying naked—and fearful. Not fearful of the sexual act but of something else, something which had no name.

He bit at her nose and whispered, "You are beautiful, Yellowhair. Only you are so white . . . even the hair between your legs is light-colored. . . ."

She closed her eyes, saying nothing, feeling the cool, damp air play over her. The tips of her breasts seemed touched with a soft flame, a new sensation, something she had never before felt. And a warmth, an insistent and growing warmth suffused itself through her loins, seemed to play over her in maddening, rhythmic pulsations of feeling, urging, urging. . . .

Big Dog drew the buffalo robe over them. He held her tightly and kissed her again.

She grew brave and suddenly thrust her tongue into his mouth and then withdrew it, half supposing he would rebuke her. But he said only. "Put your hands where a wife should always put her hands. My body hurts for you I want you so much. . . ."

She unfastened his leggings and breechcloth and heard him groan softly, then groan again as she placed both hands on his erect manhood and gently squeezed.

He breathed in sharply, held her to him.

Would she dare to do with her mouth as she had seen Pawnee Woman do, as Crooked Knife had sometimes forced her to do herself? Slowly she moved her head down, caressing his chest with her tongue, finally touching her tongue to the smooth, hard, already slippery tip of his member.

She took him into her mouth and felt at the same moment the hot stickiness between her own thighs.

Big Dog turned over upon her, his clean, strong warrior's face half illumined in the dancing firelight, and she reached down to help him slip into her.

He thrust slowly forward, and she gasped and clung to him. The intertwined sensations of pleasure and pain flooded her being. She clamped her teeth to his neck, and their bodies surged together, knew their own intelligence. They were mindless. There was no longer any need for thought, no need for anything but the hot fire of muscle and tissue and movement that was between them.

They awoke, still in each other's arms. And the rain was still falling. The thin light of false dawn filtered through the cloud cover, and the gusts of moisture shimmered nearly to silver.

Big Dog built up the fire, and once again they cooked portions of antelope meat.

Then they were on the robes again, exploring each other, discovering new things about themselves. He mounted her from behind and her knees and hands slid from the buffalo robes and onto the grainy sand of the cave floor. The strength of his powerful male body folded over her, thrusting, touching at the very core of her being. Then he shuddered to climax, groaning, and holding her breasts so hard she gasped for breath.

Still the flames of passion ran through her and she wept and moaned.

He slipped from her, his body still shuddering, and she collapsed forward. Her hair, unbraided now, flowed in a cloud around her face. Then he was urging her onto her back, spreading her legs.

He was between her legs. His exquisitely muscled shoulders hunched between her legs, his face, the black, unbound trail of his own hair covering her belly. His lips nuzzled between her thighs, and she grew fearful and moaned, "No! No! Big Dog, no!" She reached down to him to pull his face up to hers, but the male strength was determined, and his tongue thrust into her mound. Rains of sensation washed over her.

She writhed back and forth, gave in, accepted, let the current carry her, was borne away with the flood of her desire. Again and again she thought *no, no, no, you don't have to do that, I. . . .* But the waves of pleasure were mounting, and she wanted it to continue forever. Fire seemed to flow out of her femaleness, encompassing her, bathing her totally.

She screamed out. She could not control it. Her entire body was racked with spasms, and in the distance she heard but did not recognize the animal wail, the dark wail of her physical being as the cry passed through her lips.

When they awoke again, the sunlight from high in the sky was filtering through the rainfall. Big Dog kissed her on the lips and murmured, "We have gone crazy, Yellowhair. What has happened to us?"

She ran her fingers into his black, bear-greased warrior's hair and said softly, in Crow, "I do not know, I do not know...."

In the small clearing below, the two horses frisked about in the rainy sunlight, and farther off, the Gray Bull had risen once more beyond the confines of its brush and tree-lined banks.

For three days they rode, not covering a very great distance each day, and each day not starting until nearly noon. They were in a frenzy of lovemaking, neither questioning where they might be journeying or why, neither of them wishing to question anything or look beyond the present.

The evening of the third day they camped early, ate, and made love under a sky rife with stars, a whiteness scattered across the dark as if by some giant hand in a careless and last-moment act of creation. There was no moon, but a warm wind played over the land, and the earth smelled alive. Life was everywhere, birds calling in the darkness, coyotes screaming their quavering cries of mating, and wolves, farther off, howling as well.

They lay in each other's arms and, in the moments before sleep took them, they heard a long, plaintive cry like that of a woman in pain or pleasure, the scream of the mountain lion.

"The cougar honors us," Big Dog said. "She is lonely and cries for her mate. She has heard us making love and wishes to do likewise."

"Will it always be like this with us?"

"Only the mountains are always, little one. Human animals do not have always. Besides, I think we will soon love each other to death. Each time we make love, we grow smaller. The Sparrow Hawks will send out a party to find us, and when they do, we will be dead in each other's arms, and we will be no taller than a pair of jumping mice."

"That is foolish to say. I don't feel smaller at all. I feel like I've grown so that I am able to embrace all of the world."

"Even the big mountains ahead?"

"Even those."

"And yet they are all white, all covered with snow. They must be very cold when they touch the nipples of your breasts."

"No, Big Dog. The snow is fire when it touches me. But when you touch me, I am all fire."

"A white woman who lives in flames," Big Dog mused. "And yet she does not burn away. Perhaps only I will burn until I am exhausted. I will grow small, and you will carry me about in the pocket of your dress."

230

"You will not grow small, I promise that. I will always make you big."

"Even when we both lie together with Pawnee Woman?"

Yellowhair was quiet for a time.

"Do you love her, Big Dog?"

"Yes," he answered, "I love both of you, even though I love each of you differently. Is that all right, Yellowhair?"

"Yes, yes, that is all right. Together we will be able to make you very big, and you will wish to go hunting then just to get away from us."

"I will not wish that," he whispered and drifted away into sleep.

Chastity cradled his head and stared at his features. She pressed her lips to the scar over his eye. Then she too fell through the corridors of darkness and into sleep.

At the morning light Big Dog came slowly awake. He had not yet opened his eyes, but already he knew something was wrong. He reached for his Hawken, but it was not there. His hand felt slowly about. He supposed that somehow the rifle had been moved—but there was no rifle. At that he bolted upright, fully awake, rousing Yellowhair as he did so.

Six braves squatted across from their robes. Six pairs of eyes peered at them from the other side of the gray mound of last night's ashes.

"Hello, Big Dog of the Crow," one of the braves greeted him in English. "We know who you are. We remember you from the day Heavy Shield was slain by the warrior woman. You and this white woman are our prisoners. Do not get up, or we will kill you immediately. The woman we will sell back to her people after we are finished with her. Maybe her people will give us many presents. But we will have something special for you, Big Dog. You will be a sacrifice so that we will not have to mourn for so long a time. Your death will be an honor to the ghost of Heavy Shield. Then he will be happier in the Spirit World."

Chapter 12

April 1849

Their wrists were bound with rawhide thongs, and then the Sparrow Hawk warrior and the white girl were tied together at the wrists, and a lariat was attached to the binding. Thus fastened, they stumbled along on foot, their tether rope cinched to the half-saddle of a Blackfoot horse. From time to time a brave, amused by the situation, urged his mount quickly forward and jerked Big Dog and Chastity off their feet, dragging them for a short way. The maneuver was repeated several times until the leader, displeased with the brave's behavior, complained that it would not be wise to damage the white girl. She might then be worth fewer presents if they were able to exchange her back to her own people.

The brave nodded and said nothing. But as the party passed through a narrow opening between boulders, he kicked his horse forward one last time. The jolt dragged Big Dog and Chastity ahead and into the rocks.

A jagged cut opened on Chastity's cheekbone, just below the eye, and the blood streamed.

The Blackfoot warrior yipped pleasure as he pretended to control his horse.

"Cozzie, get up, get up. Pretend that nothing has happened. Be impassive—otherwise they'll drag us to death through the rocks."

"Are we going to die, Big Dog?"

"We are not dead yet. Keep moving. We must escape very soon if we can. A few hours of this and we couldn't help ourselves if they cut our bonds and told us to go. We've got to break loose while we still have some strength. How tight are your wrists? Have the thongs loosened at all?"

"I don't think so. There's blood in my mouth. . . ."

At the end of several miles, the Blackfoot drew up at the edge of the river, obviously contemplating a crossing.

"This will be it," Big Dog whispered. "Our only chance, once we're out into the water. If I can keep my footing after the brave is into the current, I may be able to jerk the lariat loose. Breathe deep, Yellowhair, and if I can pull us loose, try to get your legs around me. Let the current carry us. Can you do that?"

"I'll try. . . ."

The braves urged their horses into the brown, still-flooding river. At the point of the crossing, the river was relatively shallow but swift, breaking into white water just below and then narrowing into a foaming torrent.

Even if Big Dog succeeded in pulling the lariat loose, would they be able to survive that rush of water? There was no way of knowing.

As they stumbled forward into the icy stream, Big Dog looked at Chastity. What was the expression on her face, the long smear of blood crusted over now, the eyes distant? Trust? Unquestioningly she would put her life into his hands? It occurred to him that the girl probably had a better chance of surviving in the hands of the Blackfoot, however certain his own fate would be among them. Repeated rape and abuse of all sorts awaited her, but also a chance that the Blackfoot might indeed find a way of selling her back to the whites. But what were the realistic chances of that? They would take her back to their own lands, northward. Months, then, of constant abuse before there would be any likelihood of safety. And the fact that she had been taken prisoner with him, a well-known Crow warrior, might well encourage the Blackfoot women to demand her death as well, death under torture.

Ahead, the brave's horse had slipped down into deeper water and was swimming. Had he waited too long? Better to have caught that moment just before, when the horse's hooves were still digging at the gravel and rock-studded bed of the river.

Big Dog summoned all his strength, set his moccasined feet as best he could, and lunged backward, drawing Chastity with him and stringing the lariat tight.

The warrior shrieked but the rope did not give

way. Desperately Big Dog fought for another foothold, got it, and lunged a second time—feeling the wet rope either snap or slip loose.

Chastity was fighting to get her legs about him. He clamped her with his own legs.

And the brown current was carrying them. The water swirled about them, numb cold. They felt the swift water take them, and they tossed and bobbed about. The force hurled them against a boulder in the stream, and Big Dog thrust his legs against the rock driving them upward.

They sucked for breath, the roaring water spraying about them.

"Hold tight!" he gasped. "We're going under again."

He pushed into the current. It hit them with an iron strength, whipped them around and eddied them up below the boulder. They were pushed back into a space where the gray-white water roared above them, covering them, spinning them around but giving them space to breathe.

A ledge appeared, a place to set his feet.

"Yellowhair, are you still with me?"

"What happened?" she spluttered.

Then her head went under, and she came up coughing and gasping for air.

"The river's given us a hiding place, for a minute or two, anyhow. . . ."

Jamming his wrists against the stone, he felt the lariat, still trailing in the water somewhere, pull loose from something. It was the rope that had caught and

236

caused them to be spun around under the roaring current.

But the rock face was smooth. There were no rough edges with which to tear through the bindings. Still he ground away, tearing the skin from his left wrist. The bindings, wet and slippery now, began to give. He wrenched his wrists from his body, lifting Chastity as he did so, and then he could feel the tightness ease. He twisted again, locking his muscles, and the rawhide strip tore and came loose. He rotated his wrists, oblivious to the pain. His hands and wrists were numb, but he worked them free. Within a moment he had unloosed Chastity's bindings and had drawn in the lariat.

The Blackfoot were across the river and would be coming along the bankside, looking for them. For the moment, however, they were safe, completely hidden by the rushing current of water above them. But now a new danger presented itself. The icy water, numbing them, was drawing the strength from their bodies. They could not leave the space beneath the roaring water, but they could not stay, either. They had to get out of the water.

Big Dog and Chastity clung together, only their heads above the water, and in this position, attempted to conserve warmth. It was midday, and still hours until darkness might hide them if they could once manage to get to shore. But they would have to survive the narrow gorge first, the swirling rapids. There was no way to fight against such a current, and soon the cold water would take away their capacity to fight at all.

How long would the Blackfoot continue to search the bank? Already the warriors would have supposed them drowned. But they would wish to find the bodies, to take the scalps.

"We can't stay here," Chastity gasped.

"I know, little one. But wait—in a few minutes we will have to ride with the current. First we must give the Blackfoot a chance to convince themselves that the river has taken us, that we haven't managed to get away. . . ."

Chastity looked up at the moving arch of water above her head, the strange, wavering effect of the sunlight through the torrent of water.

Beautiful, something deep in her mind said. *Even here, it is beautiful. . . .*

She willed her mind clear again and looked back at Big Dog.

"Will we live?" she asked.

"Perhaps we will live if we want to badly enough. Can you swim, Cozzie?"

"Of course I can swim!"

"Good. When we go, we must let the water carry us. But we must attempt to angle toward the shore. That way the water may help us. Do you understand what I'm saying?"

"I think so. *Use* the current."

"Yes. You must stay close to me, hold on to me if you have to, but swim if you can. . . ."

"Do you think we can make it, then?"

"We will make it. And then I'm going to skin some Blackfoot. Not just their scalps, their whole hides."

"No. We must return to the villages, Big Dog. Forget about the warriors!"

"How will we be able to return with no horses and no weapons, not even anything to build a fire with?"

"Damn you, we're not going to die. I'm freezing. I can hardly move at all. . . ."

They waited until they could wait no longer. Then Big Dog, his hands almost without feeling, wrapped the lariat about his chest. He allowed a double arm's length of slack between the two of them, and looped the other end around Chastity's waist. Together they pushed out from under the torrent and into the high-rushing river.

The current buffeted them about, drew them under for brief periods, and swept them down through the rapids. When the water began to slow once more, Big Dog and Chastity swam clumsily toward the line of brush and trees. Still swept onward by the current, they were closing the distance between themselves and the shore.

Something loomed ahead, something strange.

It was a Conestoga, half out of the water, its canvas top shredded and torn. The current held its frame in place against a jam of driftwood. The wagon projected from the water at an angle, with the front wheels submerged and the rear wheels rising from the surface. The current swirled past the hubs and the oxen, their bloated bodies still in their traces, were jammed back against the tongue.

Big Dog reached for the iron handrail, climbed up and drew Chastity after him.

The driver was sprawled backward, his boots poking up over the seat. The gaping hole in his chest had apparently been inflicted by the ball of a buffalo rifle, delivered at relatively close range, perhaps no more than ten or fifteen feet. His mouth was locked open, as though he had sucked hard for air in his last moments, trying to draw breath into his shattered lungs. In the rear of the wagon, huddled against the storage compartment was a woman in blue and white gingham. One side of her head was blown away and a spread of blood covered the other side. Dried blood and brains had spattered the remnants of canvas that had once been the Conestoga's bonnet.

"Oh my God!" Chastity cried. "What. . . ."

Her body convulsed with retching spasms, and Big Dog took her in his arms, his hands so numb that he could barely hold her to him.

"I don't know, I don't know. . . ."

What had happened? A couple had attempted to journey westward alone. But what were they doing here, on the Gray Bull, two hundred miles north of the migration road? And how had they managed to bypass the Crow villages without being detected? The incident was without explanation, as was the nature of the fate which had overtaken them.

"The woman shot herself," Big Dog concluded, his own vision blurring for a moment, whether from the impact of this wooden island of death or from exhaustion and the aftereffects of fear he did not know.

Chastity stared at the remains of the woman. She was perhaps thirty, a dozen or so years younger than her husband—if this had been her husband. And had there been children? No children's clothing was visible, and yet everything else was seemingly intact. The two oil lanterns still hung from above, a mahogany bureau clock lay on its side near the woman's body, an axe and shovel were still in their places. The single-shot horse pistol lay on the floorboards, next to the storage compartment, where it had fallen from the woman's hand after the trigger had been pulled.

Big Dog turned the man's body over, slid it to the rear, and opened the compartment beneath the driver's seat.

He saw a Whitney percussion rifle, long-barreled, loaded, dry.

"Yellowhair! Look in the storage compartment—see if there's shot and powder and caps. . . ."

Chastity moved carefully around the dead woman, averting her gaze, and opened the latched gate to the compartment. A host of belongings presented themselves: hand tools, a small keg of nails, hammer, saw, hand level, a coil of twine, sections of dried meat, a bag of flour and another of beans, other foodstuffs. Affixed to the board walling was a steel and flint firemaker, and in one corner squatted a small chest, constructed so as to be watertight. She opened it and found what she was after.

"They're here," she said, "and the powder's not wet."

Working together, Big Dog and Chastity moved the supplies and the two bodies to the high ground above the willow tangles. Big Dog dug a shallow grave into which the two bodies were placed, side by side. Chastity turned away when the time came for filling in the hole. With that accomplished, they worked together once more, piling rocks over the mound to protect the bodies against wolves and coyotes.

Finished with the burial, they ate dried meat, jerked beef from the taste of it. The thin, salty strips were nourishing if less than substantial. It was growing dark now, and the sky, once more clouded over, seemed to promise rain, and perhaps even snow.

With their supplies wrapped in a section of canvas from the wagon's bonnet, Big Dog and Chastity walked away from the river, moving up through a tangled overgrowth of cottonwood and aspen until they came to a protected glen. Their buckskins were still soaked, but there was no way to dry them—not even if they chose to risk a campfire. They would have to wear them until they dried, otherwise the leather would tighten and no longer fit.

Well after dark, Big Dog used the flint and steel firemaker to kindle a small blaze, and they huddled close. Lacking robes for covering, they worked themselves in against a cottonwood log and slept in each other's arms.

Morning came, and with it a fine mist.

"Snow higher up," Big Dog said. "Little one, I'm going after those sons of bitches. With a rifle and an axe and a pistol, the odds are a little more even."

He spoke in English, and his voice was steady and determined.

"You think the Blackfoot killed those people?"

"The woman killed herself. What happened to the man, I don't know. If it had been Blackfoot, they'd have taken everything of use—unless something scared

242

them off just as it was happening. I suppose we'll never know."

"Can't we go back to the villages first?"

"It's two days of walking, at least. By then the Blackfoot will be over the mountains and gone—if they can get through the snows. They've probably cut north to the Shoshone. If they are still looking for us, they'd have found us for sure. Why were they crossing to the south bank?"

Chastity shrugged.

"Hunting. No other reason for it. They must think either to come back this way or move upriver and cross back."

"Big Dog. . . ."

"Are you coming with me, Yellowhair, or do you want to stay here until I get back?"

"If you get back. No. If you're set on going, then I'm going, too. When do we start?"

"Right now."

They moved upstream, staying under cover as much as possible, keeping to the high ground. Big Dog carried the Whitney rifle and the crude canvas pouch. Chastity carried the axe and the pistol.

She wondered at times if Big Dog had more than simply a hunch to go on, but she followed, unquestioning, doing her best to keep up with the long strides of the Sparrow Hawk warrior who moved along ahead of her, seemingly tireless.

The first night they walked high along the ridge side, and the mistlike rain continued. They took shelter among some boulders, ate dried meat and flour mixed with water to form a kind of gluelike gruel, and slept.

Dreams came to her that night, dreams of bodies with no faces, dead creatures drifting slowly back and forth in clear green water, not water like the river's, but nearly transparent, emeraldlike. And the woman with no face spoke her name: *Chastity Cosgrove.*

She awoke suddenly, heard herself speaking the words "No! No! No!" Big Dog, the rifle already in his grasp, realized that it was a dream, and he stroked her hair. He held her tightly, and soon she had drifted into sleep once more.

They were up and on their way before light, staying to the ridge crest. But now Big Dog stopped at intervals and surveyed the land below.

By late afternoon, a snowstorm had begun, but lightly. Only a few flakes trickled down from the gray overcast. The ridge was steeper now and dotted with evergreens, and Chastity realized they were approaching the high mountains Big Dog had spoken of. Though half a mile away, the river was louder now, the water faster and noisier, the sound drifting up.

Big Dog stopped suddenly, touched her shoulder, and pointed. In the draw below, a campfire glowed, the yellow light seeming to blink in the thin, falling snow.

"We have found them, Yellowhair. Our friends who borrowed our horses and weapons. Now we will take our things back, and a few other things also. Have you ever scalped a man, Chastity Cosgrove?"

She was more surprised by his use of her Christian name than by the nature of his question—the latter coming to her only after a moment.

"No," she said. "What are you going to do now?"

"We are both going to do this thing. My father

told me, long ago, that you were like Pine Leaf except that there was no way for you to be a Pine Leaf while you were living with the Long Knives. Now you will have your chance. This is what we must do. . . ."

The plan was simple enough. Each would crawl close from opposite sides, Chastity with the rifle, Big Dog with the pistol and axe. She was to approach no closer than a hundred feet, and she was not to fire until he had fired from the opposite side. Then they would both reload as quickly as possible and keep the braves pinned down.

"They're not expecting company," he grinned, "or they'd never have chosen a campsite right out in the open. Well, Old Man Coyote made them do it so that we could kill them. We weren't expecting company the other morning, either."

Through all of this, the reality of actually having to kill someone had not registered upon her. When they had been taken captive, the thought of her own death had seemed real enough—she had even accepted it in a rational way. But now—to kill someone? Could she do it?

"All right, Big Dog," she heard herself saying to him.

Then he was gone, slipping off into the darkness soundlessly, almost as though he were a figment of her dreaming, almost as though he had never been there in the first place.

She fought back an impulse to cry out.

Then she began her approach to the Blackfoot camp, the snowfall chilly and silent about her in the darkness. Finally she dropped to all fours and crawled forward, moving slowly, carefully, attempting to dislodge nothing, to make no sound.

When one of the horses snorted and stamped its feet, she froze. Her own horse, possibly? Had it smelled her, recognized her presence? For several minutes she did not move again—but she could see the six figures around the fire now. They were close enough for a good, clean shot. She moved forward a few feet farther and reached out to feel a slab of stone in front of her.

A good rest for the rifle, she thought and moved the weapon slowly into place. She had just started to reach down to assure herself she still had the shot and powder and caps when she heard the mating cry of a screech owl—once, twice, then nothing.

Big Dog.

She leveled the rifle, drew steady aim and waited.

She was not quite ready for what happened next. A Blackfoot pitched forward and sprawled directly over the flames, almost extinguishing the blaze. Only then did she hear the report, understood why, and fired the rifle.

She heard a cry of pain, and her target, clutching his chest, slumped to the ground.

The braves were diving for cover. One ran toward the trees at the edge of the clearing—the stacked rifles—then seemed to stumble, and fell forward. Again she heard the bark of the pistol.

She had momentary difficulty reloading in the darkness, but she tamped the ball home, fit the cap, leveled the rifle once more, and fired. Again her aim was true, and another Blackfoot fell. Though wounded, he continued to crawl toward the stacked rifles.

She was reloading when she heard Big Dog's cry—the *hoo-ki-hi!*—the Crow war cry. He pounded into the camp area, screaming, the axe lashing back and forth. She saw the blade descend and cleave the skull of one of the two remaining braves, and then the other warrior jumped him. She did not bother to finish reloading but bolted forward, ran to assist Big Dog, who was wrestling grimly with the last of the Blackfoot.

Without thinking, she too raised her voice in the war cry.

Big Dog rose up, heaved the Blackfoot above his head, and hurled him onto the snow-carpeted earth. Then, picking up the fallen axe, he drove the blade into the man's neck and severed his head from his body.

Chastity felt not horror but a blaze of excitement, the joy of confrontation and victory. Later, perhaps, she would be appalled at what had happened, but at this moment what she felt was sudden relief, a welling of spirits, a sense of profound accomplishment. Two of them against six, she and Big Dog! They had tracked down their enemies and had slain them!

She threw herself into Big Dog's arms and suddenly began weeping hysterically. Her conscious mind was angry at her for doing so, her unconscious was giving vent to fear, anger, danger, celebration. . . .

"These men should not have taken our horses from us," Big Dog laughed. "Now we will have to take their horses and guns and scalps. Big Dog and Yellowhair will hold their own scalp dance when we return to our villages!"

Chastity watched with grim fascination as Big Dog picked up the knife that the beheaded Indian had dropped during the struggle. She watched as her lover drew the tip of the blade around the scalplock and, his knee on the cheekbone of the severed head, ripped the hair loose. Then as he rose he saw that one of the braves was still alive, and he plunged his blade into the dying man's throat.

Chastity turned away and drew a deep breath.

As Big Dog took the scalps of the dead, she walked to the horses, which were nervously pulling at their tethers. She went to her own animal and caressed its nose.

A wave of nausea overcame her, and she leaned over and vomited, as though her body, unwilling to ingest this new sort of food, had chosen to reject it. She gagged, heaved, and afterwards felt much better.

Big Dog was standing behind her.

"Perhaps you will be a Pine Leaf yet," he said. "But you must get over your weak stomach. These Indians were our enemies. They would have burned me alive and raped and tortured you until you begged them to kill you. Now they have died as warriors die and are on their way to the Spirit World. It is this way, Yellowhair. It has always been this way for as long as there have been Crow and Blackfoot. We all live as long as Old Man Coyote wills it and no longer."

"I think I understand," Chastity said. "You're a heathen red devil, just like Benton says."

248

Big Dog laughed. "How many of these Blackfoot did you kill, Yellowhair?"

"One."

"No, you killed two of them. One was dying, and I helped him to leave, that is all. Two of these scalps are yours, little one."

"I don't want them."

"We will darken our lodge with the scalps of our enemies. That is the way it will be."

"Big Dog, let's leave. I want to get away from this . . . thing."

"We will not stay, in any case. I will pack up our new weapons, and we will ride out into the snowstorm, because that is the way our lives are. If you went to be a white woman again, perhaps it would not be this way, Yellowhair. But my world is a world that is ending, a world that will pass away soon. I will be dead then, and the world that comes next will not be as good as this one. It will be a world of the Long Knives, but it will not last always. The mountains will remain, but everything else will change, and then it will change again, and after that again, until all of time is used up. Then maybe time will start over. I do not know."

For a moment Chastity could see it all, Brigham Young's great dream, the New Zion, the city in the wilderness, reaching outward from its center until there was no more wilderness, the Indian people wearing the same kinds of clothing as the whites, Indians working small farms, raising cattle, irrigating fields, growing corn and beans and peas. . . .

She heard the sound of the river, a muffled sound

through the falling snow. She inhaled the odor of smoke in the air, and that other smell.

The smell of death.

Big Dog lifted her in his arms. He kissed her on the forehead and hugged her to him until she could barely breathe.

"Cozzie Yellowhair is now a warrior," he grinned.

Chapter 13

Big Dog and Yellowhair rode proudly into the camp, the string of scalps looped over the warrior's horse and the newly acquired Blackfoot horses trailing behind. The children came whooping out in droves and circled happily about, in the company of thirty or more wildly yapping dogs.

A scalp dance was held that night, for the Crow considered what had happened to be a great victory. It was more than sufficient to remove the mourning paint from the faces of those who had lost sons and husbands when Pine Leaf killed Heavy Shield.

The Dog Soldiers in particular celebrated with great enthusiasm, inasmuch as Big Dog was one of their own. Coyote Running, the chief of the military fraternity, asked Big Dog to describe for all what had happened. And so the story of their time along the Gray Bull unfolded. Much discussion ensued as to the meaning of the death wagon. One Who Strikes Three suggested that Old Man Coyote had placed the wagon and the dead white people in the river as a means of telling the Crow that the whites did not belong in the mountains and that, if they continued to come, such would be their fate. If these white people had indeed been real people, then Old Man Coyote must have caused them to go in the wrong direction and so to become lost—in which case, the meaning would be the same.

The wagon's existence was considered a great mystery, for it was agreed that no wagon had passed near the Crow encampment and that none could have passed near without someone seeing it and reporting it to the people.

Perhaps, Yellow Belly suggested, the wagon had come up from the south, had become separated from a wagon train, and had gotten lost. At the same time, he agreed, it was too early in the season for wagon trains to be passing through the Shining Mountains.

"Perhaps this wagon did come alone, then," Coyote Running said. "Perhaps the man attempted to cross the river and was shot by the Blackfoot. Then the woman took her own life. The oxen grew frightened of the gunfire and attempted to turn about, and the current carried them away and drowned them. Finally the current pushed the wagon into a log jam, up against the bank."

Once again Big Dog was asked to display the scalps, and he fastened them to his lance and raised them high, to the loud applause of all.

When the dance was concluded, Pine Leaf approached Chastity. "Yellowhair, you are a warrior now. You have fought well and bravely. I think you will be one of us, even though your blood is white. You have learned much from Benton and from Big Dog. Perhaps you will ride on other war parties?"

Chastity did not know what to say, but Pine Leaf embraced her quickly and then walked away to rejoin One Who Strikes Three and Black Panther.

"Ye've just been paid a great compliment, Cozzie," Benton chuckled. "Now Pine Leaf'll be wantin' to be your big sister. All ye've got to do now is go out and scalp three, four hundred of the enemy. It's a terrible obligation, gal."

"I do not think Yellowhair will wish to scalp that many," Big Dog said.

"Big Dog took the scalps," Cozzie explained. "I could not do that. . . ."

She and Big Dog and Pawnee Woman then retired to their lodge. Once inside, Pawnee Woman looked questioningly at the woman she called sister. Chastity, in turn, glanced at Big Dog, but his face was without expression.

There was something that needed to be spoken of, and all three were aware of it. For now, however, the previous sleeping arrangements would be resumed.

"Benton has promised the Washington Long Knife Madden that he would bring Yellowhair to Bridger's Fort. The Mormon people will meet us there," he said, turning to Cozzie. "Did my father not tell you of this?"

"He told me," she answered.

"Then you must choose what it is that you wish to do. . . ."

"I understand."

"I will not allow them to take you, Yellowhair, unless you tell me that you wish to go with them and to become a white woman once more."

"When must we go?"

"She does not wish to go, Big Dog," Pawnee Woman protested. "I can see that in her face. Her face is changed."

"Yes," Cozzie said. "Perhaps I will have a scar on my face now."

"I do not mean the cut, my sister," Pawnee Woman said, pretending annoyance that Chastity should act as though she had not understood the intended import.

"If my father has given his word," Big Dog decided, "then we will have to go. We will leave soon, for already our people are making preparations to cross through the mountains to the Little Horn and the Tongue River for the spring buffalo hunts and the reunion with the River People. When they leave, then we must also leave. Now it is time to sleep."

Pawnee Woman embraced Chastity, touched her fingers to the rapidly healing laceration, and looked into her eyes, as if ready to speak the question they both knew had to be asked.

"You are my good friend," Chastity said.

"Yes," Pawnee Woman answered. "And for that reason it is right to share things. Do you wish. . . ."

"I wish to sleep now. Lie with your husband, my sister. Tomorrow we will talk."

Outside the lodge the first noises of spring filled the night. Crickets sang and bullbats flitted through the darkness. The silver of the new April moon had disappeared behind the high westward rim of the Absaroka Range. Odors of germinating life drifted in the warm air, and far up on the ridges, coyotes were howling mouth to mouth, their voices resonating and reverberating.

Near dawn, Chastity awakened from a vision of a young city in the wilderness near a great lake. It was the New Zion of her people.

No, she thought, Brigham Young's people, not mine, not any more. Could I still be one of them? What is life here with these people, the Crow? Perpetual war, scalpings, mutilations, periods of mourning, women with fingers hacked off in honor of husbands and sons slain in battle? Am I strong enough to continue to live this life?

She turned in her robes and looked up at the faintly discernible circle of smoke in the top of the lodge, and tears came to her eyes.

But here I am alive, she thought. Here I have friends and a man who loves . . . desires me. Is that enough?

She turned once again and fell back into uneasy sleep. She did not awaken until she became aware of a scratching sound against the flap of the lodge. Big Dog, who was already up, passed next to her, saw she was awake, and nodded—then moved across to the entrance.

He opened the flap, and Pine Leaf stood there.

"Great warrior," she said. "Yellow Belly wishes to

speak to you. Madden, the strange white man who came with the bluecoats, has spoken of a treaty with the Washington chief. Yellow Belly wishes to have your advice."

Big Dog glanced back at the two women lying in their robes, and then followed Pine Leaf through the still quiet village to the head chief's lodge.

Pine Leaf pointed to a pile of branches where a blue and red butterfly perched, slowly fanning its wings in the early sunlight. A young dog stood close by, half ready to pounce, half absorbed in canine curiosity.

"The new season began last night," Big Dog said.

Yellow Belly was standing before his lodge, waiting for them. He motioned inside where a fire blazed and his wives were preparing a pot of stew and some coffee as well.

"We will leave this day for the Tongue River hunting grounds," the chief said, "but you and Benton and Two-tail Skunk will go the other way, to the Sweetwater and on toward the Big Salty. Before you leave, Big Dog, I wish to have your counsel. Pine Leaf, did you tell him what I wished to speak of?"

"Yes," Pine Leaf answered. "He knows."

"The chief of the bluecoats wishes to make an agreement with us, Big Dog."

"The Long Knives have made many treaties, but always they change their minds later. What is it they wish you to agree to?" he asked.

"I cannot agree to anything, Big Dog. Our people must agree or there can be no treaty, for I am only one among many, even though I lead our people in matters of war and hunting. And yet the people will listen to me if I speak wisely, and that is why I wish to have your counsel."

"You have spoken with my father, Yellow Belly?"

"Of course. Benton is one of us even thought he is a white man. For this reason I have listened carefully to what he has said. The part of him that is white understands the ways in which the Long Knives think, and that is important, for they do not think as we do."

"They are very stupid people," Pine Leaf asserted, "even if they have better weapons than ours. Sometimes they drag their cannons behind them and suppose they can frighten us with the big noises. And they tell us of their great villages, where their numbers are endless."

"Of that they speak the truth," Big Dog said. "I have seen some of their villages. And now they are moving across our lands and beginning to build their villages even here. What do they wish, Yellow Belly?"

"Let us drink some coffee," the head chief suggested. "Coffee also comes from the Long Knives, but we have learned to like its taste. It is good with sugar in it."

One of Yellow Belly's wives brought tin cups filled with the steaming brew, and the chief and Pine Leaf and Big Dog sipped carefully.

"This Madden has spoken of why it is not good for us to fight always with the other tribes. He thinks we should be friends with the Sioux and Cheyenne and Blackfoot. He thinks that then they would be friends with us, also."

"That is a very foolish idea," Pine Leaf snapped, shaking her head.

257

"Madden says the Washington chief will send us presents, weapons and food, if we will agree to this treaty."

"We do not need their food, and their clothing is not so fine as our own," Big Dog said.

"That is what I think, too," Yellow Belly agreed. "And we can buy the weapons we need by selling our buffalo robes. Buttermilk Thompson brings in wagon-loads of weapons and other things that we need."

"What else do the Long Knives wish us to do?" Big Dog asked.

Yellow Belly and Pine Leaf looked at each other, their eyes smiling as if at some private joke.

"They wish us to stay on the lands we have always stayed on," Pine Leaf said. "They think we wish to go somewhere else. They do not understand that Crows are in exactly the right place, with the mountains on one side and the great plains where the Buffalo feed on the other. They think we may wish to move down the Big River to St. Louis, maybe."

Yellow Belly nodded.

"What do you think, Big Dog?"

"I think these Long Knives are much stronger than we have ever believed, Yellow Belly. Benton has told me how they forced the people from beyond the Father River to move from their own lands and go to the lands to the south, where there is never enough water and game is scarce. These people had tried to live as the Long Knives live, and yet they were forced to go where they did not wish to go. Only a few were able to avoid doing as the Long Knives wished. These Long Knives claim the Washington chief is our father,

258

but his blood is not like ours, for he is not one of us. These men lie to us, and yet it is best for us to remain friends with them. In that way, in the years ahead, we may be able to keep our own lands, even though the Long Knives live among us and build their villages."

"How then would you counsel me, Big Dog?"

"I believe we should agree only to do those things which we always do and to live where we have always lived. That is my counsel."

"You speak as your father has spoken," Pine Leaf said.

"Yes, Benton and I have the same thoughts."

"I think the same way," Yellow Belly added. "When the people have crossed to the Tongue River, then we will meet our brothers and sisters, the People of the River. Then I will speak with the great Long Hair. He is old now and no longer rides the warpath, but he is very wise. He has been head chief for many winters. His people still listen to his words and respect him, even though he cannot control all of his young warriors. Our councils will meet together, and we will speak of this treaty. I will ask Pine Leaf to speak your words for you, yours and your father's, for you will be a long way away from us then. Is this what you would wish, Big Dog?"

"Pine Leaf will speak for me, but she must speak for herself also, even though she is no longer a war chief or a member of our council. Still the people respect her, and they will listen to what she says."

"Do you think it might be possible to be friends with the Cheyenne or the Blackfoot in the years which will run ahead of us?"

Big Dog squinted and drank the last of his coffee.

"We might be friends only if we should unite to drive the Long Knives from our lands forever. But even that would not be necessary, for their villages are far away still. Together with our brothers the River People and our cousins the Hidatsa we could drive the bluecoats away all by ourselves. Later, when more Long Knives have come among us, then it may be necessary to form an alliance with our enemies. The Long Knives are our friends, but they may finally be our enemies. If they should try to take our lands, then they will be our enemies, and we will have to fight them. That is what I think."

Yellow Belly nodded in a way that indicated the meeting was over.

"I know your thoughts, Big Dog, and I like them. Now you and Benton must leave to return Yellowhair to her people, though I do not think she will wish to go with them. Pine Leaf does not think so, either. When you return, you will find us somewhere on the Tongue or perhaps on the Crazy Woman or the Powder. Grandmother Earth and Old Man Coyote will protect you."

Big Dog embraced Yellow Belly and Pine Leaf, who asked, "Why do you not wish the Yellowhair to be your wife? That is what she wishes—all of us can tell that."

"That is what I wish to do, my sister."

"Then why do you not do it?" Yellow Belly questioned, raising his eyebrows.

"I must not do this thing until Yellowhair has met again with her own people and has decided that she does not want to go with them. If that happens, then I will ask her to marry me."

"You have strange thoughts, Big Dog," Pine Leaf said. "Yellowhair is already one of us."

Big Dog stepped out into the clear, warm sunlight and saw that already the wrapping hides were beginning to disappear from a number of the lodges. The women stood at ground level, supervising, and young boys scrambled about, up high, unfastening laces that had grown tight and hard during the long months of winter. Pack animals were being led in from the herds, and camp dogs were either chasing about in excitement or hanging close to the lodges, seemingly worried about the changes in progress.

By midday the entire camp had disappeared. Lodge hides were bundled and poles wrapped, all equipment and personal belongings were stored away in elkhide carrying bags or wrapped in buffalo robes. Travois rigs were loaded and made ready for the journey to the Little Horn and Tongue River country. Numerous women and boys assisted Buttermilk Thompson, whose trading post, like the other lodges, had to be taken apart. His trade goods and robes and furs would be transported downriver to Fort Alexander, and then on down to Fort Van Buren, at the mouth of the Tongue. Once there, Thompson would exchange his furs for additional trade goods and so move on up the Tongue to make contact with the Crow once more.

Two-tail Skunk, after a winter of attending to the needs and desires of his three wives, had concluded that they should accompany the people on the journey to the buffalo hunting grounds while he rode with Big Dog and Benton to Bridger's Fort. Pawnee Woman would stay with her husband and Chastity. But the lodge itself was loaded onto a travois and put into the care of Skunk's wives, who would be looked after by the old warrior Two Bears.

By late afternoon, the Crow had forded the Bighorn and were moving away northward, an exodus of perhaps four thousand in all, with an even larger number of horses and an indeterminate number of dogs. The warriors rode lead, followed by the women and pack animals. The horse herd moved behind, driven by boys and young warriors.

The other party forded the Gray Bull and rode south.

Once across the river, Chastity turned to look back at the vanished villages, the broad, open area of packed earth where now only half a dozen thin plumes of smoke rose from dying fires. A few coyotes were trotting about, curiously sniffing in an attempt to discover portions of spoiled meat or anything else that might prove edible, left behind for reasons that coyotes neither understood nor worried about. Food, indeed, would have been left for the Song Dogs, a tribute to Cirape, the smaller brother of Old Man Coyote—for then the god would see that the people had been generous and so would be inclined to be generous to them in return.

Chastity felt tears starting, and she well understood the sensation of loss. A world that had been hers for a time, and which might be again in the future, had for the moment vanished as certainly as though it had never existed at all.

Was the trip to Bridger's Fort, in fact, necessary?

Aloysius Benton had given his word, to her father, Brigham Young and Tommasen and again to Madden, the clerk from the Office of Indian Affairs. Madden had been sent out from Washington both in response to a protest that Brigham Young had lodged with the government in Washington, and to survey the general situation existing among the Indian peoples of the high plains and Rocky Mountain regions. She, then, had become in some nearly inexplicable way a concern of the federal government, a government toward which the Mormons had, in fact, scant reason for loyalty and from which they fully intended to break away and establish their own nation of Deseret.

The infinitely woven threads of circumstance, she thought. Missing in action, stolen by hostile Indians— four cows and one girl. Also several cattle killed. We demand accountable satisfaction from the government. . . . Surely the complaint had been filed in some such wording. Was Madden, she wondered, also attempting to manage the return of the cows? And perhaps a few tame buffalo in exchange for the cattle killed? So it was, she felt—she was property belonging generally to the patriarchial Mormon hegemony, which demanded its return.

And yet, she too felt a need for the return. Beside her rode Two-tail Skunk, who had become a brother to her, and ahead were Pawnee Woman, her sister, Aloysius Benton, her father, and Big Dog Benton, her lover. These people, along with other Crow—Pine Leaf and

One Who Strikes Three, for instance—had become in a true sense the only family she had ever known. Her own father seemed little more than a stranger, someone she had known and been close to once, long ago. What of Tommasen, the man she was supposed to marry? This was someone whom she did not really know at all. Nevertheless, she imagined herself once again dressed in traditional Mormon clothing, the mistress of a large house, no doubt already built by now, preparing meals, listening to the talk of the men at the supper table, herself obliged to eat silently unless spoken to, like a child. Herself bearing Tommasen's children, herself being made love to by him—that after the wild and wonderfully animal-like mating with Big Dog. The ecstasy of it, the flamings of sensation that had touched even the bones within her flesh, that had burned in her loins and her brain—had it been a dream, after all? An illusion, something that had existed because she, herself, had wanted it and had created it?

Ahead of her, Aloysius Benton was alternately cursing and crooning into Charbonneau's ear. The doughty old mare was acting up for reasons known only to her and vaguely appreciated only by Benton himself.

That horse means more to me than Tommasen, she thought. And yet I am returning—to what? If he takes me, pays for me, I will ultimately be one of several wives, for he will take others. And I will be the degraded one, the one who was forced to live with the heathen. I will be tolerated, no more. Or perhaps Tommasen will not have me in any case, and I will be allowed to live, grudgingly, with my father and his wife, avoided by the other Mormon women. I will be Tillie Ann's maid, and I will be obliged to do as she says. . . .

She stared at Big Dog and Pawnee Woman, riding side by side. Once the journey had begun, even her lover and her sister had said little to her. They seemed preoccupied with their own thoughts.

She remembered the great, powerful shoulders of Big Dog Benton, the quiet but even greater strength which animated the man. He was her lover. Once, up on the Gray Bull, he had belonged to her. It was like a dream, now. Her entire world had become nothing more than a tapestry of dreams, of illusions.

And so the days drifted onward. They rode, stopped for a noon meal, and rode once again. They camped at night, roasting fresh venison that Skunk had killed, drinking Benton's mixture of willow bark and coffee. The group of them talked together and yet always avoided the one subject most on their minds. Whatever Big Dog was thinking, he did not share his thoughts with her. And Pawnee Woman, sometimes in high spirits and sometimes distant, spoke only of domestic matters. Perhaps she would get to see the legendary Long Hair, the great chief who was spoken of in awe even by the Pawnee. Perhaps Big Dog would buy red or yellow cloth for her or a quantity of Long Knife beads which she would use with porcupine quills to decorate her clothing. Indeed, sometimes Pawnee Woman used the word *we,* but it was never certain whether she meant Big Dog and herself or all three of them together.

And when the fire died down, the coyotes howled

and sometimes wolves and owls called. And Chastity slept by herself, snug beneath the buffalo robes, but cold inside.

On the eighth day of their journey, they crossed to the Sweetwater, carefully avoiding the small white settlement at South Pass. They moved onward through the broad trench valley, which provided the primary access to the interior, and beyond which the streams flowed down into the Seedskeedee and on to the Colorado and thence to the Gulf of California and the Pacific Ocean.

Another six days or so, Benton said, and they would arrive at Bridger's Fort, where, ultimately, Tommasen and a party of Mormons would also arrive. Madden, the government man, would no doubt be among them.

They were across the Continental Divide, and when Benton called out to say so, Chastity felt a vague sense of disappointment even in this—for the land was flat, just as it had been before, and there was no reason to believe that anything was changed. Mountains rose in the distance in all directions, thick spring grass grew in places, sage and bare earth lay elsewhere, and the late afternoon sun was huge and yellow-white before them.

"Coons! We're rollin' downhill to the Pacific now!" Benton called out once more, pleased with the idea.

And it was true. Something in the tone of the old trapper's voice seemed almost to suggest that the ocean lay just beyond the next long rim of blue-purple mountains instead of nearly a thousand miles across deserts and mountain ranges.

"Where is the Great Water?" Two-tail Skunk complained. "Always when I come here, I hope to see it. I do not believe there is any Great Water—only a story the Long Knives tell each other."

"Heathen red devil! Ye don't believe nothin' you're told."

"There is no Great Water," Two-tail Skunk insisted. "Only the Big Salty and the phantoms of the deserts beyond. Benton has drunk too much coffee— his mind plays tricks on him!"

Big Dog laughed, drew his horse about, and waited for Chastity to come abreast of him.

"I will ride with you, now," he said.

"I thought you had forgotten about me."

"Sometimes I have tried to do that, but I cannot. Your own thoughts have been far away, my sister. You are thinking of the crazy people?"

"Yes. And the other crazy people also, the Sparrow Hawks."

Big Dog nodded.

"Perhaps you are right, Yellowhair. Our minds are not like the minds of the animal people, for they think only of those things which matter to them. Mr. Coyote thinks about eating Mrs. Rabbit, and Mrs. Rabbit thinks about not being eaten by Mr. Coyote. Ground squirrels think about eating sweet roots, and eagles think about eating sweet ground squirrels. And sometimes they all think about making love."

"Do the animals do that . . . make love?"

"Why do you think they have little ones, Yellowhair?" he exclaimed.

"But do the animals feel love, the way humans feel it?"

Big Dog whistled and looked thoughtful. He was silent for a few moments before he answered.

"When I was a boy, I set a snare and caught a horned owl. I built a cage for it from willow twigs and when I was finished, I pushed the bird inside with a stick. Owls have very sharp claws and are dangerous. But I intended to take the owl back to the village with me alive, and so I had to have something to carry it in. By then it was nearly the middle of the day, a time when the Owl People sleep. When I had the bird inside and the cage was fastened so that it could not get out, I looked up into the sky. There was the owl's mate, soaring back and forth in long loops. . . ."

"Was the bird you captured a male or a female?"

"I do not know. Owls look very much alike, and one can tell only if one sees two of them together, for the woman owl is larger than the man owl. She is also the better hunter, and often she leaves him to sit with the eggs or the nestlings."

"Is that true, or is this a story like one of Benton's?"

"No, Yellowhair, it is true. And the owl's mate may have been flying about at the time I was making the willow cage, I don't know. But then I looked at the owl I had captured—its eyes were blinking, and it knew that it could not escape. It seemed to be waiting for death, and perhaps it knew that its feathers would be used to decorate a battle lance—for it had very fine feathers. Suddenly I knew that I would have to let my owl go, for if I didn't, I would always remember how its mate flew about, helpless, while I took it away with me to the village. If I decorated my lance with those feathers, I would have bad medicine. The feathers would cause me sadness."

Yellowhair stared at Big Dog, not quite understanding why he was telling her the story—but understanding all the same.

"Then I opened the cage. At first the owl just looked at me, as though it did not believe what I had done. And then it was gone, up into the sky, almost as though it had vanished before my eyes. I watched them then, swooping back and forth together, like old friends who have not seen each other for a long while. They flew in circles, always closer together, and then they disappeared into the forest."

"And then?"

"That is all. I used to look for them after that, whenever I was near. Once or twice I saw them together, and then I did not see them any more. I think they went to live in a different place. Anyway, that is why I think the animal people feel love, just like the humans. What do you think?"

"Are we like the owls, Big Dog?"

"I don't know. Have you decided what you will do yet?"

"Yes," she answered.

Chapter 14

May 1849

On the night of the full April moon, Chastity left her robes and climbed the little rise to the juniper thicket where her lover and his wife were lying together.

"Yellowhair!" Pawnee Woman cried, startled at the vision of the white girl standing there, her hair full, not braided, in the silver-white of the moon flood. "Is something the matter, my sister?"

"No," Cozzie answered, "it's just that I couldn't sleep. The moon is so . . . bright. I want to talk with you, Pawnee Woman."

Big Dog slipped from beneath his robes and stood up. He looked questioningly from one woman to the other.

"I will walk in the moonlight," he said. "I will be back in a little while."

Then, thrusting his pistol into his belt loops, he

was gone, soundlessly, and Chastity spoke to Pawnee Woman.

"I'm . . . sorry, my sister. I could not sleep this night."

"We come close now to the place where you are to meet your people again, but I do not wish you to go with them."

"What does Big Dog wish?"

"He wishes you to stay with us, Yellowhair. You know that is true. And yet he believes that you will decide to go with the Mormon people. He thinks that once you have met with them again, you will wish to go with them."

"I. . . ."

"Your hair is beautiful in the moonlight, my sister. Many times since we have been together I have wished my hair were like yours. Big Dog loves you, and I love you also. You have slept with him? When you fled from the villages and were captured by the Blackfoot?"

"Big Dog has not told you what happened?"

"No. I did not ask him. But he did make love to you?"

"Yes. That is what happened."

"I thought so," Pawnee Woman smiled. "Even Crooked Knife preferred you to me, Yellowhair. I think Big Dog does also, and yet I know that he loves me. I do not mind this thing. My nose is crooked, and my hair is not nice like yours."

"He is a fool, then, my sister. In all ways that matter, you are far more beautiful than I am. I feel . . . so alone right now!"

Pawnee Woman stepped closer to Chastity, and the two women embraced. The white girl clung fiercely, crying suddenly, unable to control the sobs that racked her slim body. Then Pawnee Woman reached up and stroked Cozzie's hair, running her fingers through its length.

"I will braid your hair in the morning," she said. "I enjoy doing that for you."

Eyes closed, the tears burning her face in the chilly night air, Chastity realized once again both the warmth and the strength of this woman who held her, who had comforted her when she had been brought a captive bride into the village of the Pawnee.

"My good friend," Chastity breathed, between sobs.

"My sister," Pawnee Woman said softly, "my sister. . . ."

"What must I do, Pawnee Woman?"

Then Pawnee Woman held her at arm's length, barely touching her shoulders.

"Big Dog thinks you will go with your people."

"The Crow are my people," Yellowhair exclaimed immediately, surprised at her own words.

"They are my people, too, for they have accepted me. They accept you also, my sister, even if they do not understand why it is that you have not become wife to Big Dog."

"Is that what you wish? Will you permit that to be?"

"Does my friend not trust my words, does she not believe them?"

"Of course I do. . . ."

"Then we will both be Big Dog's wives. Our lodge will be stronger, and our husband will be even more admired among our people. Sometimes he will make love to one of us, sometimes to the other, sometimes to both at once. We will tire him out, but not so often that he will wish to escape us and go hunting or horse stealing to get away from us. That is why Two-tail Skunk did not bring his wives with him—they have worked him to death, and now he wishes to be alone so that he can regain his strength. Men tire more easily than women, and that is why we must be careful."

"Both at the same time?" she asked, her voice unbelieving.

"Men like that sometimes. Big Dog is a good man, a strong warrior. It will be good, the three of us together, just as we were before—only that time we had a bad husband. Big Dog is much different."

"Yes, yes, that is true."

"Did he please you when he made love to you, Yellowhair?"

"Yes, he pleased me very much."

"He pleases me, also. That is because he loves us. When he returns, we must tell him what we have decided. I chose him first, and now you choose him also."

The two women lay down together, close and secure in a way that they had not done for a long time.

But Big Dog did not return to the sleeping place that night. Pawnee Woman and Yellowhair fell asleep in each other's arms, and when they awoke, Big Dog was standing at the campfire, talking with Benton and Two-tail Skunk.

Benton called the two women to a breakfast of

roast duck, Big Dog having shot two of the birds just at sunrise. Both of them were so fat from eating green vegetation, Two-tail Skunk insisted, that they couldn't fly. Big Dog himself was in obvious high spirits, at one moment pounding Skunk on the back and at the next demanding that Benton go find some rotten acorns to mix in with the coffee to give it a better flavor. Then, quite unexpectedly, he looped his arms about Pawnee Woman and Yellowhair and drew them up to shoulder height, laughed, and spun them about in a circle.

"Female critters are born dizzy," Benton said solemnly. "Ye needn't be addin' to the problem, Son."

"Our husband has found a tree full of rotten plums and has been eating them," Pawnee Woman insisted, tugging at Big Dog's braided hair and wriggling about on his shoulder.

"Somethin's come over 'im, for sure now," Benton said, kneeling to remove the spitted ducks from the flames.

Whatever tension had existed since leaving the Crow camp was indeed gone, and everyone felt it. Even Charbonneau, as if sensing the change among the humans, frisked about like a colt. Laying her ears back, she nipped at the other horses, who shied and backed away from the mare's playfulness.

"That animal ain't figgered out she's gotten old," Benton explained. "Fact of the matter, mebbe she's found the secret and has been gettin' young again."

"She is growing down," Two-tail Skunk agreed. "Soon she will be only three feet tall and will wish to nurse again. What will you do then, Father?"

"Grow teats an' feed 'er, I expect. Or else stick 'er onto Cozzie and Pawnee Woman."

"My father will have to tend to his own horse," Big Dog insisted. "But I think it is just that Charbonneau wishes to get back on the trail. She is addicted to travel and wishes for us to move once more."

And so the journey continued, until they picked up the main wagon route at Ham's Fork. There they detoured around a motley-looking band of emigrants. Their wagons were in pitiful condition, one even drawn by a single ox and a pair of gray-black mules.

"Don't look like settlers to this old-timer," Benton said. "No cattle with 'em an' maybe no womenfolk either. Some ain't even got wagons—look at that! A wonder they've made 'er this far."

"They are crazier than the crazy people," Big Dog agreed. "We do well to stay away from these people."

By midday they had approached a second group of travelers, somewhat smaller than the first, but seemingly identical in all other respects. The band had drawn up in open country, to rest their animals and take a noon meal. Once again Benton signaled a detour, back away from the main wagon road and down to a creek on the far side.

"Somethin' peculiar goin' on," he said. "This coon don't figger it. Unless it be that Californy gold little Lootenant Edgeworth an' Madden was talkin' about. That's got to be what it is. Damn fools chasin' across the mountains to go diggin' out nuggets, somethin' of the kind."

"What will they do with the gold if they find it?" Skunk asked.

"Same as cash money, ye ignorant heathen. Same as buffler robes or beaver hides. Ye find some of them yeller rocks, and ye won't have to be thievin' horses from the Cheyenne anymore. Just ride up to old Leg-in-the-Water an' tell 'im ye'll give 'im some pieces of gold for a thousand horses or so."

"What would Leg-in-the-Water do with yellow rocks?" Two-tail Skunk wanted to know, his face a mask of genuine puzzlement.

"Big Dog, we got to educate this red devil. Anyone that can't see what good gold is has got to be weak in the head."

"You can use it for rifle balls, just like lead," Big Dog explained.

"What's this coon doin' with a pair of dumb-ass Injuns for sons, anyhow? Even a child could understand 'er."

"Enough gold for people to cross the mountains to get it?" Chastity asked.

"Accordin' to Madden," Benton replied, "she's lyin' all over the place out there. A Swiss-German named Sutter come across the Shining Mountains with an American Fur Company outfit back in '37. From what I hear, when the coon got to California, the Spanish give him about half of the place, an' now one of his millhands has found gold. Everybody out yonder's up in the hills, just diggin' away—Sutter hisself an' Medicine Calf too, for all I know. Anyhow, even the President of the U.S. federal goddamned gov'ment's talkin' about how much yeller stuff there is. The Greenwoods is out there an' Walker an' Carson, I guess. Meek, too, mebbe, an' old Jim Clyman, that's took to farming. If he can still hobble around, he's probably up there diggin'. Even heard that Pompey Charbonneau, Pierre's kid, was out there. All the coons. Ye never heard of any of 'em, Cozzie, but I've known all of 'em. Them was days that purely shone. All gone now, damnit. All the old trappers that ain't gone under, they're probably all out there diggin' rocks. It's a piss-poor way to end 'er."

"Our father wishes he were with them," Big Dog said.

"We should go dig the gold, too, maybe," Two-tail Skunk grinned. "Then Benton will be happy again. If we go, we can find out if there is really a Great Water, as he says. I think the world ends beyond the desert."

"Then where all these damned fools goin', ye red heathen?"

"Maybe they go out into the desert to die."

"That's what will happen to some of them," Big Dog agreed. "These people we have seen, they will not all make it across the desert. They think of the gold and forget everything else."

"Goddamn greenhorns!" Benton laughed bitterly. "They'll mark out the trail to California with their bones, sure as buffler dung."

After that Benton rode silently for a time. Then he turned to Big Dog. "Be good to see Jim Bridger again, won't it, Son? At least that ol' hoss is smart enough to stay put in the mountains."

"Where he can sell things to the Mormons and the ones on their way to Oregon and California. He is like Buttermilk Thompson, now. Soon we may all be like Buttermilk Thompson."

"Not this coot, an' ye can lay to 'er."

Just before nightfall they came upon the burned-out remains of a Conestoga. Close by the trail were three mounds of earth, one of which the coyotes and wolves had dug out. They had exposed the lower portion of a human body with a chunk of one leg eaten away, the large white bone clearly showing teeth marks. Chastity, sickened, turned away, not wanting to look at the ravaged grave. Pawnee Woman attempted to comfort her.

"Like I was sayin'," Benton shrugged. "Wonder what happened? No sign of arrows or gunshot. . . ."

"Old Man Coyote burned their wagon," Two-tail Skunk suggested. "Then he buried them when they died of fright. After that he got hungry, so he dug one up and ate a little bit."

"Well, let's cover this one up again," Big Dog said. "It's too far to carry rocks, but the least we can do is to cover the hole. Soon the flesh will stink, and then Cirape and True Dog will not be interested anymore. . . ."

The task took only a few minutes, and then the party continued on its way to Bridger's Fort. Once they were riding again, Chastity began to feel better, but her thoughts returned to the indelibly imprinted images of the death wagon in the Gray Bull shallows. Now this, another death wagon. In civilization, such things were politely taken care of, covered up, kept out of sight. But in the wilderness, the same civilized conventions could not apply. She thought of the tree-hung graves she had seen while she had been with the Pawnee and, later, among the Crow. The bodies and possessions were suspended where the animals could not get to the flesh, left to the wind and the rain and the sunlight. After a season, the bones would be gathered up. If the dead were a well-known warrior, the bones were reverently wrapped and taken to some sacred place, a repository of powerful medicine. She thought of the old ones, left alone in death lodges, with food and water for a time, but waiting to die. They accepted the inevitable, demanding that the tradition be fulfilled, the pattern completed.

"The old people have that right," Big Dog had told her once. "It would be wrong not to allow them to die in the ways of their mothers and fathers and grandparents. We do not leave them alone, for Old Man Coyote is with them. He waits with them so that he can show them the path to the Spirit World, the long path of white haze in the night sky, what the Long Knives call the Milky Way. If one has lived well, then the path is easy. If one has not lived a good life, then the path is more difficult. But all arrive at the Spirit World at last. In that place, we are all together once more."

The utter simplicity of it! Foolish and childlike, and yet was it any more childlike than what the Mormons and other Christian peoples believed? Chastity shook her head and thought, no. Somehow it is all the same.

"Perhaps the Indian way is better," Chastity mused. "There is no hell and there is no heaven. Only the Spirit World, where everyone goes. And if the good are then treated better, it is because they continue to do good. But there is no more sickness, there is no more death. And not even time matters. . . ."

That night the little party rode away from the wagon route—their usual procedure—and camped. After the evening meal, the two women and three men talked for a long while. They told stories and spoke of buffalo hunting and also of California and the strange force which called men across the continent to search for gold. They talked of who might be the next head chief of the Crow when Yellow Belly went to the Spirit World. But they did not speak of why it was that they were going to Bridger's Fort.

As they were about to retire, they heard noise in the darkness below. Men's voices sounded faint and cursing. Animals snorted and there was the scuffing pop of a steel-rimmed wagon wheel jolting over bare rocks.

"Even after dark they continue," Big Dog said in wonderment. "If they were stealing horses from the Blackfoot and wanted to get far away quickly, then it would make sense."

"They's worse than Blackfoot after 'em," Benton said, gulping the last of his coffee.

"They hear the call of death, out in the desert, maybe," Skunk added.

"Ahh!" Benton growled. "This coon's goin' to sleep for a spell. Tomorrow night we'll eat hump-rib with old Jim, if he ain't too busy to hunt for his grub."

"Not many buffalo are left on this side of the mountains," Big Dog said matter-of-factly. Then he rose and walked toward the sleeping robes. Pawnee Woman and Chastity followed him.

The three of them slept together that night, just as they had for the previous three nights, ever since the night of the full moon. No coyote sang this night. The land was strangely oppressive and quiet after the emigrants had passed, and only after the moon was well up into the sky did the crickets begin to chorus along the stream they were following.

It was an early breakfast the next day and back onto the trail. They moved along the main route once more and beside the swiftly flowing water that poured down from the high Uintas, gleaming and white, off to the south.

Late afternoon brought them to their destination. It was the way station run jointly by Louis Vasquez and Jim Bridger, with an eight-foot stockade and a corral adjoining to the north side. Inside the stockade stood four weathered cabins, their sodded roofs sagging nearly flat. One shack housed Bridger's blacksmith shop and the second his store. The third was his own dwelling, and in the fourth lived the rotund little Mexican Louis Vasquez and his wife. Surrounding it were numerous lodges of the Shoshone people, whom Bridger had long been on friendly terms with. A smaller group of lodges belonged to the Ute, friends to Bridger now because Jim was married to one of their own, Little Fawn.

No white wagon trains were there now. The party that had passed in the night had taken on a few supplies and two kegs of whiskey and had headed west to California. But there would be new traffic soon, Benton knew well enough. Of the second band of would-be miners and wagon trains to follow, some would leave the fort and head northward along the Oregon Trail. Others would take the California branch to Salt Lake City, the Mormon people to stay and settle, the others to march on, mesmerized by the lure of the distant goldfields.

A large, bearded man stood framed in the gateway.

"What goes thar?" the voice bellowed.

"Ye know me well enough, ye old thief! It's Benton an' the Crow—we're comin' in!"

Big Dog and Benton fired their Hawkens into the sky, and the group rode forward to a warm welcome. Benton was scarcely dismounted when Bridger was pounding him on the back.

"Coon, this trapper's mighty happy to see you. You've picked up a scar since last time. Friendly old white bear, was it?"

"I wanted his hide, ye see," Benton replied, "an' Ephraim was a mite jealous about lettin' go of 'er."

"Your medicine was bound to run out, 'Loysius. All these years, and you never had the ha'r of the b'ar in yuh. Guess the green's startin' to wear out. Big Dog, how you? Seems like a man could keep his pappy from tryin' to make love to bears, now don't it?"

The two men embraced.

"Gabe of the Mountains," Big Dog said, "it's good to see you again. Several winters now."

"It has been, for sure," Bridger agreed. "An' not good ones, nuther. I'll tell yuh about 'er later. Who's this with you? Two-tail Skunk, if I recollect, the pride of the Crow. An' the ladies? Which one of yuh be

Chastity Cosgrove? One looks as much Injun as the other."

"Cozzie," Benton put in, "this here's Gabe Bridger, next to me, the meanest son of a bitch in the Shinin' Mountains."

Bridger inclined his head, and turned once more to Benton.

"About that meanness," he drawled. "We'll have us a meanness contest, 'Loysius. I've got some regular, civilized playin' cards. The stakes is your meanness again' mine. Tell yuh, I ain't never lost yet."

"Ye ain't never played me for meanness, that's why."

"Be that the same bad-natured mare you've had for a hundred years? I believe it is. Time to send her off to the Spirit World, Benton."

"She'll outlive both of us. Look, Gabe, we done rode four hundred miles for hump-rib. Where's dinner, damn it!"

"Little Fawn's got summat cookin', but it ain't hump-rib. Haven't seen a buffler out here since last fall. Shoshones and Utes ate 'em all. Besides, I just got back myself, two, three weeks ago—just in time to entertain fuzz-face Edgeworth an' his bluecoats and Charlie Madden the Injun keeper. That's how I knew yuh was comin', 'Loysius. Let's get the varmits stabled and head inside. Vasquez an' his wife are here, an' we'll all have some chow an' some talk. I had bad news a spell back, but I've got hold of myself now. Let's go eat an' talk. Ladies? Little Fawn's gettin' ready to foal, this summer some time. I'll have me a new little Bridger by the fourth 'o July. Lost my daughter that was up with the Whitmans out in Oregon. Joe Meek rode in with the news last summer. Seems like the Injuns up an' murdered Doc Whitman and his wife, right in their own house. Got Joe's daughter, Helen, too. Joe found the bodies an' buried 'em. My gal, Mary Ann, the red devils carried her off an' I guess done what they always do. Anyhow, no word of her, an' I know she's gone under. No place out here for a family man, so Little Fawn an' me rode back to Kansas an' bought us a farm. But hell, 'Loysius, coons like you an' me can't stay in the settlements, even if we know we should. One month of settin' on top of black dirt, an' we was ready to head our moccasins west again. Look, I'll send off one of my Ute with a message for old Brigham first thing in the mornin'. I told Madden I would, and the Angel Moroni is expectin' word. Come on, now, let's get inside where we can talk. Ain't no point in standin' out here an' chewin' the rag. . . ."

"Right!" Benton agreed. "Let's eat."

"Now, 'Loysius, don't go splittin' a gut when yuh see what I've got inside. Genuine civilized chairs for yuh to set in. Wasn't my idee, I swear it. Looey's wife, she's a white gal from the settlements, an' damned if she didn't just insist on havin' chairs! So I hauled 'em up. Yuh don't have to set in 'em if yuh don't want, but maybe the ladies'll like 'em. Me, I always figger the damned things is goin' to bust when I do set in one of 'em. . . ."

"Ain't no way to treat guests," Benton complained. "Coon, ye be starvin' us to death."

"This way," Bridger nodded. He took two steps toward the house and then stopped and turned around.

"Benton, yuh sure this be a white gal? Yeller hair or not, she sure do look like a Crow squaw to this ol' trapper...."

Soon the introductions were completed and the dinner was served. The four women sat around a rough oak table and the men squatted around the cast-iron stove, their tin plates balanced on their knees. At the table, Pawnee Woman was attempting, somewhat self-consciously, to use knife, fork and spoon, while next to the stove Two-tail Skunk was having even less luck.

Mrs. Vasquez expressed horror at the little she had been told of Chastity's ordeal, while Mrs. Bridger, seeing things from quite a different perspective, looked from Chastity to Pawnee Woman and then glanced over at Big Dog, hunkered by the stove.

Big Dog ate silently. A knot had once more formed in his stomach, and a terrible sensation of loneliness had begun to settle over him. He imagined himself and Pawnee Woman, just the two of them, in their winter lodge on the Bighorn. He loved this woman, and she him. But their lodge was terribly empty, for Yellowhair, he had realized, would be back with her own people.

But the talk was animated nonetheless. Benton, Bridger and Vasquez rambled on about past times, the rendezvous of '26, the first *real* rendezvous, '27, when all hell broke loose, '28, after which Jim Beckwourth had been kidnapped by the Crow and had gone on to become their head chief, '29, when Jed Smith came back after being gone for two years and supposed dead, '35, when White Hair Fitzpatrick and Bridger finally gave up and joined in with American Fur, '43, the last rendezvous, with the Scot nobleman Stewart financing the final hurrah.

Even when the talk had shifted to those final years, years during which Big Dog had been an active participant, the words were meaningless to him.

Big Dog placed his hand on Benton's shoulder and said something about checking on the horses. Accompanied by Two-tail Skunk, he disappeared out the door. Pawnee Woman looked at Chastity, then rose and followed her husband.

Chastity continued talking with Little Fawn and Mrs. Vasquez. If she had attributed any significance to the departure of Big Dog and Two-tail Skunk, the matter seemed at rest when, a few minutes later, Pawnee Woman re-entered the house and once again took her place at the table.

When an hour or so had passed without Big Dog or Skunk returning, Chastity spoke to Pawnee Woman, asking in Crow, "Where have they gone, my sister?"

Pawnee Woman lowered her eyes.

"Where have they gone?" Chastity repeated.

"I am not supposed to tell you."

"You must tell me, Pawnee Woman. I have a right to know this thing."

"What is the matter?" Mrs. Vasquez asked.

"It is nothing," Chastity answered. "Only that Pawnee Woman's husband has gone out to the stables and has not come back."

"The Indian people are dancing—Fawn's people and the Shoshone. They have probably gone out to watch. They'll be back after a bit."

"The men come and go and sometimes do not tell their wives," Little Fawn agreed.

"They have left," Pawnee Woman said in Crow. "Big Dog did not wish to be present when your people came for you, Yellowhair. He and Skunk have gone toward the mountains in the south to hunt for a few days."

"Señor Benton," Vasquez was saying, "you have no idea how much gold there is in California. *Amigo,* even President Polk himself has spoken to Congress on this matter. And now that the United States has won the war with my country. . . ."

But Chastity did not hear the rest of Vasquez' words. In a moment she was across the room and out the door, running toward the stables. With a few quick words to the attendant, she was astride her mare and, checking the load in the old Hawken Benton had given her, she was on her way toward the Uintas. The waning moon, looking strangely deformed, hung over the rims to the southeast, and its light was more than sufficient.

The moon drifted across the sky as she rode along the wagon trail that led to Salt Lake City. She broke away from it where it crossed the stream and headed upstream, toward the mountains.

The stream tumbled toward her between twin walls of alder and aspen. The land appeared almost flat, but rising, tilting away southward toward the high white rim she remembered seeing by full daylight.

Several deer broke suddenly from the tree-lined edge of the stream and bounded off at a dizzying run

288

and then were away through low boulders, over a rim, gone—the only sound a trailing of pebbles down the stone face.

Brush and grass shone in the silver of moonwash.

But the mare was nervous. She pulled her head back, whinnied and resisted going onward. Chastity sang to the pony, calmed her, thumped her moccasined feet against her sides.

Still the creature resisted.

Ahead, gliding through the gray-white light were two huge wolves, dogtrotting away in the direction the deer had taken. They looked momentarily sideways at the girl on the horse, annoyed, perhaps, at having their night's hunting disrupted at the very moment they were ready to make their kill.

Then, they too were gone—gliding shadowlike up the rim and disappearing into the chaparral.

Chastity pressed upward toward the mountains. From time to time she could detect freshly kicked loose sand in the thin trail ahead. She had hoped to find Big Dog and Two-tail Skunk camped somewhere along the way, a little glow of firelight under trees, the two Crow warriors sitting around the flames. But as she rode on, the moon swept past its zenith—and still there was no sign of them.

Then the stream branched, and the trail forked also. Chastity trotted a few yards in either direction, attempting to detect fresh hoofprints, but without success.

No difficulty tomorrow, when it's light, she thought. To go on now might be to lose them, and I'd

have to re-track, spend an extra day in searching. They
. . . he isn't trying to elude me. Has no idea that I'm
following. Strange that I haven't caught up with them
yet.

She dismounted, walked her mare to the edge of
the stream, and allowed the animal to drink. She considered sleeping right here, under the cover of newly
leafed aspens, but then thought better of it. It was always best to find high ground for a campsite—Big Dog
always did that—perhaps some branching ravine, a
glade or table top higher up, away from the main
stream. Anyone riding the trail would stay close to the
creek, and a spot a few hundred yards away, with a
view back down, would provide a degree of security
and would be warmer as well. The cold air of early
morning always settled along the low ground, the bottoms of ravines, canyons, along rivers.

She crossed the meadows toward a low growth of
aspens. There was good cover there, perhaps no more
than a hundred yards from the stream.

She tethered the mare, then built a small fire and
spread her robes. Sitting next to the flames, she chewed
on a strip of jerked elk meat. She slipped into her
robes and lay awake, staring upward at the glitter of
countless stars, at the westward-descending moon. Far
off a wolf howled once, twice, then no more. She slept.

Suddenly she awoke and started. The mare was
snorting, jerking at her halter, stamping her feet. Without thinking, Chastity scrambled up, rifle in hand, and
piled some twigs on the nearly burned-down campfire.
She waited for the tinder to draw heat from the coals,

to burst into flame, and then changed her mind and blew on them, watching the flames start up.

Still the little mare was fussing. She was more than fussing, she was trying desperately to get loose.

Then she heard the scream of the puma. Again the mare snorted with fear, and strained to pull loose. The tinder was blazing now, and Chastity unfastened the mare and led her back into the circle of light where she tied her again to a hefty aspen.

She piled more wood on the fire and let the flames dance up to increase the circle of light. Her Hawken ready, Chastity waited.

She saw the great tawny cat! One moment there had been emptiness, and the next the huge cat was before her. The creature sat there, its twitching tail curled forward about its front paws. Chastity slowly raised her rifle, steadied it and took aim. But the mountain lion, as if oblivious to the threat of the rifle, abruptly sprawled on its side and rolled on its back. It turned over again, and pounced at some loose leaves, the long tail whipping back and forth.

My God, it's playing! she thought.

Her fear was gone, and she lowered the rifle. Even the mare, perhaps unable to see across the firelight or perhaps because the air had shifted directions or perhaps because she sensed that the girl's fear had vanished, seemed to relax somewhat. She no longer struggled against her tie rope, but only shifted her hooves and snuffled air through her nostrils.

The lion leaped suddenly toward an aspen, pulled itself up to the bottom branches, and kicked at the trunk with its hind feet. Then, twisting about in midair, the creature landed noiselessly beneath the tree.

"Hello, Brother—or Sister—whichever you are," Chastity called out. "Have you come to visit me? But I am looking for someone else, a man, the one who is called Big Dog. He is the one I love, and he loves me. He has run away from me because he fears that I will leave him. Does that make sense to you?"

The cat was on its haunches again, this time with its head slightly tilted, curious at the sound of the girl's voice. The amber eyes above the whiskered muzzle glinted firelight, the small rounded ears pricked forward. The terrible strength of its muscles were accentuated by the flickering firelight.

"Are you looking for a mate, big cat? You are male, I can tell that now—and you've come to court me? But I am not for you—we can visit, we can talk together, you and I, but we cannot mate. Anyway I belong to another, to Big Dog, if he will have me now. I think he is afraid of me, perhaps for the same reason that I was afraid of you. Because I did not understand you at first. You should not trust human beings, do you know that? I might have . . . shot you."

The lion began to groom its fur. The long pink tongue curled out, then in once more. The head moved slowly, and the eyes closed in contentment. The creature's whole demeanor said yes, I am a very fine cat, a fine cat indeed. . . .

Then the cougar was gone.

Perhaps Chastity had glanced away for an instant. Or else the lion had simply vanished. She was suddenly aware of gooseflesh all over her body and a prickling sensation along the back of her neck.

She built up the fire once more and sat cross-legged next to it, her rifle in her lap.

Chastity did not sleep any more that night.

Chapter 15

May 1849

She found their camp at a wooded saddle in the mountains, at a gap through which the barren desert lands beyond lay sprawled, great, broken fragments of the earth's crust tilting away in several directions. But there, at the crest, late afternoon sun flooded down warm and yellow through the stands of fir and young pine. White moths floated through the air in a slowly spiraling snowstorm of life. Wild irises, their petals thin and cream-colored and veined with blue, bunched together where a spring dripped down from a mossy bank, and the scent of mountain heather was rich with springtime.

The two war ponies, grazing sleepily on bunch grass and willow shoots, looked up. Recognizing the familiar smells of the mare and the girl, they fluttered breath through their lips in greeting, and returned to their browsing. Chastity dismounted, checked the campfire and found the charcoal still warm. Then, after exploring the camp area carefully, she lay down with her head against a thin, broken section of downed pine log and drifted into exhausted sleep.

When she awoke, several hours later, her hand flew immediately to the Hawken.

Voices and the sounds of pack animals drifted toward her.

Big Dog and Two-tail Skunk walked in, leading the animals, whose backs bore the bodies of three bighorn sheep.

"Yellowhair!" Big Dog called out. "What are you doing here? Has something happened?"

She quickly rose to her feet.

"No, only that I came to find . . . you. I also wished to go hunting."

Big Dog glanced at Two-tail Skunk, who merely shrugged his shoulders in a way that suggested he was not surprised.

"Our sister has ridden a long way," Skunk said.

Big Dog untied the pack ropes, lifted down the sheep one at a time, and tossed them onto the ground. He seemed to make a point of not looking at Chastity.

"Since you are here, you must dress out what we have killed," he ordered.

Chastity glanced at Two-tail Skunk, who shrugged once more.

This was to be some sort of test, she supposed. Why was Big Dog not glad to see her? Or was he secretly pleased—the task he had proposed for her one that carried some meaning? If she did as he said, did this mean she had at last and beyond all question accepted her role as a woman of the Crow nation? She drew in her breath and controlled her impulse to tell him that if he wanted the damned, meaningless sheep skinned out, he could do it himself.

Instead she spoke softly. "Yes, my husband."

But those were not the words she had intended to utter. The syllables hung in the air, exposed. She herself was exposed and vulnerable. Had the words registered upon him? He looked directly at her, his face expressionless.

She shifted her eyes to Two-tail Skunk, but he had turned away and was leading the pack animals across the small clearing toward the grazing ponies.

Then Big Dog also turned away, and Chastity unsheathed her skinning knife and set to work at the task.

She skinned out the first of the creatures and gutted it. Afterward, she cut out the choice portions from the rear quarter and carried these to the men, who had already built up the fire and were smoking a pipe. Big Dog accepted the meat, thrust a sharpened stick through the portions and placed the whole between two upright forked branches he had placed on either side of the fire. Chastity did not stay to watch. She returned to complete her task with the remaining two bighorns.

When the job was finished, she carefully wrapped the meat in two of the hides and tied them with deerhide rope. Into the third hide she placed the viscera and waste portions, as well as the heads of the two does, and carried these a hundred yards off across the saddle, back into the thick growth of fir. There she emptied the contents, a gift for the coyotes. She rubbed the raw side of the skin back and forth against the trunk of an aspen and returned to her work site. She carried the bales of fresh-cut meat to the fire and deposited them, then returned for the head of the big male. She knew Big Dog would wish to remove the horns, for these were prized. And this was a task for the man.

"Our meal is nearly ready, my wife," he said simply, the hint of a smile playing about his mouth.

Chastity nodded and stepped tentatively toward him.

Suddenly, he lifted her off her feet and tossed her upward. Catching her deftly on his opened palms, he raised her over his head.

"She is very light, this one," he laughed to Two-tail Skunk.

"Damn you!" she blurted out. "Put me down."

"She also has a very bad nature," Skunk said solemnly.

When her feet touched earth once more, his arms were around her, enfolding her, nearly suffocating her. His lips found hers, kissing her in the fashion of the whites.

"Damn you!" she sputtered. Then kissed him again.

"I love you, Yellowhair, Cozzie Yellowhair," he whispered into her ear and bit her gently.

"First we must eat," Two-tail Skunk insisted. "After that, Big Dog and Yellowhair may wish to eat in a different way. But right now the meat is starting to burn. . . ."

They took their meal, and never, Chastity

thought, had anything ever tasted quite so good. The three of them talked for a long while and Skunk told the story of how Old Man Coyote created the world. He finished the tale by speaking of how Old Man Coyote grew bored and even decided to make the white people.

"But that," Skunk concluded, "was probably a mistake. Old Man Coyote has made many mistakes, for otherwise we would not have rattlesnakes and mosquitoes and gnats. Also we would never get sick, and little children would not die in ways that even Ears-of-the-Wolf or One Who Strikes Three cannot help them. It was a mistake when he made the Long Knives."

"It is not a mistake if the Long Knives come to live with the Sparrow Hawks," Big Dog said, "for then we can teach them to be as we are—and we learn from them also. Our father came from the Long Knives, and Yellowhair also. They are both Sparrow Hawks now."

He looked at Chastity.

"That is true," she said. "Now I would never wish to be one of them again, for I am wife to Big Dog."

"And I am husband to Yellowhair," he replied.

"There is yet another story to tell," Two-tail Skunk laughed.

"There are many stories, my brother. And there are many nights to tell them. It would not be good to tell them all in just one night."

"There are far too many to tell in one night, anyway," Skunk replied.

"That is true," Big Dog agreed. "So now we must sleep. In a few days we must go back to Bridger's Fort, but until then you must tell at least one story each night. I forget the stories if I do not hear them often."

"You do not forget. You know them just as I do."

"My brother speaks truth," Big Dog said. "But you must tell them anyway, for when you are old, you will wish to be one of the shamans who tell the stories to all of the children. Even then Yellowhair and I will sit with you and listen. When you make mistakes, we will remind you of what is right."

"Skunk will not make mistakes."

"In that case we will be very quiet and listen and never contradict you."

Two-tail Skunk grinned, reached for a chunk of cold meat, and took a mouthful.

Big Dog and Chastity spread their robes a few yards from Two-tail Skunk and lay down together. They began to make love. She slipped her hands under his breechcloth, and he groaned softly as he began to remove her clothing. He ran his tongue over the nipples of her breasts and nibbled gently. After a time she guided him into her, and their bodies swayed together in the moonlight.

Two-tail Skunk was talking to himself out in the shadows, where his robes were spread, back away from the dying campfire. If Chastity and Big Dog had listened, they would have realized Skunk was telling the story of how Old Man Coyote had taken the power of language away from White Bear as a punishment for the bear's insisting that he, not Old Man Coyote, was the most powerful of all the creatures.

Finally Skunk grew tired of the story and finished it quickly. For a few moments he listened to the lovemaking and then called out, "I can hear the screech owls! They are making little moaning noises. Big Dog and Yellowhair, do you hear them? They make very strange sounds, these owls of the Uinta Mountains. They sound almost like a man and a woman who are making love together! Big Dog! My medicine says we should go on a horse-stealing party. My medicine says that we should go now, tonight. There is nothing else to do, my brother, and tonight would be a very good time to steal horses. Look! I see a great herd of horses down below. They are Blackfoot horses, but I do not know how it is that they have strayed so far from home. We must take these magic dogs back to our own pastures, for there they will have enough to eat and will grow very fat. Will you come now? I think it is time to go. Listen to what those owls are saying, Big Dog. . . ."

Big Dog and Chastity fell asleep with Skunk's words in their ears.

Morning came, and as Chastity built up the fire, Two-tail Skunk was grinning. He gathered wood and brought it to her.

"The Pawnee are addicted to whiskey," Chastity said. "But you are addicted to talking, Skunk."

"Words make very good whiskey, that is true. I stole many horses last night while you and Big Dog were asleep. Owls were keeping me awake, so I got up and went to steal horses. It is too bad that you and Big Dog could not come with me, but you were sleeping."

"You are like a young boy who is full of mischief," Chastity said, smiling.

"It is good that you are truly one of us now, my sister," Skunk replied.

A week passed in hunting and wandering. They rode to where the snows still lay heavy on the high peaks of the Uintas and crossed over into the desert areas beyond. Camping for a time at the wooded bottom of a river canyon, they swam in the cold, shining, green water. Chastity dressed hides as the men cut and set out to dry the meat they had taken. At length the packs were full, and the horses could carry no more.

With regret they crossed back over the mountains and came down once more to Bridger's Fort. Along the way, the old sense of distance between Big Dog and Chastity seemed to return. She attempted to break through Big Dog's silence by telling him of her encounter with the mountain lion. Two-tail Skunk laughed, insisting that the lion was looking for a mate and had probably concluded that she was a strange-looking lioness—or else it had been Old Man Coyote in disguise, intent upon testing her courage.

But Big Dog's gloom deepened as the three of them approached the fort.

They arrived about midday. While they were stabling the horses, Benton appeared behind them, his expression one of deep concern.

"Ye done worried this ol' coon half to death, damn it. Ye know that, don't ye? Me an' Pawnee Woman rode out lookin' for ye the next day, but no luck—just like ye'd vanished, slicker'n buffler grease. Finally found your campsite up in the mountains, all of ye together, an' so we guessed ye was all right. Just figgered I'd leave ye be after that."

Big Dog embraced his father, as did Two-tail Skunk.

"Ahh!" Benton snorted. "Only one I'm interested in huggin' with is the pretty one. Come here, Cozzie."

He held her and whispered, "Is everything shinin' okay, gal?"

"Yes," she answered. "The stick's floatin' . . . right."

"Okay, okay," Benton complained to all of them. "I understand how it is—a coon gets old, his family just rides off without 'im. Figger he's too slow to keep up anymore. Look, Cozzie, your kinfolk's here, your daddy an' that duck with the straight jaw, the one ye was thinkin' about marryin' with. Looks like he up an' married a couple of others while ye was off playin' Injun, so prepare yourself. Brigham Young hisself is with 'em, an' Loot Edgy an' his bluecoats an' Madden the Washington man to boot. Big Dog, ye got a handle on things?"

"I am ready to kill some white men, Father."

"Not exactly what this old-timer had in mind."

"Then I will kill the man only if he offends me," Big Dog replied darkly.

"Like breathin', for instance?"

"Like that."

"You just hold onto your temper now, ye hear?"

"I am never angry when I kill a man, Father. You know that. One should never kill in anger. There is no fun if one is angry. I heard Bridger say that many times. I was young then, so I believed him."

"Just keep a handle on 'er, Big Dog. This could turn out a mite touchy. . . ."

They followed Benton into Bridger's house and found the main room packed with people. Jim Bridger and Louis Vasquez and both their wives sat to one side. Brigham Young, Charles Madden, Lieutenant John C. Edgeworth (aged somewhat since he'd set out with Madden nearly four months earlier), Elder Tommasen and his two young wives, and Samuel Cosgrove and Tillie Ann occupied the rest of the space.

Expressions of shock spread over the Mormons' faces as they finally recognized Chastity Cosgrove. She walked to her father, hesitated, and then embraced him. She was aware as she did so that he was forcing himself to hold her in his arms. Freed from her father's embrace, she turned to Tommasen and extended her hand. Mouth slightly agape, the heavy-jowled elder finally took her hand and said lamely that he was glad to see her safe.

The Mormon women exchanged glances, and the muscles in their faces tightened.

"Yuh didn't expect 'er to be wearin' Sunday best, now did yuh?" Jim Bridger bellowed. "Hadn't been for old 'Loysius here, she'd of been a gone gosling long since."

"So you're Chastity Cosgrove?" Madden asked. "I suppose you know I've traveled across two-thirds of a continent in the hope of finding you alive and well. Somehow I missed you at the Crow village. You were out hunting, they said, and after two days I was obliged to move on to Salt Lake City. But Mr. Benton has been true to his word and has returned you safe and sound. My name's Charles Madden, at your service, ma'am."

"Hello, Mr. Madden," Chastity said, and then repeated the greeting in the language of the Crow.

Madden nodded, returned the greeting with the bit of Sparrow Hawk lingo he'd learned, and then continued. "Allow me to present Lieutenant John Edgeworth of the United States Army."

"At your service, Miss Cosgrove," Edgeworth snapped, bowing from the waist and clicking his heels together.

Chastity nodded, aware of the disgust that lay behind the lieutenant's formal manner.

"How are you, my child?" Brigham Young asked, taking her hand and holding it tightly. "The Lord has been merciful and has delivered you back to your people. Chastity, we have all said endless prayers for your well-being these past months, and now Holy God has seen fit to answer them. We welcome you back and thank the angels for their sweet intervention."

Tillie Ann averted her eyes, and Chastity decided simply to ignore her father's wife.

"All right now!" Jim Bridger boomed. "This ol' coon calls the meetin' to order. Madden's goin' to preside on account of he's the chief coon of the U.S. gov'ment. Me an' Looey Vasquez is havin' a whole deer roasted as a celebration, an' there'll be whiskey available for them as wants it, good stuff, straight in from Kansas City, an' not watered down, nuther. Of course, the saints won't be wantin' any of the arwerdenty, but we got cold milk from the dairy cows, an' it's good an' rich. Now let's get this business settled so's we can get to eatin'."

"Mr. Bridger's right, quite right," Madden agreed,

305

projecting his own rich baritone over the group and stroking back his thinning red hair as he did so. "There are certain issues which need to be resolved in the best interests of all. Actually, the Office of Indian Affairs is essentially an overseer in this matter, nothing more. As I understand it, Miss Cosgrove was kidnapped by hostile Indians, reported by Mr. Benton to be Pawnee. Mr. Benton, am I correct in this?"

"That's how the stick was floatin', sure as buffler dung," Benton said.

"Yes. And then Mr. Benton entered into an arrangement with Mr. Young and Mr. Tommasen to attempt the rescue of Miss Cosgrove, the specified stipend to be that of one thousand dollars in addition to his wages as scout and hunter, am I correct?"

"That was upon the condition that the girl be returned to us safe and well and unharmed," Tommasen acknowledged. "But those conditions have not been fulfilled. This is not the girl whom I intended to marry. This girl. . . ."

"Of course it's Cozzie, ye damned fool!" Benton yelled. "Ye be blind or somethin'?"

"Order, order," Madden insisted. "Let Mr. Tommasen finish."

Tommasen's hands were quivering. "This girl is little more than a red Indian herself. Look at her appearance! Only the Lord knows what's happened to her, what she's been subjected to. Nine months with the savages has turned her into . . . a savage herself."

Tommasen's two young wives nodded in unison.

Big Dog leaped across the crowded room, knocking Edgeworth to the floor and locked a huge arm about Tommasen's head. He held his bowie knife to the man's throat.

"You'll *think* savage," he growled, "but if you speak any more ugly words, I'll kill you and skin you and feed your hide to Bridger's hogs."

Edgeworth struggled to his feet and drew his pistol, pointing it directly at Tommasen and Big Dog.

"Sonny," Benton drawled from behind, "you pull that trigger, an' this coon's goin' to do a little shootin', too."

The Texas Paterson was jabbed into Edgeworth's back.

"Gentlemen!" Madden shouted, his face flushing. "Control your tempers, goddamn it, or I'll have you all horsewhipped."

"Be a good trick, at that," Bridger laughed. "Awright, coons! Put your toys away an' act civilized. Big Dog, let the preacher go. 'Loysius, you and the boy put your pop guns away. Ain't gonna be no goddamned killin' in my house, I'll tell yuh!"

Big Dog relaxed his grip and withdrew the blade. Edgeworth, with little choice in the matter, mumbled the words *court-martial* and holstered his pistol. Benton did likewise.

Tommasen put a trembling hand to his throat.

"Elder Tommasen," Brigham Young declared sternly, "Mr. Benton has fairly performed those actions for which we engaged him. He has acted in good faith and has brought the girl to us. For this reason we are bound by our own word, given both as gentlemen and as the Chosen of God, to fulfill our contract. I hold the thousand dollars we agreed to pay Mr. Benton and also his wages, a total of one thousand two hundred and twenty-five dollars, United States currency. Mr. Madden, if you will please pass this to Mr. Benton, with the sincere gratitude of the Latter-Day Saints."

Madden took the money and turned it over to Benton, who nodded and said, "This ol' trapper thanks ye."

"Have all conditions been met?" Madden remembered to ask after he had given the money to the old trapper.

"I judge that all conditions have been met," Brigham Young said. "Mr. Cosgrove's daughter has been returned to him, and Elder Tommasen's betrothed the same, the two being one. Elder, if you now choose not to marry the young woman, that is something which you and Mr. Cosgrove will have to settle between yourselves. I propose, therefore, that we take the girl and go, leaving Mr. Bridger and his friends to celebrate in whatever manner they choose. It is up to them if they wish to drink hard spirits. Our lives must be governed by good sense, honesty in all matters, and the will of our Father in Heaven."

"Spoke like a true coon!" Bridger joined in. "Rev'rend, I almost find myself likin' yuh at times. Crazy as a loon, mebbe, but honest—I'll give yuh that much."

"Sometimes I pray for you, James Bridger," Young said, as if wanting to smile and not quite knowing how.

"Then it's settled?" Madden asked.

"Goddamn you all!" Chastity shouted. "I don't suppose it's occurred to anyone that I might have a say in the matter? Why doesn't someone ask *me* what it is that I want to do?"

The room was ominously quiet, and all eyes turned toward Chastity.

"Daughter. . . ," Samuel Cosgrove began.

"Hesh your mouth," Benton said in a way that allowed for no disagreement, "an' let Cozzie speak her piece. Ye been bullyin' the gal her whole life long an' not givin' a buffler turd about 'er. She's worth twenty of ye or the Elder, either one. Now, what's on your mind, gal?"

Big Dog had started to turn away, but he stopped and gazed across at Chastity.

"I cannot marry Elder Tommasen," she said, her voice steady. "I am already married . . . to Big Dog Benton, the one who would have killed you on the spot, Andrew, if I had merely nodded to him. He saved me from the Pawnee. Big Dog loves me and has risked his life for me more than once. His people are now my people, and his family is my family. You are free, Andrew. You will not be disgraced among the Mormons by being forced into taking for a wife a woman who has lived among the Indians. That is my decision, and I will not change my mind. I'm sorry, Father. Tell those who are your friends that your daughter Chastity is dead. My name is Yellowhair now."

Brigham Young stared at the girl, who returned his unblinking gaze, and then turned to Madden and

Cosgrove, as if awaiting some point of clarification from either of them.

"As far as I'm concerned," Cosgrove said at last, "my daughter is indeed already dead. She is a disgrace to me and to our people."

"Trouble is, ye damned fool," Benton exploded, "ye can't tell a human being from a jackass rabbit, an' never could."

Lieutenant Edgeworth started for his pistol again and then apparently thought better of it.

"Wal, now, coons, it appears to this ol' coot that the issue's been pretty well resolved," Bridger said. "Rev'rend, what you be thinkin'?"

"Mr. Bridger," the Mormon Prophet responded, "for once we seem to be in essential agreement. I should say that Miss Cosgrove . . . Mrs. Big Dog . . . is no longer one of us in spirit, and for that reason she should be allowed to do whatever she wishes. Elder, do you see this matter as I do?"

Tommasen nodded.

"It's not a question of my being *allowed* to do as I wish," Chastity said. "God gave me this life, you people didn't. I have never truly been one of you. I have made my own choice. I will live my life in the way that I myself see fit."

"It is for the best, then," Young agreed. "We must not have those among us who are not with us in spirit. We will say prayers for you, my daughter."

Chastity glared at the Mormon Prophet.

"I am not your daughter," she said. "And I don't need your help to find my way to the Spirit World."

Charles Madden had been trying to put the whole thing together, and yet he could hardly believe what he was hearing. In a professional lifetime of attempting to intercede in behalf of the American Indian, of appreciating and attempting fully to understand the ways of these people, it had never seriously occurred to him that a thoroughly civilized white person would ever, even under the most extreme circumstances, actually choose to be one of them. There were those, like the trappers, who had in effect become Indians themselves. But such persons always came from the fringes of the white society. This girl, of course, was a Mormon, a strange breed to begin with—and if, taken at her word, she had always been something of an outsider, then perhaps. . . . Madden shook his head, as if on the verge of an understanding that he had attempted to arrive at for years, and now, faced with the reality of it, could still not quite accept.

Young's voice interrupted his thoughts. "Our business and the Lord's business, then, are finished here. Mr. Bridger, we thank you for your gracious hospitality and the offer of a feast of deer meat, but the trail ahead of us is a long one, and we will be more comfortable in the company of our own. You understand, I think? And Mr. Madden, our people wish to express their most sincere appreciation for all that you have done. Please know, and so inform the authorities in Washington, that Brigham Young will cooperate with the passage of emigrants westward in every way consistent with the laws of our church and our community. Gentlemen and ladies, we bid you a farewell. Know that you will have our prayers."

With that the Prophet turned and strode toward the doorway, the other Mormons trailing behind. Within minutes their mule-drawn wagon and horses were on their way out of Bridger's Fort.

Bursting suddenly into tears, Chastity threw herself into Big Dog's arms and was instantly joined by Pawnee Woman. Big Dog placed an arm around each of the women and stood grinning.

"By damn!" Benton chortled. "This trip didn't turn out so bad, after all. Gabe, this ol' hoss recollects ye said somethin' about whiskey, an' I've got a powerful dry."

"*Amigo,*" Vasquez said, "there is no arwerdenty. The barrels, they have run empty."

"A cryin' shame it be, 'Loysius," Bridger agreed. "Right now I expect we need us a celebration, too."

"Ye lyin' thieves!" Benton roared. Then he let out a blood-curdling *hoo-ki-hi!* and followed that with a thunderous "Hurrah for the Mountains!"

Edgeworth's nervous hand started once again for the pistol. Madden noticed and bellowed, "Lieutenant! Go tend to your enlisted men. The Ute and the Shoshone have probably scalped half of them by now!"

His world suddenly once more in order, the lieutenant clicked his heels, saluted and stalked from the room.

"Now then," Bridger chuckled, "Looey an' me'll see if we can find somethin' to wet a man's whistle."

"*Sí, sí,*" Vasquez agreed. "The señoras too will wish to drink, no?"

Chastity and Pawnee Woman looked at each

other. Neither had ever before in her life touched hard spirits.

"We are Crow," Two-tail Skunk asserted. "We do not drink the water of the white devils."

"Aw, hell, Skunk," Bridger grinned. "She's not goin' to hurt your medicine, this ol' man guarantees 'er. In addition to which, Long Hair and Yellow Belly are out on the Tongue River—they ain't watchin' yuh."

"In that case, Skunk will drink little bit. Then I will go kill all the Shoshone."

"Shoshone an' Crow are allies, have been for many winters," Bridger protested.

"I forgot about that," Skunk answered. "All right, I will drink and then kill only two, three Shoshone."

"Soundin' better all the time. Coons, bring on the grog," Benton laughed.

"As a representative of the United States government," Madden said, keeping his face serious, "I am honor-bound to protest, Mr. Bridger."

"Loosen up, *amigo*. One time can hurt very little," Vasquez said, winking at Madden.

"Even us red devils need to indulge once in a while," Benton added. "Clears the rust out of the old pipes."

"Well. . . ," Madden shrugged, his eyes twinkling.

"Sides," Benton continued, "this here's a weddin' feast, kind of. Big Dog an' Cozzie are gettin' hitched an' I got me another adopted daughter—to go along with Pawnee Woman."

Big Dog had been standing quietly, one arm about

Chastity and one about Pawnee Woman. Now he spoke.

"Bring us a keg of your good whiskey, Gabe. Now that my father has money, he will buy nothing but the best. And both of my wives must drink too. These are my words."

Everyone except Chastity and Pawnee Woman laughed. A small keg of Kentucky bourbon was brought out and the tin cups filled. They drank, and once again the cups were filled. Then the party filed outside, into the early night, where a deer was roasting over a bed of orange-red coals. A few of the Shoshone and Ute had drifted up as well, and the feast was on. When everyone had eaten his fill, Vasquez began to play the harmonica, and an extemporaneous dance began. The music drifted across to Edgeworth and his bluecoats who had just finished their own rations. The soldiers, lieutenant and all, moved toward the harmonica-playing at double time. Soon bluecoats were high-stepping with Indian warriors, and Benton, who had borrowed Little Fawn's yellow shawl and had draped it about his middle, was prancing around with Jim Bridger. Vasquez, not to be outdone, tossed aside the harmonica and joined in the dance, clasping hands with Bridger and Benton, the three of them hopping and turning in a frantic circle. The tall Shoshone braves chanted and clapped their hands to their thighs in unison.

The hours passed, and finally the exhausted dancers disappeared one by one.

Charles Madden watched Big Dog, Chastity and

Pawnee Woman slip away into the shadows, and he smiled at the night. Overhead the waning quarter-moon drifted dreamlike through the darkness, and the sky was alive with the white fire of the stars.

Epilogue

May 1849

Midmorning brought a motley rabble of men, some in wagons and some on horseback, all heading for the goldfields. Vasquez conducted a brisk business out of the trading post, while his wife alternately charmed the ragged-looking men and kept watch over her husband's tendency to forget to total up miscellaneous items, a practice which, she insisted, would turn the post into a charitable organization if not checked. Bridger fired up the smithy and replaced wheel rims and worn horseshoes. Little Fawn cooked huge pots of meat and greens, with a tin plateful selling for fifty cents. Second helpings were free.

Shortly past noon the irregular convoy was on its way westward, down the wagon road toward Brigham Young's New Zion and the Nevada desert beyond. It would journey across the burning salt flats and over the rims and down to the Humboldt River that wound on through a gray-brown landscape for nearly four hundred miles to its vanishing point in a sink. From there, Bridger said, the trail branched, one fork crossing over the mountains through the pass where the Donner expedition had starved and resorted to cannibalism three years earlier. A second fork crossed the Sierras at Kit Carson's Pass farther south, and a third fork picked up the drainage of Joe Walker's River and crossed the range at Sonora Pass.

"Mucho del oro," Vasquez said, "much gold in California. Señor Big Dog, take your father and go there, *sí,* and your brother and your wives. You will all come back *rico,* very wealthy. Gold in the stream bottoms and all over the mountains. Gabe *y mi,* we sell you supplies, you become *muy rico."*

"This Vasquez," Two-tail Skunk grunted, "he does not speak English very well. Even Skunk can speak better."

Big Dog nodded, thought once again of Pine Leaf and the missing Crow chief Medicine Calf.

"What do you think, Cozzie Yellowhair, should we cross the deserts and search for the yellow metal? We could find Pine Leaf's husband and bring him back to Crow lands."

"Do you need the gold, my husband?"

"No, we do not need it."

"Cozzie, damn ye, it ain't a matter o' need," Benton cut in. "This ol' trapper figgers Looey's got a hell of an idea. Skunk, ye really want to see the Great Water?"

"There is no Great Water. This is only one of Benton's stories," Two-tail Skunk grinned.

318

"Damn it," Benton bellowed, "I tell ye there be a whole ocean out there."

Pawnee Woman looked at her husband and then at Chastity, her eyes full of questions. What would happen next?

"Coons, I got us more than twelve hundred dollars cash money. If we use 'er right, we can get out there an' pick us up three, four pack sacks full of gold. Leapin' hogs, we could buy our horses from the Blackfoot an' not have to thieve 'em."

"Why would the Blackfoot want the yellow metal, Father?" Big Dog asked, amused at the intensity that had suddenly come over Benton.

"Ignorant red devil! I've taught ye everything I know, an' ye still don't know nothin'!"

"A long trail, and no water," Big Dog shrugged.

"Water all over the place," Benton insisted. "Hell, this time o' year the Humboldt's flooding down off the Ruby Mountains. Gabe hisself says so. What about 'er, Madden? Ye want to pitch in with us?"

"Mr. Benton," he replied, "I should dearly love to. Unfortunately, it is my lot to have to return to Washington. This entire adventure has been something of a vacation for me, but now I have to return to the drudgery of a man in government service. I wish I could accompany you, I really do."

"Coons, I'm goin' to do 'er. The rest of you with the ol' man?"

Big Dog gazed down the westward-leading wagon road, shrugged as though the proposal were hardly worth considering, then stole a glance at Benton's face.

"Come on, damn ye! Trouble is ye've got no sense of adventure."

"We'll never be able to live with him if we don't go along," Chastity laughed, squeezing her husband's hand.

"Father," Big Dog asked, "do you really think Charbonneau can make it across that desert?"

"She'll be dancin' on 'er hind legs when your pony's tongue is hangin' out an' draggin' in the sand," Benton said, annoyed that the endurance of his faithful mare should be called into question.

Big Dog thought about it. The Ruby Mountains and the great desert and the Sierra Nevadas rose up in his mind. He heard coyotes singing in the night and summer wind whispering through the tops of pines and firs. He could see green rivers flowing westward, down out of the mountains and into a broad valley bounded by yet farther mountains still to the west. And in the water, where the current coiled about great boulders, he could see lumps of gold. . . .

First in the Spectacular Series
THE AMERICAN INDIANS
COMANCHE REVENGE

by Jeanne Sommers

This is the unparalleled story of a white woman, Cynthia Ann Parker, captured by Indians as a young girl. She and a friend, Beth Hutchens, are the sole survivors of a raid that has wiped out their families and destroyed their homes. They have no choice but to follow the ways of their Indian captors.

COMANCHE REVENGE tells how Cynthia Ann learns to accept Comanche customs and how that acceptance turns to love — the love of the great chief Peta Noconi. Born of two races, their child, Quanah Parker, will ultimately rule his tribe and lead them on their path of revenge.

AMERICAN EXPLORERS #1

A cruel test, an untamed land and the love of a woman turned the boy into a man.

JED SMITH

FREEDOM RIVER

****

Arriving in St. Louis in 1822, the daring, young Jedediah Smith is confronted by rugged mountain men, trappers and bar-room brawlers. He learns all too soon what is to be expected of him on his first expedition into the new frontier up the Missouri River. Making lifelong enemies and fighting terrifying hand-to-hand battles, he learns how to live with men who will kill for a cheap woman or a drop of liquor. But he learns more. Far from the beautiful woman he left behind, in the arms of a free-spirited Indian girl, he discovers the kind of love he never thought possible. *Freedom River* is the historical drama of an American hero who opened the doors of the unknown wilderness to an exciting future for an expanding nation.

AMERICAN EXPLORERS #2

**They faced 900 miles of savage wilderness
where a young man chose between fortune and love.**

LEWIS & CLARK

NORTHWEST GLORY

Set in the turbulent 1800s, this is the story of the Lewis and Clark expedition — and of the brave men and women who faced brutal hardship and fierce tests of will. They encountered an untamed wilderness, its savage mountain men, merciless fortune seekers and fiery Indian warriors. In the midst of this hostile land, two lovers are united in their undying passion. A truly incredible tale of love and adventure.